Child of Hope

We Three Kings: Book 1

By

KIMBERLY RAE JORDAN

THREE**STRAND**
PRESS

A CORD OF THREE STRANDS IS NOT EASILY BROKEN.

A man, a woman & their God.
Three Strand Press publishes Christian Romance stories that intertwine love, faith and family. Always clean. Always heartwarming. Always uplifting.

Copyright © 2021 by **Kimberly Rae Jordan**

All rights reserved. No part of this publication may be reproduced, distributed or transmitted in any form or by any means, without prior written permission.

This is a work of fiction. Names, characters, places, and incidents are a product of the author's imagination. Locales and public names are sometimes used for atmospheric purposes. Any resemblance to actual people, living or dead, or to businesses, companies, events, institutions, or locales is completely coincidental.

Scripture taken from the New King James Version®. Copyright © 1982 by Thomas Nelson, Inc. Used by permission. All rights are reserved.

CHILD OF HOPE/ Kimberly Rae Jordan. -- 1st ed.
ISBN-13: 978-1-988409-58-0

This I recall to my mind,
Therefore I have hope.
Through the Lord's mercies we are not consumed,
Because His compassions fail not.
They are new every morning;
Great is Your faithfulness.
Lamentations 3:21-23

Chapter 1

Paige Cantor turned to look into the back seat of the SUV where her son sat. Rylan met her gaze, his brown eyes wide.

"Remember what we talked about, Ry?"

"I remember, Mama," he said with a nod, causing a chunk of hair to flop down over his eyes. He lifted a hand to brush it away. "I'll be good."

"I know you will." He was a good kid, but it didn't stop the knot of worry in her stomach from tightening. "Okay. Let's go."

Getting out of the car, she went around to the back hatch. She lifted the wheelchair out and opened it up. Even though she knew that she hadn't had any other option, she said a prayer that this wasn't a mistake.

Wheeling the chair around to the back door, she opened it and leaned in to lift Rylan out and put him in the wheelchair. The chair was a bit big for him, but when she'd bought it, it was the thought that they wouldn't be able to afford another if he outgrew it too soon.

She set the backpack they'd filled before leaving the house earlier onto the seat next to Rylan, then moved the chair back so she could close the car door. As she wheeled Rylan to the elevator, she was so grateful that the job had included a parking spot in the underground parking garage of the building where Hayden King lived. Wheeling Rylan over snow-covered sidewalks was a pain, and she always worried the chair would get stuck.

While Rylan counted the numbers as the lights flashed above the elevator door, Paige said another prayer. She couldn't afford to lose the job, and she was pretty sure that bringing her son to work might lead to that.

When they reached the floor where Hayden's apartment was, the elevator door slid open. Paige pushed the chair across the short distance to the door of the apartment. She had her own keys to the place, since Hayden rarely ventured from the two rooms he used the most—his bedroom and the theater room.

The apartment was quiet as she let herself in, which was what she'd hoped for. She pushed the wheelchair toward the opening to the right of the foyer. Though the kitchen wasn't open to the rest of the apartment, it was large and sunny, with a small dining table next to enormous windows.

That was where she wheeled Rylan since it was where he would have to spend his day. She hoped that he wouldn't get too bored. They'd brought books, crayons, some Lego, cars, and coloring books along with his tablet. Hopefully, all of it would keep him entertained while she worked.

Before she started to prepare breakfast for Hayden, she sent a text to her mom.

We're at the apartment. How is Donna feeling? Ready for the surgery?

Her mom usually took care of Rylan for her while she worked, but she'd had to help her best friend who was having surgery that day. Her mom had spent the previous night with her and then had driven her to the hospital that morning. Without a backup babysitter, Paige had had no choice but to bring Rylan to work with her.

She set her phone on the counter, then pulled out the ingredients to make pancakes. Since Hayden enjoyed them, she ended up making them a couple of times a week.

Once they were ready, she set the plate on a tray along with a small pitcher containing maple syrup. She also put a travel mug of coffee on the tray, doctored the way Hayden preferred. The last thing she added was a small bowl of berries. Sometimes he ate those, sometimes he didn't.

"I'll be right back," Paige told Rylan before she made her way to the other side of the apartment where Hayden's bedroom was located.

Balancing the tray on her arm, Paige knocked lightly on the door, then opened it. Hunter had told her to do that because there were days that if she waited for Hayden to tell her to come in, she'd be waiting all day.

The spacious room was dark, which meant that Hayden was either still asleep or not in the mood to face the day yet. He wasn't what she'd call a morning person.

The light from the hallway was enough for her to see to put the tray down on the table next to the window. She opened the curtains, then waited to see if Hayden would object to the flood of light in the room.

When she approached the bed, she saw that Hayden was awake, laying on his side facing away from the window. "Would you like to sit at the table to eat?"

"Not really hungry," Hayden muttered.

"Why don't you sit up?" Paige suggested, keeping in mind Hunter's instructions in dealing with his brother. It had gotten easier over the months. "I'll bring the tray over to you. It's pancakes, this morning."

Without waiting for his response, she returned to the table to pick up the tray, hoping that he would get himself to a sitting position while she did.

His moods could be unpredictable, but he was never abusive to her in any way. It was his unhappiness that was hard for her to see.

Her mom knew more of his story as she'd been working for him for several years before she'd quit and Paige had taken over for her. Through her mom, Paige knew a lot about the man, so she had sympathy for him, even though she didn't completely understand his mindset.

When she returned to the bed, Hayden was sitting up against a pile of pillows. It was pretty clear he hadn't had a good night. His eyes had dark smudges beneath them, and he squinted as he looked toward the window. His dark hair hung in messy waves around his face, hiding the scar on his cheek.

With careful movements, Paige set the legs of the tray over his lap, then stepped back.

Hayden looked down at it with a sigh. "Thank you."

She went back to the table and picked up the dishes from his meal the night before. Since he couldn't handle the tray on his crutches, his dinner dishes were still there each morning. "If you need anything more, just call me."

Once he nodded, she didn't linger for further conversation. They hadn't had a lot of personal conversations over the nine months she'd worked for him, so she didn't know what exactly it was that kept him up at night. All she knew was that he didn't seem to like mornings, particularly after a rough night.

She returned to the kitchen, eager to check on Rylan and make sure he was still at the table. He couldn't maneuver the wheelchair very well since it was too big for him, but he could move around a bit if he was determined.

Thankfully, he was right where she'd left him, head bent over a coloring book of cars. One hour down... eight to go!

~*~

Hayden King stared at the breakfast on his tray. His favorite breakfast meal was pancakes, but he didn't always feel like eating. He'd lost so much weight and muscle mass that he and Hunter barely looked like brothers anymore, let alone identical twins.

It was hard to look at Hunter sometimes and be reminded of what he'd once looked like—even if their hairstyles hadn't been the same since his mom had stopped insisting he get his hair cut. Now, though, their hair was the least of their differences.

Before the accident, his and Hunter's appearances had been an accurate reflection of the personalities. Hunter had been the obedient son, doing as their father said, willing to take instruction from him. He'd favored a more styled haircut along with his business attire. Hayden, on the other hand, had rejected that professionalism on every level, from his clothes to his hair.

Hunter had always been the responsible one, and he still was. The company was thriving under his leadership, and he was a husband and father now.

Meanwhile, Hayden would sometimes spend his entire day in bed. Even though he had a job at the company, which he could do remotely from that bed if he wanted, he was essentially a non-productive member of society, and he really didn't care.

Over the past few years, he'd slowly been moving toward the day when he would no longer need anymore surgeries. He wouldn't have been back to normal, but he'd hoped to at least get to the point where the pain was tolerable, since he couldn't take the stronger pain meds any longer. It hadn't been easy, and he hadn't always had the best attitude, but it had been a goal to work towards.

But his final surgery—the one that was supposed to fix the last of the damage to his left ankle, which had been crushed in the accident—had gone terribly wrong. After making it through most of the surgeries without any major issues, this one had resulted in blood circulation issues and an infection that just wouldn't heal. In the end, they'd had to amputate his left leg just below the knee.

Hayden wasn't sure what his life would have looked like if everything had gone to plan, but the amputation had seemed to be a sign that he wasn't supposed to move on from the accident. The only upside was that his pain was more manageable. He'd only had to lose his lower leg in order to get to that point.

Now, it just seemed easier to live his life in the solitude of his room, especially since he could afford to have people clean his home and cook for him. Which was how he had pancakes for breakfast that he didn't have to make.

Ignoring them for the time being, he picked up the coffee and took a sip. He leaned back against the pillows, sipping the coffee until he couldn't stand the silence any longer. Reaching over to the other side of the bed, he grabbed the remote from where he'd dropped it the night before and used it to turn on the huge television on the wall facing the bed.

He'd watch the movie series he was in the middle of later, but first, he'd see what was going on in the world. It was almost guaranteed to be bad news, but sometimes there was some good sprinkled in there.

Once the news was playing on the television, he began to slowly eat the pancakes and the fruit that Paige had brought him. He wasn't overly hungry, but the taste of the pancakes brought him a bit of joy.

After he'd finished eating, Hayden stared at the door to the bathroom. He couldn't put off getting out of bed any longer.

"Are you finished with the tray?"

He looked away from the bathroom to see Paige walking into the room with Craig behind her. Craig came each weekday to do some physiotherapy with him, trying to get him stronger so he could deal with life better. He didn't care about that, but he did it because...well, it was what his mom wanted. It was the one thing he'd been willing to give her, even though it meant dealing with Craig's infuriating attitude.

Paige lifted the tray from the bed. "I'll be back later with your lunch."

"Thanks."

He watched her leave the room, then shifted his attention to Craig.

"Time to get up," Craig said.

Hayden didn't bother arguing because he needed to use the bathroom, anyway. Craig handed him the crutches that Hayden had to use to get around.

He took his time, partly because he didn't enjoy moving quickly, but also because he knew what waited for him once he was done. Hayden knew he'd stretched it out too far when Craig knocked on the door.

"I'm coming," Hayden muttered, then moved to open it.

"Let's go," Craig said, gesturing to the far corner of the room where some workout equipment was set up, along with a massage table.

Hayden made his way over to the padded table and got up on it. Once he was lying on his back, Craig began to work his muscles. Hayden groaned as the man pushed his knee toward his chest, the muscles on the back of his thigh protesting the movement.

"Have you made the appointment yet?" Craig asked as he rounded the table to do the same with his other leg.

"No."

"Waiting's not gonna change anything," Craig said as he eased Hayden's leg to the side, working out the muscles in his hip. "Your leg isn't going to grow back."

No one else talked so bluntly to Hayden, and most of the time, Hayden didn't like it when Craig did. However, he hadn't fired him over it yet and probably never would.

"I know that," Hayden muttered.

"Then start acting like it, man." It was a conversation they had pretty much every time Craig came to help him stretch and work out. Five days a week—ever since the doctor had given the all-clear on his amputation wound—he lectured Hayden about making that appointment.

"And while you're at it," Craig said as he helped him off the table a little while later and over to the weightlifting set-up. "Make an appointment with your therapist too."

Hayden sighed as he pulled down on the bar after Craig checked the weight. Yet another topic he didn't enjoy. Craig was the only person who harped on all these things, making Hayden wonder if Hunter paid him extra to do it.

When his family tried to convince him to take steps forward, they did it much more subtly, which made it easier for Hayden to ignore what they said.

"You are so fortunate, and you don't even realize it," Craig said. "There are people out there in situations like yours who don't have the money to get the help they need. They can't afford a well-fitting prosthetic. They can't afford the mental help they need."

"Will it make them feel better to know that I'm a wealthy man who uses my wealth to get all of that? Or will they be happier that I'm suffering like they are?"

Craig shifted to stare at him, arms crossed over his broad chest. "Is that why you're not getting the help you need?"

Hayden shrugged. "I've got lots of reasons for what I do."

"And I'd venture that none of them are good," Craig said with a huff.

"I'm sure people would agree with you, which is why I'm keeping those reasons to myself." Hayden scrubbed his hands over his face. "Just trust that I have reasons that to my mind are good."

"Your mind needs help too," Craig told him bluntly. "Because there aren't any reasons that I can think of that are good enough to not do what you need to in order to live a fulfilling life."

Hayden had gone to counseling off and on for a few years, and it had done some good, especially at the start. He no longer had nightmares every single night, and he could also get into a car without having a panic attack. But then the therapist had wanted to tackle some other issues, and he hadn't been on board for that. Soon, to the dismay of his family, his visits had tapered off then stopped, and more recently, he'd refused to get a prosthesis.

He hoped that eventually, they'd accept that this stuff would happen in his time and in his way. And if that meant he never got a prosthesis, so be it.

"You have got to be the craziest person I've ever worked with."

"I bet you say that to all the sick and infirm."

Craig gave him a hard look. "I can say with all honesty that you are the first and the only."

"Well, I feel special now," Hayden said.

"You should," Craig muttered. "And now I'll leave you to go to someone who actually wants to get better."

Hayden didn't intentionally try to aggravate the guy, but Craig just needed to give up trying to convince him to do stuff.

"Try to get out of the room at some point today," Craig said as Hayden headed to the bathroom to shower. "It will do you a world of good."

Hayden wasn't sure that was true, but he nodded anyway. Quiet settled over the room when Craig was gone, leaving Hayden alone with his thoughts.

He got showered and dressed as quickly as was possible for him these days, then he grabbed his crutches to make his way to the kitchen, hoping to get himself another cup of coffee. It felt like a multi cup of coffee sort of day.

As he moved into the doorway of the kitchen, his gaze landed on a child sitting at the table.

"Who's this?"

Chapter 2

Leaning on his crutches, Hayden tried to make sense of the little boy who sat dwarfed by a wheelchair at his kitchen table. There was no reason a child—particularly a boy—should be in his apartment right then. A little girl might have made sense as sometimes Hunter brought Rachel or Heather brought Isla.

He looked away from the child to where Paige stood, a dish towel twisted in her hands and a worried look on her face.

"I'm sorry," she said. "This is my son, Rylan. My mom has been helping a friend, so she isn't able to take care of him at the moment."

"Leta's helping someone?" Hayden asked.

Paige nodded. "Her best friend had surgery and can't be on her own yet."

"That sounds like something she'd would do." The older woman had taken great care of him and Hunter over the years, so that she was helping someone else out wasn't a surprise.

"I promise I'll be able to do all my work, even with Rylan here."

Hayden frowned. Did she really think he was worried about that? He'd just been shocked to find a kid he didn't recognize in his apartment, that was all.

He released his grip on one of his crutches and waved his hand. "I don't care about that."

"I'm hoping that Mom will be able to watch him again soon."

"Seriously, Paige, it's fine if he's here." Hayden used his crutches to move to the table. He sat down in the chair across from Rylan. "What have you got there?"

"It's my math book," Rylan said as he tapped it with his pencil.

"Is there no school at the moment?"

Rylan shook his head. "I don't go to school. Mama and Nana teach me."

"Well, that's cool." Homeschooling had never been an option for him, but after hearing some homeschooled kid at church say that he didn't have to do as much schoolwork, he'd tried to convince his mom to give it a whirl. Needless to say, she hadn't. "So do you like math?"

"Most of the time," Rylan said. "Nana hates math, though."

Hayden glanced over at Paige in time to see her grimace. "I don't think my mom likes math much either. She always sent us to my dad when we had problems."

"Mama likes math, so she'll help me with that and science, if I don't understand it."

"Sounds like you have some excellent teachers."

Rylan smiled at him, his brown eyes shining. "I do."

"How about you show me what you're working on right now," Hayden suggested as he moved himself to a chair closer to Rylan.

"Did you come out here for something?" Paige asked before Rylan could say anything.

Hayden stared at her for a moment, trying to recall what it had been that had driven him from his room. "Oh. I was hoping to score another cup of coffee now that Craig has finished torturing me."

"I'll get that for you," she said with a nod.

"Do you have chocolate milk?" Hayden asked.

"Yep. I keep it on hand in case you decide you want it with your coffee."

"I think I'd like half hot chocolate, half coffee. And maybe Rylan would like some hot chocolate?"

"Can I, Mama?" Rylan asked, his eyes going wide. "I haven't had hot chocolate in a long time."

Paige glanced between Hayden and Rylan before nodding. "I'll get that for you both."

Hayden watched for a moment as she began preparing their drinks, then turned his focus back to Rylan. "Now show me what you're working on."

As he listened to Rylan explain what he was doing in his workbook, Hayden wondered why he wasn't more upset about having his space invaded by someone he hadn't given permission to. Normally, he wouldn't have been happy about it, but he trusted Paige. Her son certainly wasn't a risk to his privacy.

Though he'd heard Leta talk about her grandson, he hadn't tied that child to Paige when she'd come to work for him. He hadn't really thought about it at all, if he was going to be completely honest.

He hadn't been thinking too much about other people in the past few months. All he'd cared about when Leta had said she was going to retire was that there would be someone to step in and do her job. When she'd suggested that her daughter be the one to do that, he hadn't argued.

As far as he could tell, Paige had been doing a fine job. The food was great, and the apartment was as clean as it had ever been with Leta. All in all, he was more than happy with Paige's work.

She was also easy to be around, doing her work without disrupting his life.

"Do you use flashcards?" Hayden asked, finding that he was in no rush to return to his room. His plan had been to ask Paige to make him some coffee, then go back to his bed.

"Yep," Rylan said, turning to the backpack that was tucked into the wheelchair beside him.

Looking at the chair, Hayden wondered why he needed it. He couldn't recall when he'd last seen a child in a wheelchair, but given his limited interactions with people of late, that wasn't too surprising.

"Here you go," Paige said, setting mugs down in front of them.

Rylan pulled his mug closer and peered into it, then looked up at Paige with a smile. "Thank you, Mama."

"You're welcome, sweetie." She bent and pressed a kiss to his head. "Don't drink it too fast."

"I won't." He tilted the mug slightly toward him and took a sip. "Yummy."

"Thank you as well," Hayden said, lifting his mug.

As he took a couple sips of his mocha drink, Hayden considered the mother-son pair, who didn't look much alike. Paige had blonde hair and blue eyes, while Rylan had brown curls and light brown eyes. Leta looked much like her daughter, so Hayden assumed that Rylan took after his father.

"Here they are," Rylan said, pushing a stack of cards held together by a rubber band toward him.

Hayden set his mug down and picked up the cards. Their edges were worn, leading him to believe that they were well used.

"Do you know the answers to all of them?"

"No," Rylan said. "But I'm learning them."

"Want me to work on them with you?"

Rylan's eyes widened, then he glanced over at his mom.

"You don't need to do that," Paige said. "He knows how to do it on his own."

"I don't mind," Hayden told her. "It's not like I have a lot on my schedule."

"Okay. If you're sure."

"I'm sure." Hayden removed the band securing the cards and flipped through them to see if they were in any sort of order. When he saw that they weren't, he picked up the top one and held it facing Rylan. He could read the equation and the answer on his side of the card.

Rylan tilted his head as he stared at the card. "Eight."

Hayden nodded, then set the card down and picked up another. For the next several minutes, they worked through the cards.

"How old are you?" Hayden asked after they'd gone through about half of the deck. Rylan got them all right, though for a few of them, he had to use his fingers.

"I'm six," Rylan said. "And in grade one."

He looked small for his age, but perhaps whatever had put him in the wheelchair had impacted his growth. Although Hayden had to admit that he knew precious little about what size kids should be. The only ones he was around these days were Rachel and Isla, and they were a little older than Rylan.

"Do you like school?" Hayden asked.

Rylan frowned. "I like doing my work with Mama and Nana."

"Have you gone to school with other kids?"

"In kindergarten, I went to a school where there were other kids like me." He tapped the arm of his chair. "But then we moved here, and I didn't go to school anymore."

"Do you miss it?"

Rylan's nose wrinkled as he seemed to consider Hayden's question. "I spose. A bit. But it's hard for me in this wheelchair. I can't move around very good. And maybe the kids would tease me because of that."

Hayden thought about how he'd decided to live his life away from the public because he didn't want to deal with people staring at his scars and his need for walking aides. No one teased him, but he just hadn't wanted to have to face the fact that while at one time, people had stared at him because of his good looks, that was no longer the case.

It was bad enough that whenever he saw his twin brother, he was reminded of what he'd used to look like. He didn't need the stares of people to add to it.

"Do you like to be around kids your age?" Hayden asked.

"Not if they're mean or point at me and laugh." Rylan's shoulders slumped. "I'm nice. I never say mean things. I just want them to be like that to me too."

Hayden rubbed at the sudden ache in his chest. "Sometimes people don't know how to act around others who are different from them."

Rylan looked at him for a moment before looking back at his mug of cocoa. "Are people mean to you too?"

"I'm not around people long enough for them to be mean to me. Usually I'm just with my family."

"Like me." Rylan gave him a small smile. "Do you go to school?"

"Not anymore. I do some work for my family's company."

"What do you do?" Rylan asked.

"I work in digital marketing. Do you know what that is?"

Rylan shook his head. "I'm just a kid."

Hayden chuckled, realizing as he did that he couldn't remember the last time he'd found humor in anything. "Marketing is how we reach people to tell them about what we do or what products we have for them. Do you watch the commercials on television?"

Rylan nodded. "For candy and toys?"

"Exactly. Those companies want to tell you about their candy hoping you'll go buy it."

"Nana says they're evil, tempting her while she's on a diet," Rylan announced. "So, do you make candy commercials? Cause Nana might not be happy with you, if you do."

Hayden laughed again. "No, I don't make candy commercials."

"What do you make them for?"

Given that the boy was only six, Hayden wasn't sure he'd understand since their company was so diverse, it wasn't as simple as advertising a single product. "Right now, I don't actually make the advertising stuff myself. I oversee the work that other people do to make sure it's the best it can be."

His position in the company wasn't what his dad had wanted it to be. From very early on, they'd all known that they'd have a role in the company one day. When they'd finished high school and gone on to college, they'd each gotten degrees that could be used within the company. Hunter had taken business and finance courses. Heather had also gotten a business degree with a focus on human resources.

Hayden hadn't had a real interest in the business side of things, so he'd left college with a degree in marketing. Before the accident, he'd been in the marketing department, but he'd had a lousy work ethic. Him being responsible for the department had seemed a long way off, and he hadn't wanted to stress about it while he was still in his early twenties.

It had taken awhile after the accident to get back to it, but he'd eventually begun to do more work in the marketing department. He now had a small team that he worked with. They weren't the most experienced employees, and their projects weren't the most important, but he could manage them remotely. It was the only reason he'd agreed to take on the position.

Rylan seemed to consider his words before nodding. "Are you important?"

Well, wasn't that the question of the day? Or maybe even the year. He hadn't ever felt like he needed to be important, but now he felt like he didn't deserve to be important. "No. I'm not important."

"Hi, Mama," Rylan said, looking past Hayden.

"Are you done with your math?" Paige asked as she approached the table.

"Not yet."

"That's my fault," Hayden said. "We were doing the flashcards, then got to talking. I'll help him finish his work."

"He should be able to do it himself if he focuses." She gave her son a stern look. "He enjoys distractions a little too much."

Rylan gave her a sheepish smile. "Sorry, Mama. I'll finish it."

Paige ran her hand through his hair. "If you have questions, maybe Hayden can help you."

"Hopefully, I can. I mean, it's been quite a few years since I did first grade math, but I think I should be able to manage."

The woman gave a huff of laughter as she picked up his now-empty mug. "Do you want another cup of coffee?"

"I probably shouldn't," Hayden said with a sigh. "I think it's becoming an addiction."

"If you change your mind, let me know."

She returned to the kitchen, leaving the two of them on their own to tackle math.

Rylan showed him what he'd been working on before Hayden had appeared, and it was easy to see that he had a firm grasp of the subject.

"Mama says I have to be neat. That math needs me to be neat."

"That's very true," Hayden said as he watched him print out his answer to an addition problem. "The numbers need to line up or you might add the wrong ones together."

"It's hard to be neat sometimes," Rylan said, his head bent over the book. "I try though. Just like I try not to color outside the lines in my coloring books."

"Do you have them here with you?" Hayden asked, then realized he was distracting the boy again.

"I can show you when I'm done. Mama said I can color a page once I'm finished with these two pages."

"Sounds like a plan."

Hayden watched as Rylan continued to work his way steadily through the problems. He seemed like a pretty smart kid. He hoped that if he did go to school, he didn't run into any issues with the kids. Hayden recalled the problems Isla had had when she'd had to start a new school after going live with her uncle when her mom passed away.

Hayden remembered what it was like when he'd been in school. The new kids and the kids with differences had never been treated well. It was unfortunate to learn that none of that had changed over the years.

"Mama, I'm done," Rylan called out a few minutes later. "Can I color?"

Paige came over, drying her hands on a towel. "Did you have any problems?"

"Nope. I did perfect."

"Are you sure?" Paige leaned over Rylan to look at his book, her blonde braid sliding forward over her shoulder. She appeared to skim over his answers before kissing his head. "I'll check again at home, but it seems like it's all right."

"Yay!" Rylan punched the air with his small fist. "So I can color now?"

"Yep. One page and then you need to do some reading."

Hayden waited for him to protest reading like Isla did, but apparently, Rylan didn't have a huge issue with it because he just nodded, then dug into his backpack. He pulled out a thick coloring book with cars on the front.

"Do you like cars?" Hayden asked.

Rylan looked over at him as he put a worn box of crayons on the table. "I *love* cars."

"I love them too."

The boy's eyes went wide at his revelation. "Really? What kind of car is your favorite?"

Hayden didn't have a favorite, per se. He liked different cars for different reasons. Not sure that Rylan would understand that, he went with the one he'd aspired to own before the accident. "I'd like a Lamborghini. How about you?"

He grinned, then poked at the picture on the front of the book. "A race car like McQueen."

"I guess you've seen the movie?" Hayden asked with a laugh.

Rylan grinned. "Yes! I loved it."

"Why do you like cars so much?"

Rylan's brow furrowed for a minute. "They're kind of like my wheelchair. I just wish I zip around fast like McQueen."

Hayden watched as the boy flipped through the coloring book, thinking what it must be like to not be in control of one's own movements. At least he could move himself around on his crutches. He was pretty sure that there were powered wheelchairs available, which made him wonder why Rylan didn't have one.

Chapter 3

It took awhile for Paige's heart to settle back down to a reasonable rate. When Hayden had asked who Rylan was, Paige had visions of losing her job, which would have meant losing the medical insurance she relied on for Rylan. That would have been catastrophic for them.

Hayden seemed to have accepted Rylan's presence, but that didn't mean there wouldn't still be repercussions. She wouldn't breathe easy until they left for the day without Hayden firing her. And if her mom had to stay with Donna for another day, maybe Paige could drop Rylan off with them.

She would do whatever she had to in order to keep the job. Her mom had sacrificed it for her, knowing that Paige needed the insurance that came with it more than she did. She'd accepted the mess that Paige's life had become without complaint, welcoming them into her small house when they'd had nowhere else to go.

As she prepared Hayden's lunch, she could hear the two of them talking about cars. Rylan's favorite subject.

Once Hayden's lunch was cooking—a burger with potato wedges—she went to get Rylan's backpack. She opened it and took out the ham and cheese sandwich she'd packed for him before leaving that morning. He had also requested grapes, which was no surprise. The boy loved grapes any way he could get them. Cut up in yogurt. As raisins. Frozen. And his favorite way, just by themselves.

She had a thermos of milk for him as well. Though milk wasn't his favorite, she tried to get him to drink it more than juice.

As Paige put his food on a plate, she hoped he didn't make a comment about Hayden eating a burger and fries, especially since he didn't love ham and cheese sandwiches. He would much rather eat peanut butter and jam, but they'd run out of his favorite jam earlier in the week, and she'd forgotten to add it to the grocery order.

She took Rylan his food first, sitting in the chair next to his. "Let's say a prayer for your food."

Rylan took her hand and bowed his head. "Thank you, Jesus, for this food. May it nourish my body. Please be with Nana's friend and make her feel better soon. Amen."

"Amen." Paige squeezed his hand, then got up. She looked at Hayden. "Your meal is almost ready. Will you be eating here or in your room?"

"Oh, I'll keep Rylan company, I think."

She nodded, then went back to the stove, where she checked to make sure the burger was ready. Moving quickly, she plated it up, adding the things she knew Hayden liked, then put the potato wedges onto the plate. She carried it with a glass of water to where Hayden sat.

"Thank you," he said as he took both items from her. "Smells good."

"Hope it tastes as good."

"I'm sure it will. You haven't disappointed yet."

She was glad to hear that, since she doubted she was as good a cook as her mom. Paige glanced at Rylan, not surprised to see him frowning as he took in the burger Hayden had to eat. "Eat up, sweetie."

Rylan nodded, though the frown didn't clear from his face. She waited until he picked up his sandwich and took a bite, then she went back to clean up the dishes she'd dirtied in making the meal.

From her place in the kitchen, she could hear them talking more about the cars as they ate. Paige had never been very interested in them herself, but she always listened to Rylan when he talked about them. It seemed like something a dad would have done with a child that was interested in cars, especially if the mom wasn't a car person. But Rylan didn't have that, so Paige tried to pick up the slack.

It was nice that Hayden seemed to like cars and know what he was talking about.

When Rylan called to let her know he was done, she went and collected his plate. "Now you need to do some reading, sweetie. Go through the next story in your reader, okay?"

"Yep," he agreed readily.

For the most part, he didn't protest schoolwork too much. Which was good, because she didn't want to have to argue with him about it in front of Hayden.

After he'd finished eating, Hayden went back to his room. Paige assumed that he'd probably had all the socialization he could handle, even if it was with a child.

The rest of the afternoon passed quietly, with her teaching Rylan in between different chores around the apartment and starting Hayden's dinner.

"Pack up your stuff, sweetie," Paige told Rylan as she prepped the tray with Hayden's dinner. "We'll be leaving soon."

When she reached Hayden's room with the tray, she found him at the small table with his laptop. The TV was on, but he muted it, shifting his attention to her as she entered the room.

"Do you want to eat at the table?" she asked.

He nodded, moving his laptop to the side. She took the plate and glass off the tray and set it on the table. "Was there anything else you needed before I left?"

"No. I think I'm fine." He glanced at the plate, then looked back at her. "By the way, feel free to bring Rylan back as often as you need to. It wasn't a bother to have him here today."

Relief filled Paige. "Thank you. I really appreciate that as I'm not sure Mom will be able to take care of him tomorrow."

"Well, whether it's tomorrow or any other day, don't worry if you need to bring Rylan."

"That's a real relief, to be honest."

"No one here's gonna fault you for needing to take care of your kid."

Maybe not at Hayden's, but there certainly were some places that would. "Well, if you don't need anything else, I'll see you tomorrow."

"Have a good night."

"You too."

Back in the kitchen, she found Rylan staring out the large window. He'd been in a similar position a few times that day, entranced by the view of the city from so far up.

"So many lights, Mama," he said. "It's beautiful."

"It is," Paige agreed. After putting the dishes she'd used to prepare Hayden's meal in the dishwasher, she started it up. She did a final wipe down of all the counters, then helped Rylan into his winter wear before putting on her own.

With the time change a couple of weeks earlier, the sun was setting around five, which meant that it was dark as they left the apartment. The drive home took forever, it seemed, but thankfully, Rylan enjoyed riding in the car, so he didn't complain.

When they finally reached the small house she shared with her mom, Paige carried Rylan inside and set him on his favorite chair before returning to get his wheelchair and backpack. No scent of dinner cooking greeted them, which didn't bode well for finding her mom at home. Usually she was the one who cooked their meals, since Paige was out of the house all day.

After getting Rylan out of his jacket, she gave him his tablet, then went into the kitchen. As she contemplated what to make for dinner, she sent a text to her mom.

How's Donna?

Mom: *Still dealing with dizziness and nausea. I think I'm going to need to stay here with her for the night and tomorrow.*

That wasn't what she wanted to hear, but Paige wasn't going to make her mom feel bad about helping her best friend. She just hoped that Hayden didn't change his mind about Rylan coming to work with her.

I'm sorry to hear that she's not feeling better. Do you need anything?

Mom: *Nope. She's well stocked here. We'll be fine. How was work?*

It went fine. Rylan did great with the stuff we took for him. Hayden hung out with him for a while.

Mom: *Well, that makes me happy!*

Her mom had worked for Hayden and Hunter for several years and had a special place in her heart for Hayden. When Hayden had been injured in the car accident that had killed his father, her mom had worried endlessly about the man. Every conversation they'd had on the phone, her mom had spoken about Hayden and his struggles.

Because they'd become invested in his recovery, it was hard to see him the way he was now. Earlier that year—just after Paige had taken over for her mom—she'd seen hope in Hayden's expressions. He'd been looking forward to the surgery that was to have been the last in a long line of them.

No one could have foreseen what was to follow or the time Hayden would end up having to spend in the hospital. Paige had—at Hunter's request—continued to go to the apartment every day, even though it was empty. She appreciated that he hadn't laid her off, and she'd filled her time cleaning the apartment from top to bottom... over and over again.

I was a little worried at first, but it was fine.

Mom: *I'm glad to hear that.*

Mom: *Well, I'd better go. I need to see if Donna will eat something.*

Okay. Have a good night. Love you!

Mom: *Love you too! Give Rylan a hug from me.*

After telling her she would, Paige set her phone down on the counter. Rylan was watching a video on his tablet, happy to entertain himself while she made them supper. She was glad that he'd been able to do all his schoolwork, even with the change up with their schedules. It definitely would have been easier if he'd been in school, but that wasn't the decision she'd made.

He'd been in part-time kindergarten at a private school in Chicago that had aides to help students with special needs—whether they were physical, emotional, or mental. But after the divorce and everything that had had happened afterward, they'd had to move to Minneapolis, and she'd no longer been able to afford a private school like that.

Because she'd moved him with only a few months left in the school year, Paige had decided to just teach him herself. Then, when grade one was about to start, she struggled with the idea of putting him into a school without people who understood what was required to work with kids who had needs like Rylan had.

Because of that, she and her mom worked together to school him at home, and as far as she could tell, he was doing really well. The only problem was that she hadn't done a very good job of finding him kids to socialize with, though Rylan didn't seem to care. She did try to take him places like museums and the zoo that brought him in contact with other kids.

Paige knew it was important that he learn to function in the world, but she couldn't help but want to protect him when he was so little. He still didn't know how to move himself around very well in his wheelchair or how to take care of his own needs.

"What's for supper, Mama?" Rylan asked from where he sat. "I'm hungry."

"Soup and crackers."

"Yum!"

The rest of the evening went smoothly, and even without her mom there, they kept to their nighttime routine. Rylan fell right to sleep in his small bed in the corner of the room they shared.

It would have been difficult to hear that her mom needed to stay with Donna if Hayden hadn't said that she could bring Rylan with her. Still, she missed her mom, and with Rylan asleep, the house felt a bit empty.

Until moving to Minneapolis, she'd been able to focus on Rylan without having to worry about a job. Now, each day, she struggled with the guilt of not being there for him as she had been before. She knew her mom took excellent care of him, and she also shouldered the at-home stuff, so when Paige got home from work, she had little to do except spend time with Rylan.

With her mom gone, Paige didn't have any downtime until Rylan was in bed, and even then, she was doing some of the household chores, so things didn't pile up.

Thanksgiving was later that week, and she wasn't looking forward to it. Her main issue with the holiday was that she felt very little thankfulness again that year. The previous Thanksgiving, she'd still been trying to pick up the pieces of her broken life. In the space of six months, the world she'd been building for herself and Rylan had been totally wrecked. And just when she'd thought things couldn't get worse, they had.

Where things were going to go for her and Rylan, Paige still didn't know. She felt like she had no direction, and she had no idea where to even start putting her life back together.

The next morning, things weren't off to a good start. Rylan had had a bad night as well, waking several times. Sometimes nightmares plagued him, and though Paige had tried, she couldn't get to the root of them.

He was subdued as she got everything ready for their day, refusing to eat breakfast before they left. At least he was cooperative and did as she asked, putting on his jacket, knit cap, and mittens without complaint.

The apartment was quiet when they arrived, so Paige got Rylan settled at the table and started on Hayden's breakfast. In between the waffles she was making, she prepared oatmeal for Rylan. She added some raisins, hoping that would entice him to eat.

She had a feeling that there wouldn't be much schoolwork done that day. And from the way he was acting, he'd probably end up wanting a nap soon.

"Please eat, okay, buddy?" she said as she set the oatmeal in front of him. "I put raisins in it."

He looked up and gave her a tired smile as he grasped the spoon. "Thanks, Mama."

Paige knew that despite feeling like her world had fallen apart over the past year, she was extremely blessed to have Rylan. She was grateful, too, that he wasn't angry and frustrated about his limitations. He seemed to accept them with a maturity that was far beyond his years. Not that he didn't comment at times that he wished his legs worked, but he usually did it with more wistfulness than anger.

She bent and pressed a kiss to his hair before returning to the waffle iron. While she cooked the remaining waffles, Paige prepared the tray for Hayden.

When everything was ready, she went to his room and began the getting Hayden's day started. Thankfully, she didn't have to do anything beyond that. Though she'd cared for Rylan and his physical needs, Paige had never aspired to be a nurse.

All she needed to do for Hayden was cook his food and clean his home. If he needed any sort of medical care, a nurse came by, though that hadn't happened since the first little while after he'd come home from the hospital.

It was a job that she could do easily enough, but her heart wished for more. If she'd had to work a job, she wished that it could have been the job she'd been going to school for. At times, she longed for the dreams that had fallen by the wayside with the trauma of Rylan's birth and later the divorce and what followed. She'd had to set those dreams aside and would have to continue to do so for the foreseeable future.

Hayden was slow to wake that morning, and he had few words for her beyond a gruff greeting. Once he was lucid, she settled the tray over his legs, then left him to eat.

"I ate almost all the oatmeal," Rylan said when he saw her, tipping the bowl so she could see it.

"Good job, sweetie. Do you want to color for a bit?"

When he nodded, she helped him get his book and crayons out of his backpack. She decided not to press him on school unless he asked about it. Missing a day wouldn't hurt him, and they could do extra work on the days they were at home for Thanksgiving.

Craig arrived shortly afterwards and disappeared into Hayden's room while Paige cleaned up the kitchen. When she noticed Rylan fading, she grabbed the small blanket she'd brought in anticipation of that, then carried him into the living room.

"Why don't you try to nap for a bit?" she suggested as she settled him on the couch with the blanket. "I'll stay in here with you."

He maneuvered himself around a bit to get comfortable against the back of the big couch, then watched her with drooping eyes as she cleaned the living room. Not that it ever got dirty, since she cleaned it frequently.

By the time she was done, Rylan had fallen asleep, and Paige hoped he stayed that way for an hour or more.

She was on her way to the kitchen when Craig appeared, said goodbye, then left. They'd never really talked, and that was fine with Paige. They each had a role to play in Hayden's world, and she suspected that Craig viewed her as the housekeeper and nothing more. And he'd be right.

When her mom had started to work for Hunter and Hayden several years earlier, Paige had been thrilled for her. She'd been a housewife since the day she'd married Paige's dad and had continued to be one until his untimely death, when Paige was in her last year of high school. Her younger brother had been sixteen, and their father's death had sent him down a road that had brought much heartache for her mom.

Unfortunately, with her husband's death, her mom had needed a way to support herself. After some less than stellar jobs, landing the position cooking and cleaning for Hunter and Hayden had seemed like an answer to prayer for her mom.

Paige struggled with a great deal of guilt whenever she had less than positive thoughts about her job at the apartment because her mom had given up the job she loved for Paige and Rylan's sake.

"Is Rylan not here today?"

Paige looked up from where she was kneeling in front of a cupboard to put away the cleaning supplies she'd been using. "He's taking a nap on the couch. He didn't sleep so well last night."

Hayden frowned as he leaned on his crutches. "Does he have pain?"

She got to her feet and closed the cupboard. "Not that he's said. Usually it's nightmares that wake him up, and then he has a hard time getting back to sleep."

"How did he end up in the wheelchair?" Hayden asked.

It wasn't the first time Paige had been asked the question, and she didn't mind answering it. She'd rather they asked it of her than Rylan, as he didn't really understand it just yet.

"Birth injury," she said. "Something occurred during his delivery that paralyzed him from the waist down."

His frown deepened even further. "And it's permanent?"

"They didn't think it would be. Injuries like that can occasionally resolve themselves in time in infants—or so they told me—but that didn't happen for Rylan."

"I hope you got a good settlement," he said.

His words were like a dump of gasoline on the banked fire that constantly burned inside her. "I did, but his father decided he deserved the money more than Rylan."

"What do you mean?"

Paige hesitated, wondering how much she should share. "He decided he didn't want a disabled son, so he divorced me and gave up his parental rights, then he disappeared with all the settlement money."

Chapter 4

Hayden could hardly believe what Paige had just revealed. "He stole your money?"

"I guess he thought it was his for suffering through having a disabled son and a wife who devoted her time to their child." Her words dripped with disdain. "Apparently it wasn't how he saw his life unfolding. So he got himself a girlfriend and a divorce, took the money, and vanished to live the life he thought he deserved."

"Did the police get involved?"

"Yes. They tried to trace the money, but the trail went cold. He's an accountant, so I guess he knew how to transfer the money in such a way as to avoid being tracked. Or maybe he had help. I don't know. All I know is that he took what wasn't his."

Hayden shifted on his crutches, angry at what had been done to Paige and Rylan. "Did you hire a private detective to find him?"

Paige stared at him for a moment, her brows lifted. "I would have loved to, but sadly, I couldn't find anyone that would take cookies or coloring book pictures of cars as payment."

Hayden grimaced. Could he have been more clueless or insensitive? Of course, she'd have no money if her ex had absconded with it all. And he didn't think she was earning a ton of money cooking and cleaning for him. Maybe he should talk to Hunter about what he was paying her.

"Sorry," he said, wanting her to know that he hadn't meant to come across so cavalier. "That was thoughtless of me."

She shrugged. "You just have a different perspective on things."

"True, but that doesn't mean I shouldn't be sensitive to the situations of others. My siblings would both smack me across the back of my head for being stupid."

Paige crossed her arms but didn't comment on his remark. "Rylan, thankfully, isn't in pain."

"Does he miss his dad?"

"He says he doesn't, and that might be the truth since my ex had little to do with him even before the divorce. There was no fight from him when I asked for full physical and legal custody." She frowned. "He even signed away his parental rights with my blessing. I didn't think I'd need child support since I had the settlement, and I didn't need someone having a say in Rylan's life who didn't love and care about him."

"So he got everything he wanted," Hayden said. "His freedom and the money."

"Yep. The man not only robbed his son of the money that was rightfully his, but he happily abdicated all responsibility for him."

"I wouldn't call him a man then," Hayden said. "Because he gives decent men everywhere a bad name. From this point on, he shall be known as the scoundrel."

A small smile tugged at the corners of Paige's mouth. "I have to say that's a name I haven't called him yet, and I've called him every other name in the book for what he's done to Rylan."

"What about what's he done to you?"

Paige shrugged. "Honestly, I don't care about that. After Rylan was born, I saw a side to him I didn't much like when he seemed to reject his own son. When I'd mention it to him, he just got mad at me, and we began to fight more. He cheated more than once, so really, the divorce was a relief for me. I figured that as long as I was careful with the settlement money, Rylan and I would be fine."

"And then the settlement money was gone."

Paige's brow furrowed as her gaze shifted away from him. "Yeah. Then the money was gone."

"For what it's worth, I'm sorry you've had to deal with his actions."

"Thanks." She gestured to the kitchen. "Anyway, I'd better get back to work."

Hayden nodded, though he wanted to remind her that since he was technically her boss, he could talk with her as long as he wanted, and she wouldn't get in trouble. However, given the subject of their conversation, he imagined that she'd had enough talking for the time being.

He turned on his crutches and headed for the living room, though he'd originally been on his way to the kitchen. Moving as quietly as he could, Hayden made his way to an armchair near the window opposite where Rylan lay on the couch.

As he watched the boy sleep, he mulled over what Paige had revealed. Finally, he pulled his phone out and brought up his contacts. He found the name he wanted, then sent a text.

Hey Kent! Can you do a full background check on a Paige Cantor? ASAP would be great. Thanks!

Hayden figured that if anyone could get the information he wanted, it would be their head of security at King Enterprises. If the man couldn't get it himself, he'd know who could. Hayden trusted him completely.

Kent Security: *I'll get right on that. Anything in particular I should look for?*

Hayden considered what Paige had told him before answering. *Any information about her ex-husband would be great.*

Since she had a different last name than her mom, Hayden figured she still carried her married name. That was probably even more likely since she'd no doubt want to keep the same last name as her son.

Kent Security: *Will do.*

Hayden thanked the man, ignoring the twinge of conscience at the thought that Paige might not thank him for interfering in her life. However, he had connections that could dig deeper and in ways that police might not be able to… legally. It seemed wrong to not try to help Paige if he could.

She and Rylan deserved that money, and her ex-husband most certainly did not.

Though he hoped he would hear from Kent soon, he knew that it would take some time. Kent would understand that he wasn't looking for just a surface level inquiry. By the time the man was done, Hayden would probably have access to more information about Paige than anyone else. However, he mainly wanted to know about her ex so that he could have someone look into him.

As he continued to sit in the chair, he received a text from Hunter.

Hunter: *Just wanted to check what time you were planning to come to Mom's for Thanksgiving.*

Hayden's knee-jerk response was, *I'm not coming.* He felt like he had even less to be thankful for than he had in the past. But he knew that if he said that, Hunter would just show up and bug him until he gave in. Plus, his mom would be upset if he didn't go.

Though he liked Carissa and Rachel and Ash and Isla, it was hard to see his siblings finding love and happily moving forward in their lives. He'd thought that this year would be his year to gain a bit of happiness for himself. The year where he would finally be free of the pain from his badly fractured leg. One last surgery, and they would have been done at last.

Immediately following the accident, he'd had so much damage done to his body that it had been touch and go as to whether he'd even survive. They'd done surgery for the most life-threatening situations, but he hadn't been strong enough to undergo any other surgeries as they waited to see if he was going to pull through. Because of that, other injuries in his body healed badly, like the broken bones he'd sustained in his legs, shoulder, ribs and arms.

Once he'd healed sufficiently from his most serious wounds, they'd worked their way through the rest of his injuries. His broken body should have been made whole with this last surgery. After he'd healed from the repairs they did, he should have been able to walk without aid, though he'd still probably have limped. That would have been fine, as long as the pain was basically gone.

But apparently God had decided that he hadn't suffered enough.

Sighing, Hayden thought over the next few days, then tapped out a reply to Hunter.

Probably come over Thurs morning.

Hunter: *Are you going to stay overnight? Mom wants us all to help her decorate the tree on Friday.*

His mom liked to have them all under her roof for holidays and special occasions. Usually, that meant spending one or more nights with her. He almost wished that she didn't have enough room for all of them, so he'd have an excuse to come home. But sadly, because she still lived in their large family home—mansion, really—she had plenty of space.

He didn't enjoy spending nights away from his apartment, but he would do it for her. *I'll stay Thursday night.*

Hunter: *Great! I'll send George to get you Thursday morning.*

Hayden sent him back a thumbs up, hoping that was the end of the conversation. But of course, it wasn't.

Hunter: *Have you made an appointment yet?*

Hayden ran through several responses, including appointment for what? He knew that Hunter wouldn't buy him pretending to not know what he was talking about.

No.

Hunter: *Dude, you've been saying that for months. You have until December 31st to sort it out for yourself. If you don't get it done, I'm going to make the appointment myself and drag you to it.*

Hayden would like to dare him to try, but long gone were the days when they were fairly equal in physical abilities. Before, if they went head-to-head physically, it was a tossup which one of them would win. Not anymore, unfortunately.

We shall see.

Hayden knew shouldn't call Hunter's bluff because the guy was equal parts stubborn and determined. He didn't know what had prompted Hunter to threaten him so boldly. Usually, he was much more subtle.

Hayden shifted his gaze away from the messages and stared out the window. It was a bright, clear day, but he had no idea how cold it was. Since he rarely went outside anymore, he didn't even check the temperature. There was snow on the tops of buildings, so he knew it wasn't warm.

Rylan could probably tell him what the weather was like.

He looked at the sofa where the little boy slept. It was hard to imagine what it must be like to be so young and dealing with a disability. Had Rylan accepted it more easily because he'd never known anything different?

Hayden lifted his hand and rubbed the scar on his face that ran from his ear down by his mouth to his chin. Though no one had asked, he was sure that his family wondered why he hadn't gone to a plastic surgeon to have work done to fix the scar.

He'd gone through other surgeries because the pain had been unbearable. And while he still had some pain where the bones had been broken, it was manageable. But the scar? The stump? They didn't cause him pain. At least not physical, and he wasn't so sure that he didn't deserve the mental pain that looking at them brought him.

He'd made some progress with his therapist during the early years. She'd been trying to help him move past the mindset that he deserved what had happened to him. And for a while, he'd been willing to consider that maybe that was true.

But then, just as he was getting to where he thought that maybe she was right, everything had happened with his leg. It felt as if it had been a reminder that he wasn't allowed to move past that day. That for as long as he lived, he would remember that he was responsible for what happened on that icy highway six years ago.

Swallowing hard, Hayden had just decided that perhaps it was time to go back to his bedroom when he heard a little voice.

"Hayden?"

Clearing his throat, he looked over at Rylan to find him awake but still burry-eyed. "Hey, buddy."

"I took a nap."

"Yeah. Your mom said you didn't sleep very well last night."

Rylan frowned. "Bad dreams."

"Do you want to tell me what they're about?"

"Just monsters." His brow furrowed. "And sometimes I dream that something happens to Mama."

Hayden had no doubt that Rylan and Paige were really close, what with it being just the two of them. And losing Paige would devastate Rylan.

"Should I let your mom know that you're awake?"

"Yes, please."

Hayden got up on his crutches, then made his way to the kitchen where Paige had the entire contents of the fridge out on the counter. "Hey, Paige."

She poked her head around the fridge door. "What can I do for you?"

"Two things," he said, leaning forward to brace his weight on his crutches. "First, Rylan is awake."

"Oh." Paige moved toward the sink with the cloth she'd been using. "I'll just get him settled at the table."

"Is he doing his schoolwork today?" Hayden asked.

"Probably not," Paige said as she rinsed out the cloth. "When he's been up through the night like he was last night, it's hard to get him to focus."

"Has he seen any of the *Lego* movies? Or the *Cars* ones?"

"He's seen some of them."

"Would you mind if he hung out with me in the theater room to watch some movies? Kid appropriate ones, of course."

"You want to watch kid movies with Rylan?" Paige asked, her tone incredulous.

Hayden shrugged. "I don't have much else going on today, and honestly, some of those kid movies are highly entertaining. Even for adults."

"I mean... if you're sure..."

"I am," he assured her.

Paige wiped her hands on a dishtowel, then followed him back into the living room. Rylan had pushed himself up into a sitting position and was staring out the window.

"Hi, sweetie," Paige said as she approached him. A smile wreathed Rylan's face when he spotted his mom. "Do you want something to eat or drink?"

"A drink, please."

"Would you like to watch a movie?" Paige asked as she sat down on the couch beside him.

Rylan's eyes grew wide. "A movie? What movie?"

"Maybe one of the *Cars* movies or a *Lego* one?"

"I would love that!"

"Okay. Hayden has a movie room, and he'll watch the movie with you."

"Cool!"

"There are comfy chairs in there," Hayden said. "Unless he'd prefer his wheelchair."

"I'll carry him and see if he's okay with what's there."

Hayden wished that he could offer to carry Rylan for her. But instead, he could only lead them to the room where he spent a lot of his time.

"This is *amazing*," Rylan said, his voice hushed as he took in the room.

Hayden gestured to where he usually sat. "This is my favorite chair."

Paige set Rylan down in the one next to it. "Is this okay, sweetie?"

"It's great, Mom," Rylan said with a big grin.

She adjusted the blanket Rylan had carried in, making sure to cover his legs.

"What movie do you want to watch?" Hayden asked.

"Any movie?"

"Well, your mom has to approve it."

That didn't dim Rylan's excitement at all as he said, "I want to watch *Cars*."

"That okay, Mom?" Hayden asked with a glance at Paige, figuring it would be but checking just to be sure.

"Yeah. That's fine."

Hayden scrolled through his phone to find the movie before casting it up onto the large screen on the wall in front of them through the projector he'd set up. He didn't start it right away, though.

"Can I bring you anything to eat or drink?" Paige asked. "A cup of coffee, perhaps?"

Hayden gave her a look, then smiled a bit, feeling the scar pull at the action. "Okay. Coffee, please."

"I'll be right back."

He could hear her chuckling as she left the room. Hayden adjusted the lighting in the room, lowering it but not to the level of total darkness he usually watched movies in.

When Paige returned, she had a tray with a couple of travel mugs on it. He recognized the tall one as being one he'd used before, but the other had kid friendly colors on it.

"Coffee for you, sir," she said as she handed him the silver travel mug. "And chocolate milk for you, young sir."

Rylan giggled as he took the cup from her. "Thanks, Mama."

"And here are some cookies for you to enjoy." She set a plate on the small table between the recliners. "Let me know if you need anything else."

"Thanks, Paige."

"Have fun." She leaned over to press a kiss on Rylan's hair, then left the room.

Hayden noticed she left the door open, but he certainly didn't blame her for that. He had a feeling she'd be checking on Rylan regularly. That was fine by Hayden. Also fine by him was watching movies that allowed him to remember being a young boy again. It threw him back to a time that was full of joy and happiness.

Those memories were welcome in a way they hadn't been in a long, long time.

Chapter 5

Paige wasn't sure what to make of Hayden's offer to watch kids' movies with Rylan. As she did her work around the apartment—cleaning bedrooms that no one used—she would peek into the theater room. It did her heart some good to hear the laughter from Rylan, and even some low chuckles from Hayden.

Rylan had never had a great role model. The only male relative they had left was her brother, and unless he changed, he wasn't someone she wanted Rylan to look up to. But here was a man that she hadn't really given much thought to beyond the work she did for him, willing to spend time with her son. For all that she might not understand other things about Hayden King, she could appreciate him for that.

She also appreciated the job he provided for her, though she had to admit that there were days she was a bit bored with it. Cooking and cleaning had never been what she'd aspired to do with her life. But life didn't always end up the way a person hoped.

As lunch time neared, Paige prepared food for the pair. Once it was ready, she went to the theater room.

"Is the movie almost over?" she asked.

Both of them turned toward her, then Hayden said, "We're just starting the second one."

"Can you put it on pause while you eat some lunch?"

"Sure. We can do that." The figures on the screen froze, then the lights in the room brightened. "Let's go eat."

Paige lifted Rylan up, then Hayden followed her out of the room. They went to the table in the kitchen, where she settled Rylan in a chair there.

She set a plate with a turkey clubhouse on it in front of Hayden, then got the grilled cheese she'd made Rylan using the bread and cheese she'd brought from home. She planned to make herself one after they were done eating.

As they ate, she cleaned up the kitchen, listening as the pair discussed the movie they'd watched already. She had to smile when she heard Hayden talking about the first time he'd seen the movie.

Whenever Rylan had asked his dad to watch a movie with him, Glenn had brushed him off. She had watched movies with him, but she'd always felt bad that her husband hadn't because there wasn't a lot that Rylan could do. It was such a little thing that he could have done with his son, and yet he couldn't even be bothered to do it.

Once they were done eating, Paige knew that she couldn't let Rylan go back to watching the movie without tending to some personal stuff first. "Let's go to the bathroom before you watch the movie."

Rylan frowned but didn't argue, knowing that it was important. She put him in his chair and wheeled him into the guest bathroom.

Thankfully, it was a large room, so maneuvering the chair wasn't an issue. Once in place, she washed her hands thoroughly, then checked his ostomy bag. She was able to do what she needed to quickly, since she'd been doing it for a long time.

Rylan submitted to everything without complaint. He'd learned that when it came to things like that, it was easier to just let Paige do what was necessary. She knew that as he got older, dealing with those types of things was going to be more challenging.

But that was a bridge to cross in the future. For now, he was cooperative, and soon they were done, and he could go back to the movie room with Hayden. Paige cleaned up their dishes, then quickly prepared her own sandwich and sat down at the table to eat it.

The rest of her day passed pretty much as usual, though she took a couple of breaks to bring drinks and popcorn to the movie room. She had a feeling that Rylan would say that this had been the best day he'd had in a long time. Paige was pretty sure that he was going to ask if he could come back again. And again. And again.

Unfortunately, he still had to do schoolwork most days. Though he was only in grade one, it was still important that he do his work. If she ever hoped to have him return to mainstream schooling, she didn't want him to be behind his classmates.

"Time to get ready to go, buddy," Paige said once their latest movie had ended.

"Do we have to?" Rylan asked, his voice edging toward whining.

"Yep. We need to get home. Nana should be there." She'd texted a couple of times with her mom, and Page was glad when she'd said Donna didn't need her to stay the night.

"Can I watch more movies tomorrow?"

Paige glanced at Hayden for a moment before she said, "Maybe. We'll have to see."

Rylan frowned, but he didn't say anything more. Paige picked him up and returned him to the wheelchair in the hallway.

Hayden followed them to the foyer, where she helped Rylan into his winter stuff.

"You're more than welcome to bring him back again," Hayden said. "Anytime."

Paige flashed him a smile. "If I bring him back, no movies, though. At least not until after he's done his schoolwork."

Hayden let go of the handle of one of his crutches and lifted his hand in the air. "I promise. No movies until after the schoolwork is done."

Paige laughed as she shook her head. "We'll see."

"See you tomorrow," Hayden said with a wave of his hand.

Rylan called out goodbye as she opened the door, then pushed his wheelchair into the hallway.

All the way home, Rylan chattered on and on about what he'd watched that day with Hayden.

"He's so cool, Mama," Rylan declared from the back seat. "I like him."

"I'm glad, sweetheart." And she was—sort of—though she wasn't sure how much she'd encourage Rylan to spend time with Hayden.

She really didn't want Hayden alleviating his boredom with Rylan because what would happen when he got bored with Rylan and watching kids' movies? There was no doubt that Hayden enjoyed watching movies—he'd done plenty of it in the time she'd been working there—but that didn't mean he wanted to watch a bunch that were made for kids.

When they got home, she was happy to see her mom. Paige felt a sense of relief at having her there again. And the smell of a dinner that she hadn't had to cook was amazing.

"Why don't you tell Nana about your day?" Paige said as she wheeled Rylan to the kitchen table.

One more day of work, and then they'd have four days together. There would be a small turkey for their Thanksgiving dinner, but there would be no Black Friday shopping. At least not in the stores. She'd been keeping a few things in her cart for her mom and Rylan. And at some point over the four days, they'd decorate the Christmas tree.

When dinner was ready, they sat down, and her mom said a prayer of thanks for the food before they began to eat.

"I hear that Rylan's been hanging out with the boss," her mom said with a smile.

"He has. I wasn't sure what he'd think about me bringing Rylan with me, but he actually told me I could bring Rylan along again if I needed to."

"I think he's ready to abandon me for Hayden."

"No doubt," Paige agreed. "But he knows he has to do his schoolwork and can't just watch movies all day. Right, Ry?"

"Yeah." Rylan let out a long sigh. "How come Hayden can just watch movies all day?"

Paige exchanged a look with her mom, wondering how to answer that question. "Well, right now, Hayden isn't working in an office, so if he has the time, he can watch movies."

"I want a job like that," Rylan announced right before he took a bite of his dinner.

"I'm sure you do." Paige imagined there were a lot of people who would like a job like that.

"One of these days, Mr. Hayden needs to get back to living," her mom said.

"I dare you to tell him that," Paige responded. "I have a feeling his family tells him that on a regular basis. To no avail."

As she spent the evening with her mom and Rylan, she couldn't help but think of Hayden in his big, empty apartment. She knew that it was his choice to stay hidden away. He had the money and the means to do what was necessary for him to step out into the world. But for whatever reason, he chose not to.

Though she hadn't had the wealth the Kings did, the money she received from the settlement for Rylan's birth injury had been substantial. Because of that, she knew that money didn't take away all the difficulties in the world, and it couldn't magically cure whatever it was in Hayden's mind that kept him from embracing life. It was that mental block that made Paige feel most sorry for Hayden, and she wondered if he'd ever get past it.

Rylan seemed to have taken his limitations in stride, but she'd decided to use some of the settlement money to get him some therapy after the divorce. Unfortunately, she'd only managed to get him a handful of sessions before Glenn had stolen the money, leaving them nearly destitute.

Even with the huge settlement she'd received for Rylan, Paige had resisted living a lavish lifestyle. She hadn't known what difficulties Rylan might encounter later in life, so she'd wanted to make sure they had money to cover anything he might need to deal with it.

Because of that, she'd told her husband that they shouldn't use any of the settlement money to pay off the mortgage on the house that was still in his name, nor were they moving to a bigger home. The only money that they'd spent on the house had been to install ramps and other things that made it easier for Rylan to move around.

She'd tried to be so wise with the money, and it was all for naught. Now she wished she'd used it to buy a bunch of stuff for Rylan, like game consoles and DVDs. Stuff that she hadn't felt was a necessity then. But if she'd bought that kind of stuff, at least Rylan would have had that, and his jerk of a dad would have had less money to steal.

Taking a deep breath, Paige held it for a moment, then blew it out, knowing that getting aggravated over that situation again wasn't productive. Thankfully, the Kings paid her a decent salary so she could pay the rent on the two-bedroom house plus their expenses, including her vehicle.

She also paid for health insurance for her mom. It wasn't as great as what she'd had when she worked for the Kings, but she'd insisted that it was more important for Paige and Rylan to have the better coverage. For Rylan's sake, Paige hadn't argued.

"You can leave Rylan with me tomorrow," her mom said as they finished up their meal. "Donna seems to have gotten to where she can be on her own again."

"Can't I go with you, Mama?"

"Wow," her mom said with a smile. "Show the guy a movie or two, and Hayden's his new favorite person."

Paige chuckled. "They seemed to have a lot of fun, and all you make him do is schoolwork."

"The downside to being a teacher. We don't get to just have fun."

"I think maybe I'll take him tomorrow, and then we'll catch up on some school stuff on the weekend."

"Do we have everything we need for dinner on Thursday?" her mom asked as she got up from the table. "Or should we place an order for pickup?"

They talked for a couple of minutes about what they needed, then her mom cleaned up while Paige settled Rylan on the couch with the tablet so he could watch some videos while she placed an order to pick up the next day after work.

Finally, she took Rylan into the bathroom to give him a bath, then put him to bed. Her mom had turned on some worship music as she cleaned, and though that type of music had once been Paige's favorite, she'd only recently begun to listen to it regularly again.

After everything had happened with Glenn—from the cheating to the divorce to the theft—she'd been extremely angry. But it wasn't on her behalf. She'd actually been ready to see the last of the man after how he'd dealt with Rylan and his injury.

But after he'd taken off with the money, she'd been filled with despair over how she would provide for Rylan since she'd dropped out of college after his birth. She'd had no degree and no way to provide care for him so she could work.

Thankfully, her mom had stepped up and offered her what support she could. So they'd come back to Minneapolis and moved in with her mom. They were surviving, though, and her mom had encouraged her to not let what had happened with Glenn rob her of her relationship with God.

It had taken awhile for Paige to come around to not being mad at God for allowing the theft to happen, but she was getting there. Slowly but surely.

She had never been an angry person. Even after what had happened to Rylan, she'd been prepared to do her best to care for him and give him a good life. So the anger she'd experienced was new, and she'd hated that her ex had been the one to bring it out of her.

Lately, however, as she'd gone to bed at night, she'd tried to focus on the positive things. She wasn't always successful, but at least she wasn't going to bed angry every night like she had in the beginning.

That was a step in the right direction, and she just had to keep moving forward and keeping her trust in God. Things might not be as easy as they would have been with the money, but as long as Rylan didn't develop any serious issues, they would be okay.

Hopefully…

Chapter 6

Hayden was up and sitting at the small table of his room when Paige appeared with his breakfast tray. She paused in the doorway of his room, her brows lifting slightly, before heading over to where he sat.

"Good morning," she said as she set the tray down in front of him. "Did you have a bad night?"

Hayden shook his head and thought about asking her the same question since she had circles under her eyes, but he didn't. "Nope. Just decided to get out of bed like an adult for a change, without waiting for you to wake me up."

She gave him a quick smile. "That's progress."

"It is, isn't it?" He looked at the food on the tray, his stomach rumbling in appreciation. "This looks delicious. Thank you."

"You're welcome."

As she picked up his dishes from the night before, he said, "Did Rylan come with you today?"

She nodded. "Yep. I told him he could come for one more day."

"Is your mom's friend doing better?"

"Much. Though I think Mom was going to go by her place again today, just to check on her."

"I can help Rylan with his schoolwork if you don't want him to miss another day."

She frowned at his words. "You don't have to do that."

"I know, but I don't have much on my schedule. If it helps you, I'm happy to do it. I think I can answer any elementary level questions he might have."

"I think he'll have mixed feelings about your offer," Paige said with a laugh.

"Why's that?"

"He'll enjoy spending time with you, but maybe not doing schoolwork. I think he would rather watch movies."

"Can I tell him we'll do that after the schoolwork?" Hayden asked, hoping that Paige said yes since he'd enjoyed it when they'd done that the previous day.

"Sure. As long as you want to. I don't want you to feel like you have to spend time with him."

"I don't. I mean, maybe it's strange for a man my age to enjoy spending time with a boy Rylan's age. But since we enjoy some of the same things, I figure, why not? Hunter and I used to love it when my dad would hang out with us, doing stuff we enjoyed." Hayden paused after he said those words. "I mean, I'm not his dad. Obviously. But since his has run off, maybe I could spend a little time with him, you know?"

"I do appreciate you being willing to do that. His dad wasn't good at hanging out with Rylan even when he was around, so this is pretty new to him. Plus, I'm sure he's happy to spend time with someone besides my mom and me."

"Then I'll come out after I've finished breakfast."

"Craig isn't coming today?"

Hayden shook his head. "I told him to take the rest of the week off."

"Okay. I'll let Rylan know."

Hayden watched her walk away, frustrated with himself for not having learned more about her. She'd been working for him for months now, and he couldn't remember them ever having any sort of in-depth conversation. Certainly, they'd never discussed Rylan. In fact, the only reason he knew about Rylan at all was because Leta had mentioned him a few times. Though she'd never, to his recollection, told him about Rylan's disability.

After the accident, his life had narrowed considerably. The people he saw the most were his family and the doctors tasked with repairing his body. He'd pushed all his friends away, although, to be honest, they hadn't tried too hard to stick around.

It had been hard enough dealing with his family while he'd been grieving and in pain. His friends—the ones he'd had fun with—seemed to realize he wasn't going to be the fun-loving guy he'd once been. At least not for the foreseeable future. And maybe never again. So they'd bailed on him.

His world had expanded slightly with the addition of Carissa, Rachel, Ash, and Isla, but those hadn't been relationships he'd sought out himself. They had kind of landed in his lap by way of his siblings. Not that he regretted that at all.

In fact, he quite liked the four new additions to the family. If for no other reason than they had brought joy with them—something that had disappeared in the wake of his dad's death. Rachel and Isla, in particular, radiated happiness that brought smiles back to the faces of his mom and siblings.

As he ate, he thought of the two little girls and wondered what they might think of Rylan. Maybe he should ask Hunter and Heather to bring them over to meet him. Since they were both so sweet, Hayden knew they wouldn't make fun of Rylan for his wheelchair.

Once he'd finished his breakfast, he got up on his crutches, then stared down at the tray that contained his dirty dishes. There was no way he could carry it to the kitchen, so he'd have to leave it for Paige to pick up.

For the first time in a long time, it bothered Hayden that he couldn't do this for himself. Paige shouldn't have to come into his room with his meals, and then come back to get his dirty dishes. Maybe it was time to start sitting at the kitchen table to eat his meals.

As he left the bedroom, Hayden resolved that after the Thanksgiving weekend, he was going to make more of an effort to live like a functioning human being.

"Can't I have pancakes, Mama? They're my favorite."

Hayden smiled as he heard Rylan's question as he got close to the kitchen.

"I'm sorry, sweetheart, but the pancakes are Hayden's. I brought you some oatmeal."

There was a long stretch of silence, during which Hayden tried to process how he felt about Paige's comment. He hadn't even considered that she wouldn't feed Rylan any of his food. Though he could appreciate that she was trying to keep a line drawn between personal and professional things, it wasn't necessary at all.

"Okay, Mama. I'll eat the oatmeal."

Moving into the kitchen, Hayden looked around to see if Paige had already prepared the oatmeal. If not, he was going to tell her to feed Rylan the pancakes.

Not seeing the oatmeal in progress, Hayden said, "Feel free to give him the pancakes, Paige."

"Hi, Hayden!" Rylan said, the excitement in his voice warming Hayden.

Paige stared at him for a moment. "That's not necessary. I bring him food from home."

"You don't have to," Hayden told her. "If he'll eat what you're preparing for me, just give him some of it. There's no need for you to make two different meals."

She seemed to be reluctant to accept his offer, and Hayden wasn't sure why. He was trying to make her life a little easier, but apparently, she didn't view it the same way.

In the end, though, she said, "Thank you. Rylan really does like pancakes."

Hayden grinned at Rylan. "He has excellent taste."

"Would you like another helping?" Paige asked as he made his way over to the table where the boy sat. "I made a few extra in case you needed them tomorrow when I wasn't here."

"I'll be going to my mom's in the morning tomorrow, and there will be plenty to eat there, so we can finish up the pancakes today."

"Would you like more then?"

"Sure. Why not. They are delicious. Just give me whatever's left after you give Rylan what he'll eat. And a cup of coffee would be great."

"You like pancakes too?" Rylan asked as he leaned his arms on the table and rested his chin on them. His brown eyes were large as he stared at Hayden, but he didn't look as tired as he had the day before. Hopefully that meant he'd had no nightmares.

"I love pancakes. I think breakfast is my favorite meal of the day."

Rylan straightened and looked up at his mom as she set a plate of pancakes in front of him. "Thanks, Mama."

Ruffling his hair, she smiled down at him. "You're welcome, sweetie."

Rylan didn't start eating right away, though he eyed the pancakes with obvious hunger. After Paige returned with a plate for Hayden along with a cup of coffee, she sat down on the chair next to Rylan. He took her hand and said a prayer for his food, then began to eat the pancakes.

"I'll be back in a few minutes," Paige said over her shoulder as she left the kitchen.

Hayden figured she was going to pull the sheets off his bed, since she did that three times a week. He had to admit that it was one of his favorite things, to have freshly laundered sheets on his bed. Since he spent more time than he should in bed, having them smell fresh and clean almost felt like a necessity.

"So how're you doing?" Hayden asked as they ate.

"Good. But Mama said this is the last day I can come here." Rylan frowned as he forked up another piece of pancake. "Nana's friend is better so she can watch me again."

"Well, I'm glad your grandma's friend is feeling better. Maybe you can come visit me sometimes, even if Nana can watch you."

Rylan smiled, his cheeks puffing out. "I would love that. It's fun here."

"Do you go out a lot?"

He shook his head. "Not so much when it's winter. It's hard to move my wheelchair around."

Hayden could understand that. "Yeah. My crutches aren't much fun in the snow either."

"Sometimes Mama will take me to the pool."

"Do you like to swim?"

Rylan nodded. "I can't swim by myself, so I wear a special thing that helps me."

Hayden thought about the pool that was available in the apartment building. He'd been encouraged to use it as part of his recovery program, but he'd only been in it a couple of times. Maybe he should invite them to swim one day.

He would have to approach Paige about that when Rylan wasn't there. Hayden had learned from his siblings' experience that it was best not to ask about things that the kids would really want to do while they were actually around. He'd already kind of broken that rule with Rylan that week, but he would try to be better about it, for Paige's sake.

"Do you swim?" Rylan asked.

"Not too often."

"Because of your leg?"

Because of so many things, but Hayden didn't say that. "Sort of. I'd go swimming a lot when I was your age, though. I used to even swim in a lake."

"A lake?" Rylan asked, his eyes wide. "With real fish?"

"Yep. We have a cabin at a lake that we used to go to a lot." He wondered if they still had that cabin. To his knowledge, no one had been there since his dad's death. He would have been so disappointed if the big log building was sitting empty... devoid of life.

Hayden made a mental note to ask Hunter about it because he was curious if they'd sold it. His dad hadn't denied them some luxuries, like the large family home or the lakeside cabin. However, knowing that the building he'd spent money on was sitting empty would have bothered his dad a lot. He would have considered it a waste of money.

"So you would swim with the fishes?"

Hayden had to stifle a laugh at his question. "Pretty much. Usually they stayed away from us, though. We'd jump into the water from the dock and swim around. Sometimes we'd go water skiing with our boat."

"You have a *boat*?" If Rylan's eyes got any bigger, they were going to pop out of his head.

"We did. I'm not sure if we still do, since I haven't been to the cabin in a few years."

"You should go again."

"Maybe I should." Hayden hadn't thought about the cabin in ages. But now that he was talking about it again, he found himself wanting to know if they still owned it. And if they did... well, he wasn't sure if he was ready to go back up there just yet, but maybe... one day.

"Once you're done eating, we need to do your schoolwork. I told your mama I'd help you with that, and she said when that's done, we could watch another movie."

"Yay!" Rylan forked up a piece of pancake. "What movie are we going to watch?"

As they finished eating, they discussed their options with Rylan leaning toward *Big Hero 6*. Hayden had watched all the movies they were considering, but it had been awhile. Thankfully, he had enjoyed most of them. Even though they were geared to kids, he still found them entertaining.

"Are you finished eating?" Paige asked as she came back into the kitchen.

"Yep," Rylan said. "I'm full to the top."

"Glad to hear it." Paige cleared the dirty dishes from the table. "Now you need to do a little schoolwork."

"Show me what he needs to do," Hayden said.

Paige got Rylan's backpack and opened it up. She pulled out a few books and a notebook, which she flipped open. "Mom and I plan out his work in advance, so this will show you what he needs to do in each subject."

"That seems pretty straightforward."

"At this age, it does seem to be more straightforward than I would imagine the higher grades to be."

Paige lifted the notebook, her brows drawing together as she read over the page. "Okay. There doesn't seem to be any new stuff being taught today. He should be able to just do the work without too much help."

"That's probably good for me," Hayden said. "But I'll try my best to help if he needs it."

Paige picked up one of the workbooks and set it in front of Rylan. "Start with this, okay?"

"Yep." Rylan took the pencil case she held out to him. "I'll do it neatly."

"Good boy." She ruffled his hair, then headed back to the kitchen, where she started to clean up their breakfast.

"What subject is this?" Hayden asked.

Rylan looked up from where he was sorting through his pencil case. "It's Bible. Nana says we should start with this one because it's the most important one."

"That's good."

"Did you have Bible to do when you were in school?" Rylan asked as he set his pencil case to the side.

"Yep. I went to a Christian school with my brother and sister."

"Were the kids nice to you?"

"Most of them. I was lucky to have my brother and sister in the same class as me, so even if other kids wouldn't play with me, they always would."

"That would be cool."

"So what are you studying in Bible this week?"

"Heaven," he said, pointing to the page he'd flipped it open to. "My favorite thing I learned about Heaven is that there's no more sickness or pain. My legs will work when I get there. I will be able to run and jump and play, just like other kids. Maybe your leg will be all there again in Heaven too."

Hayden hadn't given it much thought. In the years since the accident, he had rarely gone to church. Most years, he attended the Christmas services, and Hayden supposed that he'd attend that year too. Rachel and Isla were both in their church's children's Christmas program, and they'd already told him that they expected him to be there.

They were two of the people in his life who were more than happy to make their expectations of him known, and he was loath to disappointment them. That was usually enough to get him out of the apartment to attend whatever event they wanted him at.

Chapter 7

Paige hadn't had high expectations when it came to Hayden supervising Rylan's schoolwork, but he seemed to take it seriously. Every time she came into the kitchen, she heard them talking about something related to the schoolwork.

Hayden was an enigma to Paige. For months, he had been a reclusive, often grumpy man. He'd always been respectful to her, but there were times when she could tell that he was tired and in pain. On those days, he was more likely to be a bit short during their interactions. She'd never taken it to heart because she could tell he was struggling.

Now, though, he seemed to be willing to come out of his shell for Rylan. She didn't know what it was about her son that did it, but there was no denying that he interacted more with Rylan than he did with anyone else, with the possible exception of Craig. She suspected it was their shared disability.

While a lot of people weren't sure how to approach Rylan being wheelchair bound, Hayden didn't seem to have the same issue. It was probably because he knew from his own experience that what made him different physically from others didn't mean there was anything different inside. Rylan was still just a little boy who wanted to be loved, to have friends, and enjoy his life.

Paige didn't know what Hayden might want in his life, but if Rylan helped draw him out of his bedroom, she would encourage that. It was possible that the man found interacting with a child easier than interacting with others in his life. Most likely because Rylan didn't have any expectations of him.

"Mama, I'm done everything on the page," Rylan declared when she walked into the kitchen to put away the mop she'd been using in the bathroom.

She washed her hands, then joined the pair at the table. When she saw the proud looks on both their faces, she almost chuckled. It was clear they both felt a sense of achievement over what Rylan had done.

"I checked the work that I could, and he seems to have gotten it all right," Hayden said. "He's a smart little cookie."

"I'm a cookie?" Rylan asked. "Can I *have* a cookie?"

Paige laughed as she bent to kiss his head. "I suppose maybe you've earned a cookie. But why don't you eat some lunch first. Then you can watch a movie and eat some cookies."

"Excellent plan," Hayden said as he held his fist out to Rylan, who bumped it with his own. "What's for lunch?"

"You usually have a sandwich or soup. Either of those interest you?"

Hayden thought for a minute, then said, "Do you guys like pizza?"

"Yes!" Rylan answered before Paige could respond.

"How about we order in some pizza?"

Paige wasn't going to argue with him. He was her boss, after all. Plus, it had been awhile since they'd had pizza, and she and Rylan both liked it. Most of the time when they had pizza, they made it from scratch. Which was fine, but there was something about delivery pizza that tasted that much better.

"What do you like on your pizza?" Hayden asked as he pulled his phone out of his pocket. "I'll place the order online, and hopefully it will come quickly."

"I like pepperoni," Rylan said. "No onions or mushrooms though."

"How about you, Paige?" Hayden asked as he looked up at her.

"I'm good with pepperoni and most types of meat. Even plain cheese is good."

"Do you like ham and pineapple?"

"It's not my favorite, but I'll eat it."

"How about I get one ham and pineapple and one pepperoni? Will that work?"

"Sounds good," Paige said.

When she'd considered how this week might unfold having to bring Rylan to work with her, it hadn't included Hayden hanging out with him. And yet here he was, spending more time out of his room than she'd ever seen before.

Rylan's birth might have been viewed as tragic for most people. His disability something to be pitied. She'd never thought of it that way. Yes, for his sake, she wished that he hadn't suffered the injury that had landed him in a wheelchair. However, she chose to be thankful that he'd survived at all. They hadn't been sure he would at first.

He'd had kids point at him and laugh, and adults had even ignored him. She'd seen the hurt in him because of that. But now there was Hayden. He'd not only been willing to acknowledge Rylan, he'd been willing to spend time with him. It was honestly kind of amazing.

Her perception of Hayden was changing, but she wasn't sure that was necessarily a good thing. She knew that Rylan needed a good male role model in his life, and it was likely that he was going to latch on to Hayden for that. What would happen when... if... Hayden lost interest in hanging out with Rylan?

They cleared away the schoolwork, returning everything to the backpack, then Paige set out plates and cups for their lunch. While they waited for the pizza, she took Rylan to the bathroom to check him over. The buzzer went just as they were headed back to the kitchen, so Paige let the delivery guy in the downstairs security door, then pushed Rylan to the table so she could return to wait for the pizza to arrive at the apartment.

"If that's my pepperoni pizza," Rylan said, pointing to the large box she'd opened. "Then where is yours, Mama?"

Before she could respond, the little boy began to giggle, apparently finding his own joke quite funny. Paige couldn't help but smile. Rylan had always laughed easily, but he hadn't laughed as much in the time since they'd had to leave their home in Chicago and move in with her mom.

"I guess I'll have to share mine with her then," Hayden said, a grin lifting the unscarred side of his face.

Rylan's eyes went big as he looked at the pepperoni pizza again. "I think it's okay if she has some. I can't eat all this by myself, and Mama doesn't eat a lot. You probably eat more than we do."

"Sometimes," Hayden said as he lifted a piece of pizza and put it on his plate. "Pizza is something I enjoy, and I don't have it very often."

Hayden didn't start eating right away, and Paige realized he was waiting for them to give thanks for the food. At her nod, Rylan bowed his head and prayed.

Once he was done, they began to eat their meal. Rylan and Hayden eagerly dug in, and Paige had to admit that the pizza was some of the best she'd had. Of course, Hayden hadn't ordered from a franchise pizza place. Though she enjoyed the pizza they ordered from those places, it would be hard to go back to after eating this.

"Are you going to your mom's for dinner tomorrow?" Paige asked.

Hayden nodded. "I told Hunter that I'd be there in the morning. Mom wants us to help her decorate the tree on Friday, so I think I'll probably be staying at least one night."

Paige was glad to hear that. Even before they'd begun to interact more, she'd hoped that the man would spend time with his family over the Thanksgiving weekend. She, her mom, and Rylan would probably have much the same sort of family time as the Kings, only on a much smaller scale.

"Do you plan to go shopping on Black Friday?" Hayden stopped chewing the bite he'd taken and lifted a brow as he stared at her. Paige couldn't help but chuckle at his response. "Not a shopper, huh?"

"Not normally," he said after he swallowed his bite. "And definitely not on Black Friday. How about you?"

"Nope. The only Black Friday shopping I plan to do is online."

Hayden nodded. "I don't know what people did without online shopping. I know I couldn't have survived without it."

"You might have had to actually get out of the apartment more," Paige pointed out.

"I know, right? That would have been just terrible."

Paige gave a shake of her head. "I do have to say that I am glad for grocery pickup and delivery."

"That's how you get them delivered here, isn't it?"

"Yes. I place an order based on what the menu looks like for the week, then they bring it by. It's wonderful."

"I don't like to go shopping," Rylan said with a frown.

"Why's that?" Hayden asked, lowering the piece of pizza he held to his plate.

"People stare at me."

"I understand," Hayden told him. "They've done that to me too."

"Is that why you stay in your apartment?" Rylan asked.

"Part of the reason, yeah."

Paige could see their connection growing. And though it seemed right then it was a good thing for them both, she wasn't sure that in the long run, it would be. She didn't want Rylan to get too attached to the man, only for Hayden to lose interest in him over time.

Sooner or later, she was pretty sure that the man would tire of his life within the four walls of his apartment. Once he began to venture out, Rylan wouldn't be of interest to him anymore.

Still, she was happy that, for a few days, Rylan had something new in his life. The movies had been a highlight for him, and Paige was glad about that.

Rylan ate one entire piece, and then they shared a second. Hayden polished off a couple. Once everyone was full, Paige got Rylan settled in the theater room with Hayden before she cleaned up their meal.

She did her afternoon chores, checking in with the pair periodically. As she moved around the apartment, their combined laughter drifted out through the open door of the theater room.

The afternoon passed quickly, and once Paige had finished making Hayden his dinner, she went to the theater room, hoping they had finished their latest movie.

When she stepped into the room, the lights were up to their full strength, and there was no movie playing. The two of them were chatting, and they both looked her way when she walked in.

"It's time to go, sweetie," she told Rylan.

"Okay, but maybe I can come back?"

Paige ran a hand over his hair. "I'm not sure, since Nana can watch you again."

Rylan sighed as he bobbed his head. "I'm glad she can do that. I just wish I could come back again."

Hayden stayed silent as the two of them spoke, and Paige found she was both relieved and disappointed. She was glad that Hayden was letting her handle this, but she knew that Rylan was going to be disappointed that Hayden hadn't said that he wanted to spend more time with him.

Rylan was quiet as they gathered up their things, but as they approached the door to leave, with Hayden following behind them, he finally spoke up.

"Thank you for watching movies with me," Rylan murmured. "And thank you for being nice to me."

Paige swallowed hard against the sweep of emotion at Rylan's words, and when she looked at Hayden, she saw that he wasn't unmoved.

"You're very welcome," Hayden said. "Thank you for hanging out with *me*. I had a lot of fun."

Rylan smiled. "I did too."

Paige opened the door, and as they stepped into the hallway, Hayden said, "See ya around, buddy."

She hoped that was true, but there would be no promises made to that effect. As they drove home, Rylan talked about the movies they'd watched. There was no doubt that the time he'd spent in Hayden's apartment would be something he'd talk about for a long time.

~*~

The apartment was terribly quiet after Paige and Rylan left, and Hayden found himself restless in the silence, pacing as best he could on the crutches and ignoring the meal Paige had left for him on the table in his room.

He heard his phone beep somewhere and looked around to find out where he'd set it down. When the text alert went again, he zeroed in on where it sat on the coffee table.

Picking it up, he put it in the pocket of his sweatpants and made his way to the bedroom. Once he was seated at the table, he pulled it out to read the message.

Hunter: *Just checking to make sure you'll be at Mom's tomorrow.*

I said I would be.

Hunter: *Do you want me to pick you up or just send George?*

Though Hayden missed a lot of things from before the accident, one of the biggest was the ability to drive. Not that he went anywhere, but sometimes he wished he could just get in his car and go. Get out of the city and just drive.

Since it was his left foot that was missing, he knew that he could drive again. After the surgery he'd had on his right leg had been successful, he'd been looking forward to driving again once he finally got his last surgery. But after everything that had transpired following the surgery on his left leg, he'd set it all aside.

Unfortunately, that had left him reliant on people like Hunter and George, the family's driver, to get around. *Whatever is most convenient.*

Hunter: *I'll be there at nine.*

Hayden sent him back a thumbs up, then closed out the text window. He brought up one of the apps he used to stream and scrolled through the shows and movies.

Since choosing to lose himself in the world of television and movies in recent years, he'd watched his way through a good portion of several streaming services. Because of that, he'd watched some genres he'd never thought he would. The cooking competition shows had become a favorite, though he wasn't about to tell Hunter or Heather that. They'd tease him mercilessly.

He was happy to see that the newest season of a show he'd enjoyed was out, so he clicked to cast that one onto the screen. As the intro rolled, he went to his contacts and brought up Paige's information.

Hey Paige, this is Hayden. I didn't want to say anything in front of Rylan, but I wondered if he'd be interested in going swimming. There's a pool here in the building that my two nieces like to go in sometimes. I could invite them to come too. They're real sweet girls and would be kind to Rylan.

The message was long, but he'd just wanted to get it all out. There wasn't a response right away, so he set the phone down and turned his attention to the dinner Paige had left him.

It was almost an hour later when his text alert went. He paused the show and picked up his phone.

PaigeCantor: *He does love to swim. When were you thinking?*

I can talk to Hunter and Heather tomorrow to see what might work for their girls. Is there a time that's better for you? They're still in school, so maybe on the weekend.

PaigeCantor: *The weekend would be okay for us.*

Great! Let me talk to Hunter and Heather tomorrow, and I'll get back to you.

PaigeCantor: *Thank you for entertaining him this week and for helping him with school.*

He's a great kid. And smart!

PaigeCantor: *Thankfully, he has never struggled with school. Doesn't always like to do it, but when he puts his mind to it, it goes smoothly.*

Hayden hoped that Rylan would have the opportunity to pursue whatever interested him in the future. Unfortunately, people would probably underestimate him and not make his journey easy. The idea of that made Hayden want to rage, but at the same time, it also made him want to be there when Rylan proved them all wrong.

Chapter 8

Hayden had set his alarm for seven-thirty to give himself enough time to get ready without having to rush. Things never went well when he had to hurry. At least he didn't have to worry about breakfast. He knew that Essie would insist that he eat when he got there, even if he'd eaten before coming.

He hated getting dressed because it was the one time when he absolutely couldn't ignore his missing lower leg. The bare stump drew his attention even when he didn't want to see it, and then once he had his pants on, he had to deal with the leg so that the bottom part didn't just flap around.

After he was dressed, he used his crutches to get to the bathroom so that he could brush his hair. It had gotten pretty long since he didn't bother to get it cut. There had never been a point in his life when he and Hunter had looked more dissimilar.

Bracing himself for the day ahead—one which had, in the past, included sharing what they were thankful for—Hayden headed out of the bedroom. He'd just reached the living room when his phone buzzed. A glance at the screen confirmed it was Hunter letting him know that he was in the basement garage.

He tugged on his coat and put his boots—boot—on before leaving the apartment for the elevator, which would take him straight down to where Hunter and his car waited.

"How're you doing?" Hunter asked when Hayden settled himself in the SUV a few minutes later.

"Same as usual," Hayden replied.

It was a question he got frequently, but he rarely answered it honestly. Hunter was probably aware of that, but then he really didn't need Hayden to vocalize things in order for him to know them. They'd always been able to convey things to each other without having to say a word.

Hunter skillfully guided the SUV up the ramp that led from the underground garage to the street in front of the building. Hayden blinked at the sudden brightness and the way the sun gleamed off the snow that covered the ground.

"What have you been up to this week?"

"I've been babysitting."

"Say what?" Hunter glanced over at him. "Who on earth would you be babysitting? Isla?"

"Nope. Leta's been helping a sick friend, and she is Paige's babysitter for her son."

"Paige has a son?"

"Yes. A little guy who is paralyzed from the waist down, so he's in a wheelchair."

That bit of information gained him another glance from Hunter. "That's interesting. I didn't know that."

"I didn't either until I walked into the kitchen and saw him sitting at the table. They homeschool him, so I took a turn at helping with that too."

"What else did you do?"

"Watched movies," Hayden said.

Hunter gave a laugh. "Of course."

"Hey, the kid loves cars, so we started with that movie, then watched a bunch of other animated kids' movies."

"I guess that broke up the monotony for you," Hunter observed.

"It was actually quite fun. But Leta's friend was feeling better, so Paige probably won't need to bring him to work with her anymore. I asked if she wanted to bring him to swim in the pool. I thought maybe Rachel and Isla might like to join us."

"I'm sure they would. Those girls love swimming in the pool. I'll let you line that up with the ladies, though."

"I'll talk to them today."

They drove in silence for a couple of minutes before Hunter spoke again. "Not that I want to tick you off, but I have to say it's great to hear you talking about something you've obviously enjoyed. I'd like to meet this kid."

Hayden couldn't deny that he'd enjoyed having Rylan around, so he didn't bite Hunter's head off. "I think you'd like Rylan. He seems to be a smart little guy."

"How did Rylan end up paralyzed?"

Hayden paused for only a moment before sharing everything Paige had told him about their situation. She hadn't asked him not to tell anyone, plus Hunter wasn't one to gossip with just anyone about something like that.

"Have you talked to Kent?"

A grin lifted the corner of Hayden's mouth. "Great minds think alike."

"Let's talk more about this later," Hunter said as he pulled the SUV into the long driveway of their mom's house. "See if we can come up with some ideas to help Paige and Rylan, especially if we're not successful in coming up with information on her ex."

"If she's willing to accept help," Hayden added. "She might not be."

"If she's anything like Carissa, she may want to reject offers of help, but for the sake of Rylan, she'll accept them."

Hayden was sure that was true, but at the same time, he didn't want her to feel backed into a corner. It seemed she'd been at the mercy of other people's actions recently, and he didn't want her to feel that way about them—even if they wanted to help her.

She was already in a vulnerable position financially because of what her ex had done, so it was likely she wouldn't do anything that would jeopardize her job. That likely meant she'd agree to stuff whether or not she really wanted to.

"I don't want her to feel like she has to accept it, or her job would be at risk."

"I think we can handle it with sensitivity," Hunter said. "I mean, somehow we convinced Carissa and Ash to let us into their lives."

Hayden considered his words for a moment. The situation with Paige was nothing like what Hunter and Heather had found themselves in with Carissa and Ash. His siblings had both been romantically interested in the people they'd been trying to help. That wasn't the case with him and Paige.

Not that he thought Paige wasn't worth his interest. However, she was clearly still recovering from what she'd experienced over the past year. Plus, he was so far from being a good catch that if Paige had any sense at all, she'd steer clear of him in that way.

Once at the house, Hayden greeted his mom with a hug and kiss, tolerating the concern in her eyes because he knew that he could do things that would ease it. If he didn't want them to be overly concerned about him, he needed to get his act together and take the steps necessary to move his life forward.

"Hi, Uncle Hayden!" Rachel called when she saw him.

She and Isla raced to where he stood, each of them giving him a tight hug. From the moment he'd met them, the girls had seemed to not even see his scars and injuries. They'd had questions about it at first, but once they'd had an explanation, they'd just accepted that was how he was. Their love for him was refreshing, since it was free of worry or judgment.

"Grandma says that we're decorating the tree tomorrow," Rachel informed him. "It's going to be awesome!"

Hayden didn't feel the kind of excitement he once had for Christmas decorating. As a kid, he'd always enjoyed it, but that had been a long time ago. Now, he was content to sit back and watch the others do the work.

"Essie made cinnamon buns," Isla said. "Are you hungry?"

"I'm always hungry for Essie's cinnamon buns," Hayden told her.

As he greeted the others in the family, he wondered what Paige and Rylan were doing. Hopefully, they were enjoying their Thanksgiving with Leta.

Leta had been a great housekeeper over the years. She'd taken good care of the apartment and of him and Hunter. He'd been surprised when she'd decided to retire, but since she'd recommended Paige for the job, it had been a relatively smooth transition.

As he considered the situation now with the knowledge of what had happened to Paige, Hayden had to wonder if there had been more to Leta's decision than just not wanting to work anymore.

Those thoughts stayed with him as the day progressed. There was plenty of food. Plenty of conversation. And plenty of laughter.

In the past couple of years, there had been a return of joy and happiness to their family. There would always be a gaping hole in their family where their dad should be, but his mom and siblings seemed willing to find joy through embracing the things his dad would have loved. They were also sharing more of the memories they had of him, especially with the new members of their family who hadn't known him.

Unfortunately, he had memories of his dad that his family didn't. When he'd woken after the accident, he hadn't immediately remembered what had happened. Eventually, he'd recalled the accident, but he hadn't shared all of those memories with them. He'd passed on messages from his dad, but he'd also kept some things to himself.

Even though sharing those memories might have helped his family to understand why he struggled the way he did, Hayden kept what had transpired in the hour before the accident to himself.

Hayden stared at the fire flickering in the fireplace, his mind slipping away from the room filled with warmth and laughter. Soon he was caught in a world of fire and ice. Freezing and burning. And pain. So much pain.

Tell your mom I love her, son, and I want her to be happy. Pain filled his dad's voice, and Hayden was sure he'd see it on his face if he could see more than the shadow of his features in the tomb of their car. *Tell Hunter and Heather that I'm so proud of them, and I love them. Always and forev—*

Any further words had been silenced by the truck that slammed into theirs, taking Hayden's pain to a level that robbed him of consciousness and ending the life of a man who had deserved to live for many more years. The tremendous loss wasn't just for the family, but also for the world that his dad had worked hard to improve, believing it was what God had called him to.

So why had God taken his dad before he was done touching the lives of the people who needed him?

"Hayden." A hand gripped his shoulder and gave him a little shake. "Honey?"

He took a shaky breath, mentally trying to free himself from the emotions that lingered from his traumatic trip down memory lane. It never got any easier.

Looking up at his mom, he tried to smile. "I'm okay."

She didn't look convinced, but then, she rarely did when he said that. But rather than argue with him, she just took his face in her hands, holding him gently as she pressed a kiss to his forehead. "Love you."

"Love you too, Mom."

Hayden tried not to let those emotions take over him again as the evening progressed. He would have preferred to head home, but that wasn't going to happen since he'd already said he'd stay the night.

When it was time for bed, he ventured down to the rec room where he'd sleep on a fold-out bed. It might have been uncomfortable if it wasn't a top-of-the-line piece of furniture. At one time, he would have had Hunter for company. But since his brother had tied the knot with Carissa, he was done sharing space with Hayden.

Ash had offered to sleep in the rec room instead of Hayden, but Hayden had turned him down. When he couldn't sleep at night, he liked to have the option of watching TV or playing video games on the big screen television that was there. He'd be relegated to a much smaller screen in one of the bedrooms.

That night, as he lay on the bed, watching a movie on the TV, he found his attention wandering. He could not stop thinking about Rylan, but also Paige. Had they had a good Thanksgiving that day? He hoped so. If it wasn't so late, he might have messaged her to find out.

Instead, he'd wait to contact her the next day, hopefully with a date for her to bring Rylan over to go swimming with the girls.

"You want the girls to come swim at the pool at your apartment building?" Heather asked the next morning once they'd all eaten breakfast, and the girls had disappeared off to play together.

"They've done it before," Hayden reminded her. "And they seemed to enjoy it."

"Oh, they did," Heather agreed. "I just wasn't sure that you had."

Hayden frowned. "I didn't hate it."

"There's a long road between enjoying and not hating something," Carissa pointed out.

"You *were* my favorite sister-in-law," Hayden groused.

"I'm your *only* sister-in-law, so even if you say I'm not your favorite, I still really am."

Hayden couldn't argue with her logic, especially since he was pretty sure that there wasn't anything she could do to truly remove herself from her favored status. She'd been a wonderful addition to their family, just like Ash would be once they tied the knot in a few weeks.

"*Annny*way," Hayden dragged out. "If you'd rather them not come, that's fine."

Heather narrowed her eyes at him. "Okay. Tell me why you *really* want them to come over. Is there a woman you're trying to impress?"

Hayden gave her an exasperated look. "No. It's not that. Paige—my housekeeper—has a son who is paralyzed and in a wheelchair."

He took a few minutes to explain how he'd met Rylan and his situation, hoping that would convince Heather and Carissa to bring the girls for a swim.

"Wow. Well, sure, we can bring the girls," Carissa said. "Right, Heather?"

"Of course, I'll have to ask Ash, but I'm sure he'll agree. When were you thinking?"

"Maybe Saturday afternoon?"

"This Saturday?"

"Yeah."

"Let me ask him," Heather said as she got up from her seat. Hunter and Ash had headed out to the garage to look at something, so Heather disappeared through the door that led out of the kitchen.

"I'm sure the girls would love to meet Rylan," Carissa said.

"I hope so. He doesn't have a lot of friends apparently, so he might be a little shy at first. At least until he knows for sure that they're going to be nice to him."

"I understand that. It's just too bad that he's had to learn so young that people can be not-so-nice to those who are different." She gave him a curious look. "Do you think your own differences made it easier for the two of you to connect?"

Carissa had never been one to avoid talking to Hayden about what he was going through, and for some reason, from her, he really appreciated that. He didn't usually like it when his siblings would do it, however.

"I'm sure that's part of it," Hayden agreed. "But I connected with Rachel and Isla without them having to be disabled."

"That's true," Carissa said with a nod. "Hopefully, Rylan's connection will end up extending to the girls, but that can really only happen if they're able to spend time together. Will his mom be okay with that?"

"I think she will be after she meets the girls and sees how they treat Rylan. She's taking a chance that I'm telling the truth when I say that the girls will be nice to him. Only time will tell for her."

"It's all decided," Heather announced as she joined them at the table again.

"What's all decided?" Hayden asked. There hadn't been anything to ask beyond if the girls could come over Saturday afternoon.

"We'll be there Saturday afternoon at two o'clock."

"We as in who?" Hayden asked. "I only invited the girls."

"It's not like they can bring themselves," Heather said. "We've just decided we'll all come for a swim."

"We have?" Carissa asked with lifted brows.

"Your husband has." Heather grinned. "Take it up with him if you don't want to come."

Carissa just shook her head and laughed.

"Fine." Hayden knew it was best to pick his battles. "I'll let Paige know what works for you all and see if that's okay with her."

"I can't wait," Heather said, rubbing her hands together. "I really do love the pool at your place."

Hayden wondered if he should warn Paige that the girls weren't going to be the only ones there with them.

Chapter 9

Paige parked her car in her usual spot in the underground parking lot at the apartment block, then sent a text to let Hayden know they were there. He'd told her to do that so he could come down and go to the pool with them, since apparently it needed a special card to gain access to the area.

While she waited for him to arrive, she got Rylan out of the car and into his wheelchair. She hung the bag with their swimming stuff in it on the handles of the chair, then closed up the car and moved toward the elevator. She still wasn't entirely convinced this was a great idea, but Rylan loved to swim, and they hadn't been able to go for a while.

When the elevator arrived, the doors slid open to reveal Hayden inside. He gave them a quick lopsided smile and reached out to press the button to hold the door open so Paige could get the chair in.

"Good afternoon, you two," he said.

"Hi, Hayden," Rylan replied with a huge grin.

She hadn't told him of the plan to go swimming until that morning, knowing that Rylan would be thrilled. If she'd told him too soon, he wouldn't have been able to contain his excitement and would have driven her and her mom crazy.

"Heya, bud. How's it going?"

"It's going *great!*"

Paige really hoped he felt that way after he met the two little girls that Hayden had said were coming to swim with them. He seemed quite certain that they would be nice to Rylan, and she hoped that was true. She'd only seen them in passing during the time she'd worked for him so had no personal experience.

"There are family-style changing rooms at the pool, but if you'd feel more comfortable changing in my apartment, we can go there first."

Paige had changed Rylan in all kinds of places, so she was pretty sure that the changing rooms in a luxury apartment building would be just fine. When she told him that, he pressed a button, and the elevator began to rise.

She had thought they'd stop on the second or third floor, but it went up to the floor right underneath the one where Hayden's apartment was. They walked out into a small foyer area which had a wall of glass that showcased the pool on the other side. And on three sides of the pool were floor to ceiling windows that revealed a spectacular view of the city.

It was a huge area with a large pool as well as a smaller one and what appeared to be some hot tubs. There appeared to be some people there already, but it was by no means packed.

Hayden explained how to get into the changing rooms and then into the pool area. After that, they parted ways to change.

Paige helped Rylan into the special suit that he wore for swimming because of his bladder and bowel issues. Thankfully, when she'd found the suit, she'd bought a few in increasing sizes back when she still had his settlement money, since they'd offered her a deal if she bought more than one. Thankfully, that meant she'd have suits for him for a while yet.

After he was dressed, she turned his wheelchair to face the door while she quickly changed into her own swimsuit. She put their clothes into the bag, listening as Rylan chattered on excitedly about swimming with Hayden. She had told him about the girls, and while he hadn't been *as* excited about that, apparently being with Hayden was enough to offset that.

When they were finally ready, she followed Hayden's instructions to get out to the main pool area. He was already there and made his way to where they stood.

It was weird to see people in bathing suits—it was weird to *be* in a bathing suit—when she could see snow on the buildings through the windows that surrounded the pool. Hayden wore a T-shirt and sweats, though she suspected that was just until he actually got in the water.

One side of his mouth lifted as he approached them. "Ready to get in the water?"

"Yes!" Rylan punched the air with his fist. "I can't wait."

Paige had a special ring that she used with him to keep him upright, but it also allowed him a little freedom in the water. He could move himself around just using his hands and arms if he wanted to.

Hayden led them over to a set of chairs were there was already a bunch of bags and towels. "You can leave your stuff here."

Paige took off the towel she'd put around her waist and draped it over the handles of the chair. She then inflated Rylan's ring and fitted it around him before she lifted him up and carefully carried him to the steps that led into the pool. By the time she and Rylan were in the water, Hayden had removed his extra clothes and was seated on the edge of the pool, his crutches just behind him.

"Are you getting in too?" Rylan asked as he propelled himself toward where Hayden sat. Paige followed behind him, just to be safe.

"Time to get in, Uncle Hayden," a little girl's voice chimed in.

Paige turned to see two little girls bouncing toward them in the water. It was shallow enough that it didn't come above their shoulders as they moved.

"Yeah, I know." Hayden slid himself off the edge, keeping hold of it as he adjusted his balance in the water.

"Rylan, these two are my nieces," Hayden said as the girls came to stand beside him. The littler one wrapped both hands around Hayden's arm. "This is Isla, and this is Rachel."

"Hi, Rylan," Rachel said with a beaming smile. "I'm glad you could come swim with us."

"Do you like to swim?" Isla asked.

Rylan nodded. "I do."

"Why do you need a wheelchair?" Thankfully, Isla's curiosity seemed to be genuine and not motivated by meanness.

"My legs don't work," Rylan told her. "They were broken when I was born."

"That's good you have a wheelchair then," she said.

Rylan nodded. "But I like being in the water because then I can move around by myself."

"I like your swim ring," Rachel said as she reached out to touch it.

By that point, they'd been joined by four other adults that Paige knew from sporadic contact with them since she'd started working for Hayden.

"Hi Paige," Hunter said with a smile. "It's nice to see you again. How're you doing?"

"I'm good, thank you."

"You know Carissa, Heather, and Ash, right?" Hayden said.

She nodded. "Yep."

"They all decided that they wanted to join us for our swim." Hayden sent a glare at his sister, but Heather just grinned in response.

Before long, the girls were encouraging Rylan to join them as they swam back and forth across the shallow end. Though Paige kept an eye on him, she wasn't too worried because the ring had always kept him safe, and it didn't appear that the girls were interested in doing anything too acrobatic in the water. Still, she was glad that they stayed close by in the shallow end.

"How's your mom doing, Paige?" Hunter asked.

"She's doing good. Been busy helping a friend of hers. She's over there this afternoon, actually."

"Remember when I got so sick?" Carissa asked as she peered up at Hunter. "And you had to help me out?"

"Oh, I do," he said with a grimace. "I think you scared a few years off my life."

Carissa entwined her arm with his and leaned her head against his shoulder. "I'm so sorry for that."

"Well, while I'm not happy you ended up sick, I'm glad that it meant you came to live with Mom for a bit. That meant we could get to know each other and finish falling in love."

"Finish falling in love?" Heather asked.

"I was already halfway in love with her before that," Hunter said as he leaned down to kiss the top of Carissa's head.

"How about you, Cari?" Heather asked. "Were you halfway in love with Hunter when you got sick?"

"I don't know if I was *halfway*, but I was definitely on the way, even though I thought it was a futile emotion."

"Love is never a futile emotion," Heather told her.

"It sure felt that way when I was convinced that he'd never love me in return."

"Why would you think?" Heather frowned at her. "You're very easy to love."

Carissa laughed. "Thank you, but all I could see were the inequalities in our lives. I felt like all I did was take from your family. Who would want to be with someone who was needy like I was?"

"We're all needy in different ways," Hunter said. "We needed you and Rachel in our lives, and I especially needed you in mine."

Paige listened with interest as they talked about how the other two people had come into their family. Ash was a man of few words, but she could see that he was devoted to Heather, sticking close to her in the water.

"Are you beginning the adoption process right away?" Carissa asked Heather.

"As soon as the wedding is over." Heather smiled. "We haven't told Isla. We plan to surprise her when it's all completed."

Carissa glanced over to where the girls were swimming around with Rylan. "I'm sure she'll be thrilled."

Paige couldn't help but notice that Hayden wasn't contributing to the discussion anymore than she was. Given her own track record with love, she had absolutely nothing positive to add.

She wished that she had chosen a better man to pledge her love to, not even for her sake, but for Rylan's. He needed a man who was willing to be there for him in the good and bad times. Her son deserved someone who saw value in him, even though he might be different and less physically abled than other boys. She could only hope that Rylan didn't carry the wounds left by his father's abandonment into adulthood.

It was her hope and prayer that he would be as loving and caring as an adult as he was as a child.

"Well, I'm going to go hang out in the hot tub," Heather said. "Feel free to join me."

Ash, unsurprisingly, trailed after his fiancée, and Hunter and Carissa followed the pair. Paige might have enjoyed going into the hot tub, but she wasn't going to go that far away from Rylan.

"You can join them," she told Hayden. "You don't have to stay here with me."

"I know, but I'd like to. I can hang out with them anytime." He turned to look at where the trio were playing together. "They seem to be getting along."

Paige couldn't help but agree. Rylan was smiling and laughing as the three moved around in the water. Did she dare hope that these girls might become his friends?

"Thank you for inviting them to hang out with Rylan," Paige said.

Hayden looked back at her, his expression gentler than she was used to seeing on his face. "I want him to know that not every kid will be mean to him. I didn't plan for their parents to crash the party, though."

Paige laughed. "You didn't think they'd want to tag along?"

"I thought maybe they'd take advantage of me watching the girls and go for a date or something."

"Do they not get to go on dates very often?"

"Oh, they get to go on plenty. My mom would watch the girls every single night if they'd let her. As it is, I think they spend most Friday nights with Mom."

"Rylan spends every night with my mom," Paige said, and she felt an absurd sense of accomplishment when Hayden chuckled softly.

"That's a good one."

"I thought so." Paige lowered herself into the water so that it covered her shoulders. "This pool is so much nicer than the one we go. It's warmer, and the view is amazing."

"It is," Hayden agreed, moving to lean against the side of the pool. "I'm just surprised that it's not busier."

"Rylan really enjoys swimming, so this is great for him."

"We can swim whenever you'd like. Just tell me when, and I'll make the arrangements."

"I don't want to impose."

"You're not imposing if I'm offering." Hayden turned his attention to the kids. "It's not as if I have a lot going on in my life, and even if I did, I'd make time for this."

Paige fought to ignore the rush of warmth Hayden's words filled her with. She was seeing a side to the man that she'd never seen before. He'd always been courteous toward her, but there had been no personal conversations. She had made some assumptions about him and the way he lived his life, but now Paige wondered if she'd been wrong.

"I do hope that you'll feel comfortable to bring Rylan with you any time you'd like."

"Hey, Hay!" Heather called from the hot tub. "Ask her about the party."

"Oh. Sure." Hayden turned to look at her. "Our company has a children's party each year, and you and Rylan are welcome to come."

"I don't work for your company, though," Paige reminded him.

"That doesn't matter. Carissa brought Rachel before she and Hunter even knew each other that well. And Heather invited Isla and Ash last year."

"Are you proposing to me?" Paige asked.

Chapter 10

Paige tried not to laugh as Hayden's eyes widened. "What?"

"Well, has it escaped your notice that apparently inviting someone to the children's party is a precursor to a relationship?"

Hayden gave a huff of laughter. "Well, yeah, I can see that it seems to have worked that way in the past. But I'm not sure I'm in any condition to contemplate a relationship, let alone a marriage."

"I think that makes two of us," Paige said, relieved that they were on the same page.

It wasn't that she'd sworn off men or anything. She knew that her ex wasn't representative of all men. Any time she was tempted to think that way, she remembered her dad, who had been a wonderful man. And she thought that perhaps Hayden would also be considered a good man, given how he'd been with Rylan.

"So do you think you could make it?"

"When is it?"

"Next Saturday afternoon."

"I suppose we could come." She knew that Rylan would probably enjoy going to something like that.

"Santa will be there, giving presents out to the kids. Heather asks for the parents to give her an idea of what their kids might like in the twenty-five dollar range."

"You buy presents for all the kids?"

"Well, I don't *personally* buy the gifts," Hayden said.

Paige gave him an exasperated look. "You know what I mean."

"To answer your question seriously, yes, the company covers the cost of the party and the gifts. It's something my dad started several years before he passed away. He used to play Santa himself."

"That's amazing."

Hayden shrugged, the water rippling around him with the movement. "My dad has always loved kids, so he saw this as a way to do something for the children of the people who worked for us."

"Do you usually include non-company kids?"

"I don't think it's something Heather or Hunter seek out," Hayden said, rubbing a hand over his shoulder, drawing Paige's eye to the puckered skin of the scars on his arm. "But if a situation presents itself, they'll include other kids."

Hayden's gaze moved to the windows, though Paige had a feeling he wasn't looking at the view.

"My dad used to pray each day that God would bring people across his path who he could do something for. Nothing made him happier than being able to help people."

"Was there something that made him want that?"

Hayden looked back at her. "Lots of different things, I think. He was raised by a single mom who struggled to make ends meet. That's why Hunter wanted to help Carissa. She and Rachel needed a place to live, among other things. So he and Heather did what they could to help them."

"She seems really nice," Paige said. "And Rachel too."

"They're great. I hadn't spent much time around kids until I met Rachel."

"And Ash and Isla?"

"Ash rescued Heather on the side of the road. Isla's mom—Ash's sister—had died of a drug overdose, and Ash had only had custody of her for a few months. Heather felt drawn to help him with Isla, teaching him things like how to braid hair."

"And they fell in love?"

"They sure did, though I think it was a struggle for Ash to accept a relationship with Heather, even though he loved her."

Paige didn't even have to ask why the man might have had reservations about dating a woman from a wealthy family like the Kings. But like with Carissa and Hunter, love had obviously overcome whatever obstacles had been in Heather and Ash's way.

"And you like Carissa and Ash?"

The side of Hayden's mouth tipped up. "I do. They've been very tolerant of me and my issues, which is a big mark in their favor."

"I'm sure that makes family get-togethers easier."

"It does. Plus, being triplets, the three of us are close, so it was almost necessary that the significant others fit in with all of us." He hesitated, then said, "Do you have any siblings?"

Paige grimaced at the question. "I have a younger brother."

"Are you close?"

"No. He's kind of made a bunch of bad decisions that have landed him in jail off and on."

"I'm sorry to hear that," Hayden said. "I'm sure that must be hard for you and your mom."

"It is very hard for her, especially because she doesn't have my dad to help shoulder that burden."

"Have you seen your brother recently?"

Paige shook her head. "The last time we saw him, he wasn't exactly nice to Rylan, so I decided to not spend any time with him until I saw some significant changes in his life. Rylan doesn't need that kind of person around, especially someone who should be on his side because of their relationship."

"Well, I'm glad that you were able to put some boundaries in place."

"I had to," Paige said. "I'm Rylan's advocate, and I have to say that I'm also my mom's advocate. She had a hard time putting boundaries in place with Pete, so my putting one in place for Rylan helped her as well."

"Paige and Pete? Are you twins?"

Paige laughed and shook her head. "Nope. Just how it worked out for us."

"It's too bad you don't get along better with your brother. I don't know what I would have done without my siblings. They've been a tremendous support." Hayden gave a huff of laughter. "Also a pain in my butt sometimes, but I know they're only doing what they do out of love."

"Are you talking nicely about us, Hayden?" Heather asked as she slid back into the pool near them. "Because if you're telling mean stories about me, I can also share a few about you."

"I would never say a bad word about you," Hayden said, his half-grin making a fleeting appearance. "Now Hunter, on the other hand, is fair game."

Since Hunter remained in the hot tub with Carissa, he couldn't defend himself. Paige enjoyed seeing a different side to the siblings. Most of the time, she saw the protective sides of Hunter and Heather. They usually showed up at the apartment because they were concerned about something going on with Hayden.

"Mama!" Rylan called, making Paige move in his direction.

"What's up, sweetie?" she asked as she grabbed onto his ring and pulled him closer. Thankfully, he didn't look upset.

"Can I go to the Santa party with Rachel and Isla?"

The two girls looked at Paige with expectant looks on their faces that matched the one on Rylan's.

Assuming it was the same party that Hayden had talked to her about, Paige nodded. "I think we'll be able to go."

"Yay! They said that Santa comes and brings presents! But I have to write a letter to Santa."

"We can do that," Paige said, though she hadn't really been too keen to focus on presents from Santa that year. She wasn't sure what she'd be able to afford to get him, so she hoped that the items on his list weren't too lofty.

Of course, the one thing she wanted to give him more than anything was so far out of her reach right then, she wasn't sure if she'd ever be able to give it to him. Once things had settled down from the divorce, she'd been preparing to get him his first power wheelchair.

The one she'd been considering had a minimum age/weight that he hadn't met yet at that time. Until that point, they'd been using a manual one. Unfortunately, before she could place the order, Glenn had absconded with the settlement money, and she'd worried about spending what little she had left on an expensive wheelchair when she had to think about food and shelter for them.

The power wheelchair was also something Rylan desperately wanted. He struggled to manage the manual chair since he wasn't super strong.

"When we get home later, we'll write a letter to Santa."

"I'm so excited," he said, clapping his hands. "They said that I can decorate cookies there too."

"That sounds like fun," Paige told him.

"It is," Rachel said. "We even make decorations for the tree. It's so much fun."

"And there's food too," Isla said. "Lots of yummy food!"

"Rylan can hang out with us," Rachel told her. "We'll make sure that he has fun."

"Do you have other friends who attend?" Paige asked, wanting to make sure that Rylan wouldn't get shoved aside if they had friends they'd rather be with. If there was any chance of that happening, she'd rather it just be her and Rylan at the party.

Rachel shook her head. "Most of the kids have parents who work at my dad's company, so we don't really know them. None of our friends from school or church are there."

That kind of made Paige feel a bit better about the idea of going. "Then I guess we'll see you there."

"We'll have lots of fun," Isla said with a big smile, her blue eyes sparkling.

Heather and Hayden had joined them, while Ash had lifted himself up to sit on the edge not far away.

"Did you girls convince Rylan to come to the party?" Heather asked.

"Yep," Isla said.

"And he's going to write a letter to Santa," Rachel added.

"That's great." Heather smiled at Paige. "Just give the letter to Hayden, and he'll make sure that it makes its way to Santa."

"We'll work on it tonight," Paige said.

"That's great. I look forward to having you both at the party, and feel free to bring your mom too. I think Hunter and Hayden would be happy to see her again."

Paige had to wonder if Hunter and Hayden had thought all that much about her mom once she'd retired. Not that she thought they hadn't liked her. She just got the feeling that what they'd really cared about was having someone to cook and clean for them. They'd treated her very well, giving her time off when she'd needed it, and probably paying her more than she would have received for the job working for someone else.

Of course, the most appealing thing about the job for Paige had been the health insurance they'd offered. Because of Rylan's special needs, she had to make sure he always had access to good medical care. She *had* been paying for good insurance with the settlement money, but that had been another thing gone with her ex's theft.

When her mom had offered to give up her job to Paige, she hadn't been sure they'd hire her. However, they seemed more than willing to skip the interview process and hired her strictly on her mom's recommendation. Thankfully, she was used to cooking and cleaning. She hadn't wanted to let her mom down, nor did she want to give Hayden or Hunter any reason to fire her.

"I'll ask Mom if she wants to come," Paige said. "She might just want to enjoy the quiet with us out of the apartment."

Heather laughed. "Yeah, I understand that."

Paige hoped she wasn't making a mistake by accepting these invitations from the Kings. They all seemed eager to include her and Rylan in things. But for how long? It had been a long time since Rylan had had something to be excited about, and she was loath to take that from him. So, for the time being, she would accept these invitations, and hope that when they stopped, Rylan wouldn't be too disappointed.

Chapter 11

Hayden frowned at Heather. "I'm not sure I can do that."

"You don't have a choice," Heather said as she packed Isla's wet things into a bag.

They'd returned to the apartment after swimming, though Paige and Rylan had left for home already. It had been a fun time, and Hayden hoped that Paige and Rylan would join them again.

"I don't like going to social events," Hayden said. "You know that."

"Tough luck." Heather straightened as Ash took the bag from her. "You issued the invitation, so you need to be there. Rylan seems to be drawn to you, though *why* is a mystery to us all. So, you need to bring yourself to the party and leave your grumpy attitude at home."

Hayden sighed, but he didn't argue with her. He had a week to make up an excuse not to go, though he wasn't sure Heather would accept anything short of his death as a reason for him not to attend.

On the following Friday night, he tried for the last time to get out of going. Heather answered his call, said *be there*, and hung up. She wasn't even giving him a chance to plead his case.

He'd done his part in inviting Rylan and then had forwarded the boy's letter for Santa to Heather. Hayden didn't want to go to the children's party where he'd be stared at. And it wasn't the kids he cared about staring at him. Their curiosity was natural. It would be the people who hadn't seen him in the years since the accident whose stares he didn't want to deal with.

Hayden was pretty sure that his mom would get mad at him if he scowled at their employees when they stared at him. It was unlikely that he'd be able to smile at them like he used to, especially considering the scar on his face. Why wouldn't Heather accept that it really wasn't a good idea for him to go to that party?

It wasn't that he hadn't enjoyed the parties in the past. Before his dad's death, he'd had fun going and seeing him dressed up at Santa. However, since the car accident, he hadn't gone even once. And this was the first time that any of the family had insisted. Heather had probably been waiting for an opportunity to force him to go.

On Saturday, just before noon, Hayden got himself ready for the party. It took far too long to choose clothes to wear. The dark green shirt he decided on was as close to being in the festive spirit as he was going to get.

He didn't have a lot of dress pants. The ones he'd had before the accident were all big on him now. Even though he wasn't getting much exercise, he'd lost a lot of weight following the accident, and he'd only managed to put a bit of it back on.

Finally, he settled on a pair of black pants that, even though they were a little big, looked okay with a belt on. It took time for him to pin the leg up so that it didn't look horrible. There was no way to disguise that he was missing the lower part of his leg, so he'd just have to deal with it.

Hayden ignored the voice in his head that told him there *was* a way for him to disguise it. In his mind, he deserved the stares he got when he ventured out of the apartment, which was why he didn't like to go out or to be around anyone but family. And Paige and Rylan. He had grown comfortable with them too, surprisingly enough.

When the call came from Hunter to let him know they were waiting for him in the garage, Hayden took a deep breath and blew it out. He was doing this for Rylan. If the boy was brave enough to venture out into a world of strangers who would likely stare at him, Hayden should be willing to do it too.

Rachel greeted him enthusiastically, and he smiled, always happy to see her. Knowing that three of the kids who would be present there were important to him helped to keep from slipping into the grumpiness that Heather had instructed him to leave at home.

When they reached the hotel where the party was taking place, Hunter let them out at the front door, then went off to park.

Hayden followed Rachel and Carissa as they walked through the doors. From Rachel's chatter on the way over, he knew they had been there earlier that morning to check things out. It had sounded like his mom had had everything well in hand, however, which was no surprise since she'd been a part of planning the party for many years.

"There's Isla!" Rachel exclaimed, then took off running toward her friend and soon-to-be cousin.

"Did you tell Paige to let you know when they got here?" Carissa asked.

"Yeah." Hayden glanced around the large foyer area, just in case they'd beaten them there, and she hadn't texted him yet to let him know. Unfortunately, there was no sign of them. "We're a little early, so I suppose they'll be here soon. I offered to send a car for them, but she said she'd rather drive."

By that point, they'd reached Ash, who had Isla with him. The man greeted him with a nod.

"Ready for the bedlam?" Hayden asked, knowing that Ash had only come to the party the previous year because of Isla. Now that Heather had forced him to come, Hayden had a better understanding of how the man had probably felt.

"I tried to get out of it, but Heather wouldn't listen to me," Ash revealed.

"Yeah. She wouldn't listen to me either. She'd answer when I called, but all she'd say was, *be there*, and then she'd hang up."

Ash chuckled. "Yeah. I heard a couple of those calls."

The two of them moved off to the side as Carissa, Rachel, and Isla headed for the hallway that led to the ballroom where the party was being held. People dressed as elves had come out to the foyer and were directing kids and their parents or guardians to where they needed to go.

Hayden knew he couldn't hang around outside for the whole party, but he was going to wait until he knew that Paige and Rylan were there before going inside. And maybe he'd get lucky, and they'd arrive late.

"Ready for the wedding?" Hayden asking, glancing at the man who'd won Heather's heart.

Ash laughed. "I guess so. I told Heather just to give me the info on the time and place, and I'll be there in whatever she chose for me to wear."

"Brave man," Hayden told him.

"Not really. I just want your sister to be happy. I also want to get married, so I'm fine with whatever she wants in order to make that happen."

Though the gruff man wasn't the type of guy Hayden had expected his sister to end up with, they appeared to be happy together. From his own interactions with him, Hayden had found Ash to be hardworking and dependable. Just two of the many qualities that he was sure his dad would have found admirable about the man, if he'd had the chance to meet him.

His dad wouldn't have found much to admire about him since the accident. Even before that, his dad had already been after him to be more responsible and to take his position at the company more seriously. In fact, his dad had been speaking to him about that very thing when they'd become part of the tragedy on the highway.

"I'm glad her expectations are low for the rest of us," Hayden said. So far, all she'd said was that she'd provide him and Hunter with pants, a shirt, and a tie since they were Ash's groomsmen. Their mom and Carissa were her bridesmaids.

"I had braced myself for something much more grandiose," Ash confessed. "So when she told me she wanted to keep it small, I certainly didn't argue with her."

"So not only brave, but smart," Hayden said with a laugh. "If she had decided on a big wedding, I'm not sure you would have been able to convince her otherwise."

"She's very eloquent in her arguments," Ash agreed. "But she isn't dismissive of my opinion, which I appreciate."

Before Hayden could respond, he spotted Paige, Leta, and Rylan coming in the entrance. He excused himself and made his way over to them. Paige had moved Rylan's wheelchair off to the side, and she was looking around as if trying to get their bearings.

"Hey there," he said as he reached them. "Glad you made it."

"Hi, Hayden!" Rylan smiled broadly.

Hayden gave him a high five, then turned to greet Leta with a smile. "It's so good to see you again, Leta."

"You too, Hayden. Thank you for inviting us."

Paige gave him a smile, though he could see concern on her face. He understood it because he was feeling a bit concerned about the party himself. Just like him, Rylan had things that would make him stand out. All he wanted was for people to leave them alone and let Rylan enjoy the party.

"Shall we go inside?" Hayden asked.

"Yep! Let's go!" Rylan was definitely excited, and Hayden was glad for that. He just hoped nothing dimmed the boy's excitement.

"The boss has spoken," Paige said.

Hayden fell into step beside them as Paige pushed Rylan down the hallway toward the wide doors that led into the party room. The noise level escalated the closer they got, and Hayden got his first glimpse of the decorations that his mom, Carissa, and Heather had organized.

"Wow," Rylan said, his head turning back and forth as he took in the room's décor. "So much Christmas."

"I have to agree with Rylan," Paige said. "This is a lot of Christmas."

"It's absolutely beautiful," Leta added.

"Are Rachel and Isla here?" Rylan asked as he looked at the groups of kids and adults wandering around the room.

"Yep. They're here somewhere."

Before he could say anything more, Rachel and Isla appeared, dressed in Christmas attire with big smiles on their faces.

"Hi, Rylan," Isla said. "Do you want to decorate a decoration? Rachel and me are gonna go do that."

"Yep. I want to do that too."

The girls led the way, then the three found a spot where they could sit together. It frustrated Hayden that he couldn't help move the chair to make space at the table for Rylan's wheelchair. Instead, Paige and her mom had to do it.

The elf supervising the table came over to the kids and got them set up with decorations and supplies to add to them. While

Leta stayed close to the kids at the table, Paige came to stand next to Hayden, her gaze on Rylan.

"Thanks for inviting Rylan," Paige said. "He's been so excited about it."

"Was he bugging you this morning?"

She glanced at him and laughed. "Yeah. But honestly, it was nice to have something that he was looking forward to so much. It's been awhile."

Hayden understood that. It felt like a lifetime since he'd had something that made him really excited. Even the weddings of his siblings had left him with mixed emotions. He was happy for them, but there wasn't really any level of excitement for him. Watching them move on to new phases in their lives made him even more aware of how their lives were moving on in a different direction than his.

Hayden kept his attention on the three kids, not wanting to see the people who might be staring at him. He couldn't trust himself not to scowl at them.

"The only thing that Rylan has talked about more than this is you."

Hayden looked over at Paige. "Me?"

"Does that surprise you?" Paige asked with raised brows.

"I don't know," Hayden said honestly.

"Well, you add a lot of excitement to his life when I bring him to your apartment."

"I'm glad he has fun. I really enjoy it too."

"I know you offered that I could bring Rylan with me again," Paige said. "Were you serious?"

"Sure. I'd like to hang out with him again."

"I was wondering if maybe I could bring him one day a week. If that would be convenient for you."

Hayden laughed. "You know that my schedule is pretty much wide open. Aside from the odd appointment and Craig, my days are fairly flexible. And if I need to do some work when he's there, he can always watch a movie while I deal with it."

"I talked to my mom, and we figured that maybe if she added a little extra work for Rylan each day, he could just have a four-day school week."

"You know, I wouldn't mind teaching him one day a week. I found I actually enjoyed it."

"You enjoyed it?" Paige asked. "Really?"

"I did. I mean, I'm not going to suddenly become a teacher or anything, but working with Rylan was fun."

"I'll talk to my mom and see what she says."

"Also, if you could free up one of your afternoons, we could go swimming. Maybe I could teach him, or we could watch movies in the morning, then we could swim in the afternoon."

"I could probably do that. If I added a bit more work to each day, that would free up a couple of hours."

"How about we see if we can do that on Friday?" he suggested. "Give it a try and see how it works."

"I'd like that," Paige said. "I haven't been able to offer Rylan much variety to his days with his homeschooling, so this would be nice."

"It would certainly add variety to mine as well."

"If it's not something you want to continue to do, promise to tell me."

"I will," Hayden assured her.

"Hey, Mama," Rylan called out, twisting in his chair so he could see her. "Look at this."

Paige moved toward Rylan and bent to look at what he was holding. Hayden stayed where he was, his thoughts on the new event he could look forward to. He still wasn't sure why he was so willing to spend time with Paige and Rylan.

It wasn't like he'd been a kid person before the accident. Or at any point in his life, really. And yet here he was, not just offering to spend time with Rylan but actually looking forward to it. Would he have been as willing to do that if he hadn't had a disability and if Rylan hadn't had a disability?

Hayden could admit that his curiosity had been what had first drawn him to the boy, but now he knew there was so much more to Rylan than his disability. It was one thing they shared, however, and he had a feeling that commonality appealed to Rylan as much as it did to Hayden.

He found that he was already looking forward to the next Friday, and he wondered if Paige and Rylan—and maybe Leta—would be interested in going to the children's Christmas program at their church. The previous year, it had just been Rachel taking part, but this year, it would be both girls, and he thought Rylan might enjoy it.

Maybe he'd broach the subject with Paige later. He hoped she'd say yes, since he'd love to have them both with him at the program.

Chapter 12

When Rylan turned his attention back to the decoration he was working on, Paige looked around. Her mom stood talking with Eliza, appearing completely at ease with the other woman, despite their very different levels of wealth.

"Mama," Rylan said, drawing her attention to him again. "Can I make another decoration?"

"Did you finish the other one?" Paige asked.

He nodded and held it up for her to see. "This one is for our tree. I want to make another one for Hayden's."

"Uh..." Paige glanced at Hayden.

"I don't have a tree," he muttered.

"What?" Rylan turned to the other way so he could see Hayden. "Why don't you have a tree?"

"Yeah, Hayden," Heather said. "Why don't you have a tree?"

Hayden scowled at his sister, but his expression softened when he looked back at Rylan. "I usually go to my mom's for Christmas, so I don't need to have one at the apartment."

"But..." Rylan frowned down at his decoration. "Everyone should have a tree."

Paige hadn't explained to him yet that not everyone celebrated Christmas, but a children's Christmas party wasn't the place for that conversation.

"I think it's time for you to get a tree, bro," Hunter said.

"Yes, it's definitely time," Heather agreed. "Tomorrow afternoon we'll be at your place with a tree and all the trimmings." She turned to Paige. "And we'd love you guys to be there, too. After all, Rylan is going to make a decoration for the tree."

Paige looked at Hayden, not too surprised to find him shooting angry looks at his siblings. He was definitely being steamrolled, but she had a feeling that was the only way his siblings could get him to do anything.

"So can I make a decoration for the tree?" Rylan asked, glancing around at them.

"Yeah," Hayden said. "Make a decoration for my tree."

Rylan grinned. "Yay!"

Having a sibling who'd annoyed her plenty over their growing-up years, Paige felt a pang of sympathy for Hayden. However, she also thought it was good that they were going to get him a tree. She thought that his apartment could do with a bit of Christmas cheer, and though she wasn't sure that she and Rylan needed to be there, she'd probably end up accepting their invitation.

"We'll order some food, and all have dinner together," Eliza said. "I'll tell Essie that she can either have the night off with George, or they can join us, but she's not cooking."

"Oooh, I can't wait," Rachel said. "I'm going to make a decoration for Uncle Hayden's tree, too."

Isla held up a decoration. "Me, too!"

Paige wondered if the trio were just going to spend the rest of the afternoon making decorations for Hayden's tree. They seemed up for the challenge.

"Is Rylan taking part in a Christmas program this year?" Heather asked.

Though it took some effort, Paige managed to keep her expression smooth when she answered the woman. "Not this year."

She wanted to point out that with Rylan being in a wheelchair, onstage performances didn't often work, but she didn't. In a way, she appreciated that Heather didn't just assume that he couldn't be part of something.

There definitely wasn't a school program. And a church program? Well, that would require her to actually take him to a physical church. While they had attended one regularly in Chicago, and she'd had friends there, since coming back to the Twin Cities, she hadn't tried too hard to find a new church.

Her mom attended a small church, but it hadn't been accessible for Rylan's wheelchair. Though, honestly, Paige hadn't really tried to make it work. Her anger at God over what had happened had meant that she hadn't been all that interested in church. If she felt the urge to attend a service, she would log into the livestream from her old church. The comfort of the familiar faces helped to ease the anger and hurt a bit.

"If you're interested, Isla and Rachel are part of a kids' program at our church, and you both would be welcome to come."

Paige wasn't sure what to do with that invitation. Part of her wanted to accept, and she was sure her mom would want that, but she was reluctant.

"I'm not sure," she said, not wanting to reject the invitation outright.

"That's fine." Heather gave her a smile that was friendly, without any sort of reservation. "I'll text you the information, and if you can make it, great. And if not, that's fine too."

Paige wondered if Hayden planned to attend. Since she hadn't been working for him the previous year, she didn't know if he usually attended Christmas events or not. She didn't even know if he went to church with his family, since she wasn't around on the weekends.

Would she be more interested in going if Hayden had been the one who extended the invitation? She didn't really want to think too hard on that question, so she shoved it aside.

As it turned out, the kids only did a couple more decorations before Isla decided she wanted to decorate cookies. It took a few minutes for them to gather up the decorations and then get situated at another table, which had platters of sugar cookie cutouts and an abundance of frosting and sprinkles.

"I love decorating cookies," Rylan said as he took a star from the elf supervising the table. "But I love to eat them more."

Decorating cookies had been something she and Rylan had done frequently, and not just for Christmas. Pretty much every holiday, they would make and decorate cookies. And at Christmas, they usually worked on a gingerbread house.

They hadn't done that yet, and she honestly hadn't felt much like doing it at all. But seeing how happy he was decorating the cookies there, Paige knew that she needed to get over the anger and resentment that was still bogging her down. Those emotions just made her want to ignore the happiness of the holiday, but that really wasn't fair to Rylan.

Sighing, she crossed her arms as she kept an eye on Rylan. He had seemed to take everything regarding divorce and his dad's disappearance in stride, even saying a few times that he was glad the man was gone. She hadn't explained exactly why they'd had to move out of the home they'd both loved and into her mom's small house. Like she'd done from the moment he'd been born, Paige had protected him.

"I should probably make some cookies for him this week, huh?" her mom said.

"Or make the pieces for the gingerbread house."

"You make a gingerbread house?" Hayden asked.

Paige turned to find him at her side, leaning on his crutches. "Yeah. We used to make one every year. I didn't do it last year, and I haven't really thought much about doing it this year, either."

Hayden nodded, clearly understanding why she might not be feeling in the mood. "I cannot even imagine what Isla and Rachel would do with houses. The amount of icing Rachel put on the roof would probably break it. She *loves* icing."

"Rylan has gotten better at decorating the houses over the years. We did our first one when he was just a year old, so it was only up from there."

Hayden let out a huff of laughter. "I bet he still enjoyed it."

Paige nodded. "He did."

She had to keep her own emotions from spilling over on the traditions she'd celebrated with him over the years. If anything, she should be doing what she could to make this year even more special, to help him cope with all the changes in their lives.

"Maybe we should get gingerbread houses for the three kids, and they could decorate them sometime."

Paige lifted her eyebrows at his suggestion. "Are you volunteering to host this event?"

His brows drew down for a moment before he shrugged. "I suppose I could, though someone else is going to have to figure out the gingerbread houses and all the stuff needed to decorate them. That's definitely not my thing."

Paige was a bit surprised by his response. Considering they had already forced him into having a Christmas tree, she wouldn't have expected him to be eager to do anything else related to the season.

"If you're serious," Paige began, giving him a chance to back out if he wanted to. "I suppose I could get everything to make it happen."

Hayden turned his focus on the three children for a moment, then he gave a decisive nod. "Do it."

"Ooookay. So, do you have a day in mind? A time?"

He didn't respond right away, but after a minute, he said, "Next Friday. We'll have pizza and decorate gingerbread houses."

"Now, this *we* actually includes you too, right?" Paige asked.

He scowled at her. "Have you secretly been friends with Hunter and Heather all this time?"

Paige laughed. "Nope."

"That just sounded like something they'd say. They're mean."

"Are you saying I'm mean?"

"Well... since you cook my food, I'm going to go with... no. You're not mean. You're the sweetest person I've ever met."

"Except when I open the curtains in the morning."

He nodded. "Yeah. Except for then."

"Look at my first cookie, Mama!" Rylan lifted the star over his head.

She bent over to look at his masterpiece, then dropped a kiss on his head. "It's very sparkly, buddy."

He tipped his head back and grinned at her. "Just like a star."

"Just like a star," she agreed.

After a brief discussion with the girls and the elf, Rylan moved on to a tree. Paige looked at the other kids at the table, noticing that while a couple of them were eying Rylan with curiosity, no one said anything.

It made her wonder if she'd made the wrong decision to homeschool Rylan. Or maybe it was her reasons that were wrong.

When they'd had to leave Chicago halfway through the school year, it had just made sense to school him at home rather than send him to a new school midway through the year. And when it had gone fairly well, she'd just stuck with it for the next year.

But had it been the right decision for him? She hadn't even given him a chance with a new school because she knew she wouldn't be able to afford to send him to a school like he'd attended in Chicago.

It wasn't the time to ruminate over it in the middle of a children's Christmas party, though. She needed to set all the negative stuff aside and focus on the season that had always been her favorite. The previous year had been horrible as she'd been trying to come to terms with the theft, but she needed to buck up and move past that.

Being with her mom for the holiday was a definite blessing. Glenn had always insisted that they celebrate with his family in Chicago, even though his family hadn't been any happier with Rylan than Glenn had been.

"You okay, darling?" Her mom slid her arm around Paige's waist.

Paige nodded. "Just... thinking."

"Save it for later," her mom said gently, knowing Paige's tendency to think hard over things—especially negative stuff. "Enjoy this wonderful moment."

"We're going to have more of them, Mom," Paige promised her. "Rylan deserves them."

"And so do you."

Paige glanced over to where Hayden had moved closer to the kids, talking to them about what they were doing. "We all do."

Her mom squeezed her waist. "I'm not pleased with the circumstances that brought you back home, but I'm so glad you're both here."

Paige found that she could echo her mom's sentiment. It wasn't what she'd planned for their future, but there was no denying that being with her mom again was an unexpected blessing on several fronts.

"Shall we get some food?" Heather asked once the kids had each finished two cookies. "They can come back and decorate more after they've had some food."

"I could go for some," Hayden said, though Paige suspected that he just wanted to sit down.

Again, it took them a few minutes to get the kids and their cookies gathered up along with the decorations from earlier, then they went to a table on the other side of the room. Eliza disappeared, and when she returned, she had three elves with her, each carrying a couple of platters. They set them on the table, and Paige could see that the platters held an assortment of finger foods.

Eliza set down a stack of paper plates, and Paige wondered if they'd brought food to the table in deference to Hayden, who would have a difficult time serving himself from a buffet style table while on his crutches. Others in the room were going up to the long tables set with food.

Paige was just as happy not to have to wheel Rylan through a line, so she wasn't going to complain about special treatment. As they settled into seats at the table, she noticed that Hayden had taken the seat next to her, while Rachel and Isla were seated on the other side of Rylan.

He seemed to be happy to chat with the girls, and Paige knew she was doing him a disservice by not finding kids for him to be friends with. These little girls had been a start, showing her that there were kids who wouldn't make a big deal out of the chair, but who also wouldn't just ignore Rylan's disability.

A couple of people stopped by the table, greeting Eliza, Hunter, and Heather and casting curious glances at Hayden. When an older man and woman approached the table, Hunter got up and shook hands with him.

"Stan, I'm so glad you could come today."

"It was the first year we felt our granddaughter was old enough to appreciate it."

"Has she had a good time?" Eliza asked.

Stan's wife smiled and nodded. "She's loved every minute it of it."

"The best is yet to come," Hunter said with a wink.

Stan's gaze moved to Hayden, and he smiled. "It's great to see you, Hayden."

"Thanks, Stan. It's good to see you again too."

The older man didn't make a big deal out of it, turning his attention to Carissa. As he spoke with her, Paige glanced at Hayden, who was focused on the food on his plate.

She shifted toward him. "You okay?"

He glanced up and met her gaze. "You know I don't go out much."

"Do you not usually attend this event?"

After a moment, he shook his head. "I haven't come since the accident."

Paige let the significance of that sink in. "Did you come just for Rylan?"

Chapter 13

Hayden wasn't sure how to answer Paige's question. The way she asked it made it seem like it would have been a bad thing if he had.

"Heather said that since I issued the invitation, I should attend as well."

Paige frowned. "You didn't have to come just because of that."

Hayden shrugged, then took a bite of a cocktail sausage wrapped in puff pastry, contemplating how much he wanted to talk about that stuff as he chewed. "This was my dad's big thing each year. He was Santa."

"And you used to come?"

Hayden nodded. "I was even an elf for a couple of years. Heather and Hunter refused to dress up, but I thought it was fun."

"I... just can't image that."

He lifted a brow at her. "Not many one-legged elves running around."

She rolled her eyes at him. "I was thinking more about your demeanor."

"Never met a grumpy elf?"

"Can't say I have."

"I wasn't always grumpy," Hayden said.

She gave him a considering look as she ate something off her plate. "Does being grumpy make you happy?"

He almost tried to laugh off the ludicrousness of the statement, not wanting to discuss his state of mind, ever, but especially not at a party. Paige seemed to understand that because when he didn't answer, she didn't push the issue. He appreciated that because he knew the others might not have let it go so easily.

"So Santa shows up at some point?" she asked.

"Yeah. It's kind of the last part of the party."

"Rylan hasn't visited with Santa before."

"Don't they make sure that he's accessible at those mall places? I mean, Rylan's not the only kid in a wheelchair."

"Maybe they do." Paige sat back and glanced over at Rylan, who was still chatting with the girls. "I guess I never wanted to take the chance. He didn't seem to care."

"Have you told him that Santa is here today?"

"We did discuss it, but he didn't seem overly excited."

"That's okay. I think he'll get excited once the big guy arrives today. Last year, Isla wasn't sure if she wanted to believe in Santa or not, and she was still a little leery, even after meeting him. She's definitely on board with the idea this year, though."

"My brother hated Santa. Every single year, my mom would take us to get pictures, and Pete would scream. She finally stopped taking us when he was five and kicked Santa. We probably would have been banned if she hadn't decided that we weren't going to go anymore."

Hayden chuckled. "I think my dad would have been devastated if one of us hadn't liked Santa. He was dressing up for us before he ever started dressing up for this party."

Though he'd been dreading coming to the party, it wasn't going as badly as he'd thought it would. Sure, there were people staring at him as they realized who he was, but for the most part, he was able to ignore them. The people who had gone the extra step and greeted him had been friendly without overwhelming him with questions.

It was entirely possible that he had overestimated people's reaction to his appearance with his family. Still, there was a pit in his stomach that he'd been trying to ignore that seemed to be present in varying degrees, starting during the time leading up to the anniversary day of the accident and lasting into January.

That stretch of time, more than any other, was a harsh reminder of what their family had lost. The hole left by his dad's death was more noticeable during the holidays because it had been when his dad had been the most excited and larger than life. His excitement had been contagious, and even if they hadn't really been in the mood, it had been impossible to not succumb to their dad's excitement.

For four years, that lack of excitement had led to low key holiday celebrations. But over the past two years, the excitement had crept back in, brought by two little girls who loved the holiday in a way that would have made his dad so happy.

Hayden had even been changed by the past couple of years, though they had been reluctant changes. He'd already been attending church on Christmas Eve, just for his mom's sake. But with Rachel around, he'd found it harder to say no when more and more reasons to go to church popped up.

"It's almost time," Heather said from where she sat on the opposite side of the table, a couple of seats down.

"We usually have our kids go last," Carissa said to Paige. "But if you'd like to have Rylan go sooner, that's perfectly fine."

Paige shook her head. "It's probably better for Rylan to just wait and go with the girls."

"Excellent." Carissa smiled as she got to her feet, with Heather and Hunter following suit. "We're just going to check and make sure everything is ready to go."

Once the three had left, Rachel and Isla's conversation got even more animated as they told Rylan about what was to come. The girls' excitement—and now Rylan's—dragged forth memories that Hayden had hoped would stay long buried. Memories of a time when their family had been whole and happy. Back before he'd played a role in removing such a vital person from their lives.

"Does anyone know what time it is?" Hunter's voice came from the sound system in the room.

All the kids began to shout and clap in response. It seemed like a good chunk of them had been there in previous years. Rachel and Isla joined in while Rylan just looked around curiously.

Soon, Santa appeared at the door with a couple of elves in tow as *Santa Claus is Coming to Town* was pumped over the sound system. He waved as he made his way to the big chair they had set up for him next to a huge Christmas tree.

Children quickly fell in line with their parents. Though Rachel and Isla obviously knew the drill since they stayed at the table, their attention was on the activity around Santa.

"Is he giving them presents?" Rylan turned to ask Paige. "Or is it just for pictures?"

Paige glanced at Hayden, so he answered for her. "It's for both. Santa has a present for each child, plus they can have their picture taken with him if they want."

"Am I going to see him, Mama?"

"Yes. We'll go up with Rachel and Isla."

The girls smiled at him, and Rachel said, "He's really nice, and he gives us presents that we really like."

Hunter almost laughed at the skeptical look Rylan gave his mom, but the little guy didn't say anything. Upbeat Christmas music continued to play, and the kids in line danced around as they waited their turn. Though Santa couldn't spend a long time with each child, they had his undivided attention while they were with him.

Heather and Carissa returned to the table, and Heather said, "Do you guys want to go talk to Santa?"

When Hunter came back to the table, Rachel took his hand along with Carissa's and they headed for the line. Heather smiled at Paige and Rylan. "Ready?"

Rylan glanced at his mom, then at Hayden. "Are you coming with us?"

Hayden hadn't planned to, but he found it exceedingly difficult to spit out the word *no* in response to Rylan's question. "Uh... sure."

As he reached for his crutches, he glanced at Heather and Ash to find them looking at him in surprise. Ash gave him a quick smile that Hayden assumed was supposed to be encouraging. It just made him want to punch the guy. Lightly... in the arm... of course.

While Hayden situated himself on his crutches, Paige got up and took hold of the handles of Rylan's wheelchair and pushed him toward where the others had gotten into line. She moved slowly enough that Hayden could keep pace with her.

"Sorry you got roped into this," Paige murmured.

"I could have said no." Technically, that was true. In reality, however, that hadn't been the case.

"Do you know what Santa got him?"

"Nope." Hayden had seen the list Rylan had put together, but he had no idea what Heather and Carissa had settled on.

When it was Rachel's turn, she skipped to where Santa waited and, with Hunter's help, settled herself on the arm of the large chair. They held a brief conversation, then posed for a picture. With her gift bag in hand, she came to where they waited with a big smile on her face.

Isla wasted no time leading Ash up to Santa, her reluctance from the year before clearly gone.

"You'll come with me, Mama?" Rylan asked, obviously seeing how the parents of the girls had stepped back while they had their conversations with Santa.

"I will, sweetheart," she assured him, taking the hand he lifted up and holding on to it.

When it was Rylan's turn, Hayden walked partway with them, but then stopped to lean on his crutches as Paige pushed him the rest of the way. He pulled his phone out of his pocket and snapped several pictures. Rylan didn't hold a long conversation with the man, but he did smile broadly for the official picture once they were done talking.

Rylan had a gift bag that was almost bigger than he was on his lap when Paige pushed him back toward where Hayden waited.

"This is huge!" Rylan exclaimed as they got close to Hayden. "I can't wait to open it."

Hayden met Paige's gaze, and she widened her eyes at him, like she couldn't believe the size of the gift bag any more than Rylan could. He just shrugged, then gratefully made his way back to his seat at the table.

Since Santa was the last event of the party, the crowd was rapidly thinning out. Several people came by the table to speak to Hunter, Heather, and their mom as they headed out of the room.

"Can I open this now, Mama?" Rylan asked, eyeing the girls who were looking into their gift bags.

"I guess it's okay," Paige said as she settled into her chair.

Hayden watched Paige as she held the bag open so that Rylan could pull out the tissue paper that covered whatever was inside the bag. The little boy crowed in delight at what he saw.

As Hayden sat there, he felt a bit like he was coming out of the fog of despair that had swept over him when he'd realized that he was going to lose part of his leg. He hadn't thought he'd ever get to this point, especially so soon, and perhaps he wouldn't have had he not walked into the kitchen and seen a little boy sitting in a wheelchair at his table.

He was truly seeing Paige for the first time, too. She'd been a constant in his life over the past several months, just like her mom had been for years before that. But he'd been blinded to anything but the role she played in his life. She had been a silent figure in his life, caring for him when he hadn't cared enough to do it himself.

Now, however, he saw her as a mom, but more than that, he saw her as a woman. A strong, determined woman who had taken a few hard hits in life. Hopefully not literally, Hayden thought with a scowl. She hadn't said anything to indicate that her husband had been physically abusive. Just that he'd been neglectful. And a thief.

He appreciated how she'd pushed forward despite the obvious setbacks she'd faced. Thinking about all that, Hayden made a note to contact Kent to see if he'd found anything. The background check had given him the name he'd needed, and after Hayden had explained what had happened, Kent had promised to pass the information on to the right person. So now he was just waiting to hear what they discovered.

"Look at this, Mama," Rylan said as he struggled to pull a large box from the bag.

Paige leaned over to help him, and a smile tugged at the corner of Hayden's mouth when he saw the familiar logo of the Hot Wheels that he'd loved as a boy. From the size of Rylan's eyes, it was something that thrilled him to no end.

He wished he could talk Paige into letting Rylan set it up at the apartment, but he knew that Rylan wouldn't be spending as much time there now that Leta could watch him again. The boy would want to have the track where he could play with it, and Hayden couldn't blame him for that.

Of course, that didn't mean that Hayden couldn't buy a similar track to set up at the apartment. Hunter would probably think he lost his mind if he showed up at the apartment to find a Hot Wheels track set up on the living room floor. But given that Hunter already thought Hayden had lost his mind, perhaps it didn't matter.

Maybe he'd spend some time on the web, checking out what was out there for racing tracks.

"Did you see this, Hayden?" Rylan asked, pointing at the box. "It's amazing."

"It is. I think you're going to have a lot of fun playing with it."

Rylan nodded vigorously. "I will."

"Did you know they were getting him that?" Paige asked.

"How would I have known?" Hayden pressed a hand to his chest. "Santa doesn't consult me about gift purchases, even for people I know. He just reads the letters they send."

Paige gave him an exasperated look as she shook her head. "Somehow, in this case, I think he might have."

Hayden felt the urge to grin, but that didn't work like it used to, so he just gave her the smile he used now that only lifted one side of his mouth. "I will say that Heather probably has Santa's ear. Or maybe it was Carissa. So if you're really wanting to have a discussion about the gift, they're the ones to talk to."

Her gaze went to where Heather stood with their mom and Hunter, talking to a couple who stood there with their young son. "I think I'll just leave it well enough alone."

"Are you scared of them?" Hayden asked. "Because I can guarantee that neither of them bite."

"I'm not... scared."

"Well, don't be intimidated or anything like that, either. Heather and Carissa are two of the sweetest women you'll ever meet. And if I'm actually saying that about a sibling, you've got to know it's true."

A quick smile crossed her face. "I guess so."

"Seriously, though, just enjoy the gift. That's why Santa brought it, after all."

"I know."

"Did you not believe in Santa as a child?"

"We kind of let Santa fall by the wayside after my brother's freak outs about him. Mom didn't want Santa-induced upset at Christmas. I didn't tend to focus too much on Santa for Rylan, either. He didn't seem to care that the presents he got didn't come from Santa."

Hayden understood that. Even after they all knew that Santa wasn't real, his parents had continued to have gifts from the big guy under the tree. "I think Dad pushed the idea of Santa because he liked to be able to act like him. Being Santa allowed him to give in a way that people more easily accepted, you know?"

"Which is what he did here," Paige observed with a glance around the room.

"Yep. This was definitely the highlight of his year."

"But neither you nor Hunter have taken up the mantle of the red suit, so to speak."

Hayden scoffed at the very idea. "Santa isn't crippled, and I don't think Hunter has the same passion for Santa that my dad did. At least, not yet. He might get to that point now that he has Rachel."

"Well, even if you're not going to follow in his footsteps by being Santa, you're still carrying on for him by continuing this party that was important to him."

Hayden let his gaze wander the room that now held more elves than guests, trying not to let Paige see how her words had pierced him right to his soul. She was right that his dad's legacy was being upheld, but it certainly wasn't any thanks to him.

His siblings and his mom had soldiered on, moving forward in ways that would have made his dad happy. While he, on the other hand, had languished in his self-pity. Sure, he'd been in pain, but he hadn't needed to wallow in it the way he had.

And while Page hadn't been there since the accident, she'd seen how he'd dealt with things over the past several months. He could only imagine what she thought about him.

When he looked at her, he saw a strong, competent woman. When she looked at him, she probably saw a weak, self-absorbed man. That wasn't a good look on anyone.

Chapter 14

Paige wondered if maybe she shouldn't have mentioned Hayden's dad because his mood seemed to turn somber after she did. That hadn't been her intention, but probably being reminded that his dad wasn't around anymore hadn't been a great move on her part. Especially at an occasion that was supposed to be happy.

From the way the room was emptying out, it looked like the party was over anyway, so maybe it was time for them to go. She glanced at her mom to see her talking to Eliza once again. Hayden's mom gestured to the table, and soon a couple of elves showed up with some flat boxes.

Her mom looked at her, then shrugged, leaving Paige perplexed over what was happening. She got up and walked over to her mom. "What's up?"

"Eliza wants to send some food home with us."

Paige looked at Hayden's mom. "Really?"

"Sure. We have plenty, and we've sent some of it home with some of the other guests already. You'd be helping us out."

"There's only the three of us, though, so probably not too much," Paige said. It had all tasted great, however, so she knew they'd happily inhale anything Eliza sent home with them.

"Perfect!" Eliza beamed like she'd just been given something instead of her giving something to them. "You can freeze some of the food as well, so if we send you with too much, just put it in the freezer for another day."

"Thank you so much, Eliza," her mom said. "You've been very generous, especially including Rylan in your Christmas party. I think he's really enjoyed it."

Paige glanced at Rylan, who was still chatting with the girls while they showed him the gifts they'd gotten from Santa.

For all that she'd been reluctant to come to the party, Paige was glad they had. It had been fun for Rylan, and she couldn't deny that she'd enjoyed seeing Hayden again outside of her work environment.

"What's wrong?" Hayden said as she sat back down next to him.

She watched Rylan tilt his head back as he laughed at something one of the girls said before turning her attention to Hayden. "He's really enjoying himself."

"And that's a problem?" Hayden frowned at her. "I mean, I'm not a pro at understanding women or anything, but I would think the fact that he's enjoying himself would make you happy."

Paige gave a huff of laughter. "It does make me happy."

Hayden nodded. "Yep. Makes perfect sense."

"I think we're both ending this party on a high note, huh?"

He met her gaze for a moment, his blue eyes serious. "Yeah. But you know, as long as the kids are happy, that's the important thing."

"It is important," she agreed, then looked over to where her mom now stood with two large flat boxes on the table in front of her. "I think we're going to go soon."

"Are you coming tomorrow to decorate my sister's tree at my apartment?"

Paige grinned at his description. "You act like a little Christmas spirit is going to kill you."

"I enjoy Christmas spirit, as long as it's at someone else's house."

"But what if I'd like my workplace to filled with holiday cheer?"

"Hmmm. Guess I never thought about that." His gaze narrowed at her for a moment. "Has the lack of Christmas décor been bothering you?"

"No. But you know, having decorations might make you feel better."

He didn't look convinced. "Doesn't matter one way or the other. Heather has decreed that the apartment shall become a Christmas wonderland, so it shall be."

"We might show up," Paige said.

Hayden looked at Rylan. "I think you'll be there."

Paige should have been annoyed that after basically not interacting with her on a personal level for months, he thought he knew her that well. Except that... maybe he did. Rylan had enjoyed decorating their tree, so she knew he would have a lot of fun decorating Hayden's, especially if the girls were there.

"Yeah. We probably will be."

Laughter lit Hayden's gaze for a moment, fading only when his scar prevented him from fully grinning at her. He reached up to touch his cheek, then lowered his hand, his brows pulling together. No doubt he thought that he didn't look very attractive with the scar on his face.

Why he hadn't gotten cosmetic surgery for it was as much a mystery as to why he didn't have a prosthesis. Something held him back mentally, because there was no doubt he could afford to pay for both, if he was so inclined.

"It feels... bad," Hayden said, frowning as he stared at Rylan and the girls.

Paige was lost as to what he was referring to. "What feels bad?"

"You've been working for me for months now, and it's taken this long for me to actually get to know anything about you."

Oh. "You've been dealing with a lot."

He frowned at her. "That's no excuse. I was over the worst of things physically three or four months ago."

Paige hesitated, trying to figure out how best to word her response. "I think perhaps the physical adjustment wasn't what you struggle with the most."

Hayden angled a look at her before focusing back on the kids. "Maybe."

Well, at least he hadn't gotten upset with her observation. Frankly, she hadn't cared too much about the fact that he wasn't connecting with her personally. Her own life felt like a dumpster fire, so in some ways, it was nice to not have to hear from him what was going on in his. She'd been as bad at connecting as he had.

Though she hadn't exactly hated cooking and cleaning, she hadn't really loved it either. And perhaps that had been part of what had held her back as well. She was seeing parts of him now that hadn't been apparent in their limited previous interactions.

"Are you ready to go, darling?" her mom asked, laying a hand on her arm.

Paige nodded. "Let me just get Rylan into his stuff."

Rylan protested at first, but when she promised he could see the girls again soon—without being too specific about the next day—he relented and cooperated in getting his jacket on. He could manage his mitts and knit cap, so she focused on her own jacket.

Hayden stood, balancing himself on his crutches. "So tomorrow?"

"We'll be there. Just text me the time."

"I will. Thanks for coming today."

"I believe we should be thanking you for inviting us. This was great." She went to where Heather stood with Ash's arm wrapped around her. "Thank you for including Rylan. He really had a lot of fun."

Heather smiled. "I'm just glad you could make it. Hopefully, we'll see you tomorrow."

"I think we'll plan to be there."

If possible, the woman's smile grew bigger. "Wonderful! Be sure to remind Rylan to bring his decoration for Hayden's tree."

After promising that she would, Paige said goodbye to the others there, then she pushed Rylan's chair from the room with her mom at her side.

"That was just lovely," her mom said. "I'm so glad you talked me into coming."

"I'm glad you came too."

"Eliza told me to come tomorrow as well if you decide to go."

Paige glanced over at her mom. "I already told Heather and Hayden that we'd be there."

"I'm glad."

Once they were in the car on the way home, her mom said, "I was so pleased to see Hayden there today. Perhaps he'll begin to embrace life again."

"I think he only came because of Rylan," Paige told her.

"God uses unexpected people sometimes. Perhaps a child was needed to lead Hayden out of the darkness he's been living in. Hayden still has so much to offer the world, and it's been hard to see how much he's struggled over the years."

Since she'd been living in Chicago while her mom was working for Hayden, she'd only heard about the man in passing when her mom mentioned him during their weekly chats. All she knew was that her mom prayed for Hayden on a daily basis, and that she cared for him.

That care and concern had made it difficult for her mom to leave the job, but she'd still insisted that it was the best for their situation. That she was happy to turn her time and attention to Paige and Rylan.

Paige was a bit chagrined to have to admit that while her mom had seen caring for Hayden as more than just a job, Paige had approached it as a necessary—but not really enjoyable—job. Its positives for her were that it paid well and provided her with the type of insurance Rylan needed.

Now, however, she didn't think she'd ever be able to go back to viewing Hayden as just the man she cooked and cleaned for. They'd crossed a line—at least in her mind—and surprisingly enough, that didn't bother her.

It was weird to knock on Hayden's door, but Paige didn't feel it was right to walk on in, even though she had a key, since she wasn't there in an employment capacity.

When the door swung open, Hunter stood there with a smile on his face. "Hey! I'm so glad you could make it."

He stepped back as the girls came running to the door. They greeted Rylan with happy squeals, which made Paige smile. It warmed her heart to have the person she loved the most be greeted so enthusiastically.

Over the next couple of minutes, they got out of their jackets and boots. Her mom went into the kitchen, while Paige pushed Rylan's chair into the living room. Without even thinking about it, her gaze sought out Hayden, and she frowned when she didn't spot him in the group gathered in the room.

She parked Rylan's chair next to where the girls were looking through some bags, then after greeting Heather, Carissa, and Ash, she went to the kitchen. Her mom was there with Eliza and a middle-aged woman and man.

"Paige," Eliza said with a smile. "Have you met Essie and George?"

Though she'd never met them, she was well aware of who they were. "Nice to meet you."

Essie's smile was warm as she greeted Paige, as was her husband's. Hayden was fortunate to be surrounded by such caring people. Except that right then, he wasn't anywhere to be seen.

Excusing herself, Paige returned to the living room. A quick glance showed that Hayden still wasn't there. Given that he hadn't seemed all that excited about the prospect of having them decorate a tree at his place, she wouldn't be completely surprised if he was hiding out in his bedroom.

"This tree is huge, Mama," Rylan said as she sat down on the couch next to his wheelchair.

Paige looked up at the tree that now stood in front of the large window. She was mildly surprised that it wasn't a real one. For some reason, she assumed that if people could afford a real tree, they'd have one.

"Have you two decided which one of you is up on the ladder to string the lights?" Heather asked, glancing back and forth between Ash and Hunter.

"I don't understand," Ash said slowly as he looked from his fiancée to the tree. "Why do we need to add more lights when the tree already came with lights?"

"My question *exactly*," Hunter said.

Heather crossed her arms. "You can never have too many lights on a Christmas tree."

"We didn't add more lights to our tree," Hunter said.

"That's because I decided to take it easy on you since we're still essentially newlyweds." Carissa smiled as she took his hand. "But you just wait until next Christmas. It's all on you then."

Hunter frowned. "Fine. But how are we supposed to reach the top of the tree?"

"No worries!" Heather clapped her hands. "I had George bring a ladder. It's in the hallway."

"I'll get it," Ash offered, then headed to the hallway that led to the bedrooms.

"How do you feel about the light situation, Paige?" Heather asked. "What's your opinion?"

Paige held up her hands. "I have no opinion."

Heather gave her a skeptical look. "I doubt that. But since this is the first time you're decorating a tree with us, I'll let you get away with it. Next year, all bets are off."

Paige wondered if they'd actually still be in the Kings' lives in a year's time. It wasn't that she had plans to quit working for Hayden, but she knew all too well that a *lot* could change in a year. Within a twelve-month period, she'd gone from what she thought was a stable life to being divorced and nearly broke. So yeah, who knew where they'd be next Christmas.

Heather glanced toward the hall when Ash didn't return right away. Underneath the lighthearted subject that Heather was focused on, Paige could see some concern. Maybe she wasn't the only one wondering what was up with Hayden.

"When can we start decorating, Auntie?" Rachel asked as she held up a decoration from one of the bags. "I want to put this one on. It's really cool."

"What is it, lovey?" Carissa asked.

"It's a book." Rachel skipped over to show her mom. "I love books."

"I know," Heather said. "That's why I got some book ones for you. I also got some art decorations for Isla, and little car ones for Rylan."

There was no way that this was the spur-of-the-moment suggestion it had seemed to be the previous day. Even with all her money, Paige was sure that Heather wouldn't have been able to find those types of decorations in less than twenty-four hours.

"We need to get the lights put on the tree first," Heather said. "Then we can hang the decorations."

Eliza entered the living room with the others and looked around. "You haven't started yet?"

"We're just waiting for Ash to get the ladder so we can string the lights."

George frowned, then headed for the hallway. He returned a minute later with the ladder, but Ash was nowhere in sight. Without commenting on that, Heather guided George on where to set the ladder. She and Hunter went to work unboxing the lights, then Hunter climbed up the ladder to work under his sister's direction, with a little input from their mom.

Paige shifted in her seat, itching to head to the kitchen to make Hayden a cup of coffee and take it to him in his room. Was this how he was on the weekends when she wasn't there to make him breakfast, open his curtains, and get his day underway?

When Ash returned a short time later, Heather swung toward him, a question in her eyes. Without her even having to voice it, Ash said, "He'll be out in a few minutes."

Heather made her way to Ash and slipped her arm around his waist, leaning her head on his shoulder for a moment. "Thank you."

Ash brushed a kiss against her head. "You're welcome."

Paige felt an ache in her chest as she watched the affection between the couple. It was what she'd hoped she'd have with

Glenn, but nothing could have been further from the reality of their relationship.

There'd been some of it at the beginning of the relationship and early marriage. Though looking back now, she realized it had been less about the emotional connection and more about the physical one. Glenn had no trouble squeezing or patting certain parts of her body, stating that he loved how hot she was. That wasn't the type of interactions she saw happening between Ash and Heather or Hunter and Carissa.

A fleeting thought about how Hayden would be with a woman he loved flitted through her mind, but Paige didn't grab onto it to mull over. It didn't matter to her, so she didn't need to spend any time dwelling on it.

Still, it didn't keep her from wondering about the man and hoping that he was okay. As an employee... Just like she would wonder about him if this happened during the week when she was there to cook and clean for him.

An employee. Nothing more.

Chapter 15

Hayden stared out the window next to the table in his room, wishing he'd had the guts to tell Heather no when she'd suggested decorating his apartment. His night had been restless. Phantom pains. Nightmares. Thoughts of a lost future. All of it had led to too few hours of sleep and too many hateful inner thoughts.

He knew that it had been triggered by attending the party and the memories it had brought up, along with the memories of his dad. And all his mind had attached itself to were the reasons why the man was no longer with them.

He hadn't yet moved to the point in his grief that Hunter and Heather had, where they could look back on the memories of their dad without the intense mourning. These days with them, a mention of their dad often brought smiles and laughter. That still wasn't the case for him, though, and he wasn't sure if it ever would be.

If this had been a weekday, he would have spent it in bed or, more likely, the theater room where he'd play video games or watch movies to distract himself. But unfortunately, he was going to have to deal with his family, who would look at him with worry and concern.

Maybe if he'd been a stronger person, he would have been able to bluff his way through their visit. But he wasn't able to hide his current mental state when he was exhausted on top of everything else.

A light tap on his door drew him from his thoughts, and he wondered who had decided to try to pry him from his room. His first guess would be Hunter or his mom.

"Come in." He glanced over to see his door swing open to reveal his soon-to-be brother-in-law. He hadn't seen that one coming, even though he considered Ash a close friend. The man seemed willing to just let him be, never forcing conversation on him. "You draw the short straw?"

Ash gave him a small smile as he made his way across the room and folded himself into the chair opposite Hayden. "No straws were drawn. I was sent to fetch a ladder so we can put lights on a tree that was purchased with some already attached."

"And you decided to make a run for it. I get it," Hayden stated. "Unfortunately for you, I don't think Heather will let you get away. She'll probably chase you to the ends of the earth."

Ash's expression softened. "As I would do for her."

Hayden scowled at him. "If I wanted to deal with sugary sweetness, I'd ask Paige to make me cookies or something."

"Not gonna apologize for loving your sister, bro," Ash said with a serious look.

Hayden regarded him for a long moment. "Nor should you. I think I'd probably smack you around if you did."

"And I'd let you."

Hayden shifted his gaze to the window again. The day was sunny and bright, a slap in the face of his decidedly un-sunny mood.

"You know that your family wouldn't hold it against you if you didn't make an appearance."

Hayden was sure that was true. They'd cut him all kinds of slack over the years. Probably more than they should have.

The thing was... his thoughts were of a little boy and his mom. He didn't want to disappoint Rylan, and even though he'd shown plenty of weakness to Paige over the months that she'd worked for him, he didn't want to do it that day.

After a couple more minutes of shared silence, Hayden finally looked at Ash. The man had been staring out the window as well, but at his movement, Ash also turned away from the view.

"I'll be out in a bit. I just need to get cleaned up."

Ash nodded. "I'll let them know."

He got to his feet, then rested his hand on Hayden's shoulder, squeezing gently before he left the room. Hayden rubbed his hands over his face, then reached for his crutches. Moving slowly, he headed for the bathroom, hoping a shower might wash away the lingering negativity from his night. Though maybe that was hoping for a miracle, since it had never worked before.

When he finally approached the entrance to the living room a short time later, Hayden felt physically better, if not mentally. He'd put on a pair of worn jeans that were soft enough that he could pin them up, along with a black turtleneck shirt. Black in deference to his dark mood, though he hoped that it wouldn't hang around once he saw the girls and Rylan. And Paige.

As soon as he turned the corner, his mom spotted him and smiled. She got to her feet and came over to give him a hug. After stepping back, she reached up and cupped his cheeks, urging him to bend down so that she could place a kiss on his forehead. She didn't bother to ask how he was, no doubt not wanting to force him to lie.

"Look at this decoration, Uncle Hayden," Rachel said as she skipped up to him. "It's a book!"

He looked at her decoration, then at the one Isla came over to show him. Rylan had one too, so Hayden made his way to his chair to check it out before sitting down on the couch with Paige.

Her brows drew together as her assessing gaze swept over him. It probably wasn't the first time she'd looked at him that way, considering she'd seen him first thing in the morning after many of his roughest nights. But like his mom, she didn't ask him how he was.

"Looks like you're getting a child-themed Christmas tree," she said.

Hayden leaned his crutches against the end of the couch. "I'm not going to complain about that. These kids love the holiday so much, it's only right the tree should reflect that."

She smiled at him then. "It's a good thing you feel that way. Hope you also like lots of lights."

"Even if I didn't, I wouldn't protest. If I dared voice my displeasure, I'd probably wake up to a million fairy lights strung throughout the apartment. So I'll accept a tree heavily loaded with them instead."

Paige smiled. "You think Heather would really do that?"

Hayden let out a huff. "Have you *met* my sister? Of course, she would."

"You need to change your locks, then you wouldn't have to worry about your siblings exacting revenge on you."

"And you wouldn't let them in if they tried to convince you it was in my best interests?" Hayden asked with a heavy dose of skepticism.

Paige crossed her arms and glanced at Hunter and Heather, where they stood near the tree, supervising the kids. "Ummm... No?"

"Haha," Hayden said, a grin briefly lifting one side of his mouth. "They will prey upon your weakness. First rule of sibling club. Never let them see your weakness."

She seemed to consider his words for a few moments before she said, "But the first rule of keeping my job club is always obey the boss."

"And you don't think I'm your boss?" Hayden asked.

"Well, considering Hunter was the one to hire me and pay me, I figured that made him boss."

"Okay. You've got me there." He would have suggested that maybe it was time he took over that responsibility, but he liked the idea of not being her actual boss.

"Still, I would think twice before letting them in, depending on the circumstances," she said. "Just in case you ever do decide to change your locks."

"Why would you want to change your locks?" Heather asked as she dropped down on the couch beside him, making the cushions jostle. "Were you robbed?"

"Not yet. But maybe, like changing passwords, changing locks regularly is a good idea."

"You're crazy," Heather said. "But as long as I get a copy of the key, I won't comment too much on your craziness."

"That kind of defeats the purpose, if my goal is to keep out the riffraff."

"What*ever*," Heather muttered. "Personally, I think the riffraff already *lives* in the apartment."

Paige didn't even bother to hide her laughter. "The three of you must have driven your mom around the bend."

"Probably," Hayden agreed. "But it was a really fun trip for us."

Hayden hadn't thought anything would lift his mood, but being around Paige and the others seemed to lighten things for him. The kids were having a blast putting their decorations on the tree, along with the more generic ones Heather had bought.

"Can you lift me up to put one of my decorations on the top of the tree?" Rylan asked Hunter.

"Uh... sure?" Hunter glanced over at Paige. "Is it okay if I lift him?"

"Yep. You just have to be aware of his bag." Paige got to her feet and went to help Hunter lift Rylan up, showing him where to be careful of putting his hands.

Hayden frowned as he watched his brother do something for Rylan that he couldn't do for the little boy. Rylan hadn't even asked him, well aware that Hayden wasn't up to the task.

For the first time in a long time, it pained him to be found lacking by someone he cared about.

No one in his family had any expectations of him—or at least none that they'd voiced to him—and he'd always been glad of that. Rylan also had had no expectations of him, but for some reason, Hayden wanted him to. And on top of that, he wanted to be able to at least attempt to fulfill those expectations.

His lifted spirits began to sink again as he watched Rylan hang his decorations, then give Hunter a hug before his brother carefully lowered him back into his chair. Hayden was glad that Rylan was happy, but it was hard to realize that because of his own decisions, he had to accept that others would make him happy in ways Hayden couldn't. Not unless he was willing to make some changes in his life.

"The tree looks amazing," his mom said as she approached the kids. She gave each of them a hug. "What a great job you've done. I know Hayden is going to really enjoy it."

When she glanced at him, Hayden forced a smile and gave them a thumbs up. "Yep. It looks great."

Paige sat down beside him again. "I think Rylan is thrilled to be able to decorate two trees this year. He's only ever decorated one at Christmas."

"I'm glad he's having fun," Hayden said. "That's what it's all about, right? The kids having fun."

"I suppose," she agreed. "But I think it should be a time of year when we're all happy and having fun."

He slanted a look at her. "Are you?"

"Am I what?"

"Happy and having fun."

"Oh. Well." She frowned for a moment, then shrugged. "I figured this Christmas would be much like last year. I tried to make it happy for Rylan, but my heart definitely wasn't in it because of everything that had happened in the months before."

"And it's different this year?"

"It seems like maybe it is," she said. "Rylan is certainly enjoying himself immensely already. And it hasn't escaped my notice that is thanks to you and your family."

"Since Christmas was my dad's favorite holiday, being around our family at that time of year would inevitably result in people being drawn into our celebrations."

"I'm thankful that you've continued that tradition, since we've been beneficiaries of it."

Hayden gave her a lopsided smile. "In the interest of full-disclosure, it's been Hunter and Heather that have been responsible for that."

"Not everything he's enjoyed has been centered around Christmas," she reminded him. "You've watched movies with him, which he loved. You invited him to swim, something else he really loves. So I have to say, you *have* played a role in making this a memorable holiday for Rylan."

"And the holiday isn't over yet."

"So I've heard," she said. "Heather mentioned something about a children's program."

Hayden nodded. "Both girls are in it."

"Is the church accessible?"

"It is. They've made sure everyone who wants to attend can."

"That's good." She hesitated. "When we moved here, I didn't really look for a church to attend."

"I get that," Hayden said. "Regular church attendance hasn't been my thing since the accident, but I go at Christmas time, and other times that seem important to my mom and the girls."

Hayden looked to where his mom and Paige's mom were talking with the kids. He wondered if Rylan's other grandparents had anything to do with him. Paige hadn't mentioned anything about them, so perhaps they were of the same ilk as their son and not deserving of being in Rylan's life.

Not that he believed every parent of bad kids was also bad, or vice versa. But if Rylan's grandparents were like their son, Hayden hoped they didn't get anywhere near him.

He was starting to care too much. No. Scratch that. He *already* cared too much, which didn't bode well for him.

When he looked at Paige and Rylan, he wished he were in a place in his life where he'd be good for them. It didn't escape him that it was one hundred percent his fault that he *wasn't* in that place. If he'd been working on his issues all along like his family had wanted him to, he would have been there already.

"I think we're done," Hunter said. "If we put another decoration on that tree, it's going to collapse."

The tree didn't match the perfection of most of the trees at his mom's house, but it looked like a happy tree. Hopefully, whenever he looked at it, he'd feel some measure of joy.

"Now we need to clean everything up," Heather said as she began to collect the packaging that had held the decorations she'd brought.

"The food should be here any minute," his mom announced. "I hope you're all hungry because we got a lot of it."

Paige got up to help Heather, gathering up bits of garbage while Heather stacked up the packaging that they'd re-use when they removed the decorations after Christmas. Ash sat down beside him on the couch, and Isla ran over to climb on his lap.

"I got to do four trees this year," Isla exclaimed while she held up her fingers. "Four!"

"How did you manage four?" Hayden asked.

"One at our house. One at Grandma's. One at Rachel's." She poked up a finger for each place. "And now one here. Four!"

"Well, thank you for helping me with mine."

She beamed at him. "You're welcome."

"Are you excited about the wedding and the new house?" Hayden asked.

"Yep! I've never been on a plane before, and I got to pick my favorite color for my room in the new house."

He hadn't been keen on the idea of a destination wedding that Heather wanted, but at least he wasn't going to be plagued by intense pain like he had been in the past. And he couldn't deny that a break from the cold would be very welcome.

"Are *you* ready for the move?" he asked Ash, knowing that he'd been reluctant to move at first, assuming that Heather would want to live in a mansion similar to their family home.

"Yep," Ash said with a nod as Isla slid off his lap and abandoned them to their boring conversation. "It's not like I'll be taking much from my old place. Mainly just our personal stuff. Not that it's any loss. The furniture I had was ancient."

"I'm just glad you two found some middle ground. I was worried."

"You shouldn't have been," Ash told him. "We each knew where the other was coming from. We just needed to talk it out."

"And you're truly happy with the house?"

"Once we found something that fell between my small house and the mansion, I was happy. Plus, it has a huge garage which makes me even happier."

"And Isla will be able to go to the same school as Rachel?"

"Yep. We're going to switch schools as soon as we get back from the wedding. Though she hasn't had as hard a time this school year as she did last year, she was more than happy to switch mid-year if it meant she'd be with Rachel."

"I'm sure they'll be happy to see each other every day."

Ash chuckled. "Well, they're already on video chat every evening. But yeah, they'll see each other in person."

Though he was happy that things were coming together for his siblings with people he not only liked but admired, it was just another reminder of how stagnant he was in his own life. He'd been very focused on the past, barely existing day to day. The only time he'd looked to the future had been when he'd been anticipating another surgery.

But now he had nothing to look forward to. His surgeries were all done. There was nothing except maybe some cosmetic stuff left, but he wasn't focused on that at all.

Was that really enough to justify his life going forward? Or was he just going to be someone not really contributing much to life or society?

His dad would absolutely look at him in disappointment if that's what he ended up doing. And his mom, though she might try to hide it, would no doubt feel the same way.

"Thank you for letting me help decorate your tree, Hayden."

Rylan's voice drew his attention, and Hayden found the little boy had approached the couch with the help of his mom.

"I should be thanking you," Hayden said. "You did an amazing job. I don't think it would have looked as nice without your help."

Rylan grinned, his whole face beaming, and Paige stood beside his chair, watching her son with obvious love and affection. Seeing them so happy brought him happiness as well, but he was quite sure that it wouldn't last. The momentary blips of happiness he experienced never did.

But as Paige looked at him and smiled, Hayden wished that this particular moment of happiness could last forever.

Chapter 16

Paige found that she was keeping an eye on Hayden more than she was Rylan. She had no worries about Rylan. He was having a blast with Rachel and Isla, and he hadn't hesitated to inhale all the food she put on his plate. She didn't think he'd stopped smiling since they'd walked through the door. Hayden, on the other hand...

From the moment she'd arrived to find that he hadn't made an appearance yet, she had a feeling that he wasn't having a great day. When he'd first come from his bedroom, he looked like he'd had a rough night. But then he'd engaged with her and the others, and she thought things would be fine. That didn't appear to be the case, however.

The pendulum of his emotions was something she struggled to understand. For most of the time she'd known him, she hadn't dwelt on it. Paige had known that if she asked him how he was feeling, he'd just brush her off. So, she hadn't expended the effort.

Now, though, against her better judgment, she'd come to care for the guy. Paige worried about him, and she wanted to know if there was anything she could do to make him feel better.

"Want some dessert?" she asked him. "Your mom ordered some yummy looking chocolate cake."

He looked up at her from where he sat at the table next to Rylan. They were all seated around his large dining room table instead of the smaller one in the kitchen. "Sure. Thanks."

"Coffee too?"

A corner of his mouth tipped up. "Why not?"

"Can I have cake too, Mama?" Rylan asked. "And coffee?"

That got a chuckle out of Hayden, while Paige just shook her head. "Yes, on the cake. No, on the coffee. I've heard that coffee makes you stop growing."

"But wouldn't that be a good thing, Mama?" he asked. "Cause then you'll always be able to carry me when I need you too."

His words hit her in the heart, but she tried not to show it. "Nope. You need to grow up healthy and strong. So, no coffee for you."

"Milk?"

"Milk is fine." She tousled his hair, then went into the kitchen without making eye contact with anyone as her emotions took a pendulum swing of their own.

She didn't like to think too far into the future, especially now that she didn't have the funds to make sure that Rylan's every need would be taken care of. As he grew, she knew that he'd learn how to take care of himself more, but it would be harder without the money to buy him what he'd need to accommodate his limitations.

"Here you go," she said a few minutes later as she set plates with cake on them in front of Hayden and Rylan.

After she'd given them their drinks, she went back to the kitchen to help clean up. Her mom was already there and slipped her arms around Paige and gave her a tight squeeze. She didn't need to ask if Paige was upset. More than anyone else, she would understand why Rylan's comment hurt her heart.

"Love you, Paigy." She gave her another squeeze before stepping back and fixing her with a firm look. "Don't borrow worry from tomorrow. It won't change a *thing*, and it will only rob you of the joy of today."

"I know, Mom. I know." And she did, but all it took was an innocent comment to have her mind in the grip of worry once again.

"If you forget, I'll always be here to remind you." She gave her a broad smile. "Now let's clean this up."

Eliza and Essie came in to help them, but Paige sent them back out again. "You just go enjoy your visit. We'll take care of this."

"But you should be enjoying your day off," Essie said with a frown.

"From what I've heard, you never take a day off."

Eliza laughed. "She's got you there, Essie darling."

Essie let out a huff as she shook her head. "Fine."

The two women left the kitchen, and Paige was relieved. She didn't want to have to keep her emotions hidden right then. Her mom knew what she needed and chatted about everything and nothing, prattling on in a way that didn't require responses from Paige.

By the time they rejoined the others in the living room, she was back in control. Hunter and Carissa were the first ones to gather up their stuff to leave. After that, it was Eliza, Essie, and George who left. Heather and Ash didn't appear to be in a big rush, and Isla seemed happy to hang out with Rylan, talking about pictures they liked to color.

"How is the program going at the garage?" Hayden asked as Ash settled in the armchair next to him.

"Really well. We've got a couple of new people starting in January. One is a teen who is interested in car mechanics as a career. The other is a woman who actually has some experience in the garage, but she's had trouble finding work."

"Because she's a woman?" Hayden asked.

"Possibly. She's applied lots of places, but no one will hire her."

"Maybe you should hire her yourself, instead of her just being part of the program."

Ash shrugged. "Maybe. Depends on what I see of her work ethic and knowledge. I don't really need another employee, since we have plenty of work for me and the two guys I have now."

"Good thing I'm getting you locked down," Heather said. "Wouldn't want you to decide you'd rather be with someone who speaks the language of the garage."

Ash chuckled. "Never gonna happen. I love the language you speak."

"No mushiness allowed," Hayden said with a wave of his hand. "This is a mushy-free zone."

"You're just jealous," Heather teased, going in a direction that Paige wouldn't have thought she would.

"Hah. I don't think so."

"We should probably go," Ash said. "Before the two of you get into it, and I have to call Hunter back to deal with you."

"Yes," Heather agreed. "School day tomorrow. That's the only reason we're going. Not because I'm scared of Hunter or anything."

Paige knew that they should probably go, too. It had been a good day, but she was ready to head for home and put some distance between herself and Hayden. She was fairly certain that he'd be in the kitchen for his breakfast the next morning instead of waiting in his room. Hopefully, she could shore up her defenses before coming back to work.

"We should go too," Paige said. "I gotta work tomorrow."

Heather laughed. "And your boss is probably a real meanie."

"I would have to say he is," Hayden agreed. "Paige and I decided earlier that Hunter is actually her boss."

That comment made Ash chuckle. "How I wish you'd said it was Heather."

Heather reached out and pushed at Ash's shoulder, making the man laugh again. "I'm going to tell Essie you're not allowed to have dessert for a week as punishment for that comment."

"Essie likes me," Ash said with a smirk. "She'll still feed me dessert."

"Yeah. Probably," Heather agreed with a sigh. "That's because after our cooking classes with her, you're better at it than I am."

"Who would have thought that would be the case?" Ash mused.

"Well, I think it's proof that you should do all the cooking after we're married." Heather's smile was so big that Paige had to chuckle.

Ash sighed. "If I'd known that was going to be the result of excelling in the classes, I might have put a little less effort into things. Although, I think it's got me desserts for life."

Paige hadn't spent much time around Hayden's siblings and their significant others until recently, and she enjoyed the banter they shared. It reminded her of how her parents had been together.

"Have a good week," Heather said when she stood at the apartment door a few minutes later. "It was so much fun having you here tonight."

"It was fun being here," Paige told her. "Thanks for including us."

Isla gave Rylan a wave, then took Heather's hand as they left the apartment. Once they were gone, Paige checked to make sure the kitchen was clean, and that there were no dirty dishes sitting around. While she did that, her mom and Rylan chatted with Hayden.

Once that was done, Paige went back to the living room. "We should probably go."

Hayden looked disappointed, and it made her want to stick around, knowing that once they left, he'd be alone. That had never really bothered her before, since she'd never gotten the feeling that he cared one way or another if she was there or not. So much had changed in the past few weeks.

"I'll see you in the morning," she said as they stood at the door a short time later with their coats on.

Hayden leaned on his crutches. "Yep. Thanks for your help with the tree, Rylan."

The two high-fived, then Paige pushed the wheelchair from the apartment and followed her mom to the elevator. She was glad that they had parked in the basement earlier, so once they got to the car, she didn't have to worry about the cold as she got Rylan into his seat.

"It was so nice seeing the boys again," her mom said as Paige drove them out of the underground garage.

"Boys." Paige laughed. "They're not boys, Mom."

"They are to me."

"Well, regardless, I'm glad you got to spend some time with them."

"Hayden seems a little better. I never would have imagined him wanting to be part of stuff like the party yesterday or decorating the tree tonight."

Paige decided not to tell her that she thought maybe Rylan played a role in that. "Would be nice if it meant he'd look at getting a prosthesis. Not sure what's been holding him back."

"That would be wonderful, and a definite sign that he is healing in all ways from that accident."

Only time would tell if that was the case. Paige wasn't sure if Hayden's willingness to be present at stuff like that was just because of the time of year. If he continued to be this way into the new year, perhaps it was a change of more permanency.

The next morning, the apartment was quiet when Paige let herself in, and she felt a pang of disappointment. Though what she'd been expecting, she wasn't sure. It wasn't likely that he'd have the television in the living room on or be banging around in the kitchen. Of course, it would be quiet.

She hung up her jacket and took off her boots before heading into the kitchen to start breakfast. As she mixed up the pancakes, Paige's thoughts went to Rylan, who had been so disappointed that he couldn't come with her that day.

Even though there wasn't a problem bringing him, she didn't want him to get even more attached to Hayden than he already was. It was important to Paige that Rylan view time with Hayden as a special event, not a daily thing. She was beginning to wish that she only had sporadic contact with him herself.

Once the pancake batter was mixed, she started the coffee that Hayden would want. Soon the smell of pancakes cooking mingled with the aroma of the coffee brewing.

She cut up some strawberries into a small bowl, then put the pancakes on the plate. It didn't take her long to put everything on a tray, planning to carry it to Hayden's room as soon as she took the rest of the pancakes off the pan.

Before she even picked up the tray, however, Hayden appeared in the doorway of the kitchen. He wore a pair of sweatpants and a long-sleeve T-shirt, and his hair looked like it hadn't had its daily meeting with his hairbrush yet.

"I smell coffee." Though he didn't look as bad as she'd seen him some mornings, he did look like he was barely awake.

"You must be imagining things," she said as she turned back to the tray, trying to hide her smile. "No coffee around here."

"Hah. You lie like a rug." He made his way to the table by the window. "Ugh. Looks miserable out."

"Yeah. Driving wasn't a whole lot of fun."

"You know that if the roads aren't good, I don't expect you to come here. I'd rather you be safe."

Paige nodded. "It wasn't too bad, as long as I didn't drive fast like some people on the road."

"Bad conditions can be risky when there are idiots on the road."

Too late, Paige recalled the accident he'd been in had been because of poor road conditions. The slick highway contributing to the pileup that took the lives of Hayden's dad and Carissa's parents, as well as several others.

"Just…" Hayden cleared his throat. "I'd rather you be overly cautious than take the risk of coming here if the roads are bad. I can fend for myself if I have to. You've left food in the freezer, or if need be, I can order stuff in."

She carried the tray over to the table and set it down. "I won't take any risks."

He looked up at her as she unloaded the tray. "Thanks. I'd really hate for anything to happen to you, just because you felt you had to come to work."

"I'll be careful." Paige rested her hand on his shoulder for a moment, feeling the bones in his shoulder. "Promise."

Hayden let out a sigh as he picked up his mug of coffee. Moving her hand, Paige returned to the kitchen to clean up the mess she'd made.

"The pancakes are good as usual," he said after he'd taken a couple of bites. "How's Rylan?"

"Rylan is fine." Paige filled a glass with water and took a sip. "He had such a good time this weekend. He talked about it until he fell asleep last night, then mentioned it again this morning when he woke up."

Hayden chuckled. "That's great."

"He recounted the whole weekend over and over again, like Mom and I hadn't been there with him for everything. If he'd been going to school today, his teacher probably would have gotten sick of hearing about it."

"I remember being like that after a particularly fun weekend. The teacher would say to me *why can't you be more like Hunter.*"

"Well, that's kind of mean."

"Do you know what I told her? That I didn't want to be like Hunter because he was boring." Hayden's mouth lifted in a lopsided smile as Paige laughed. "And that's still how it is today."

Before she could reply, she heard the apartment door open.

"I'm in here, Craig," Hayden called out.

Craig appeared in the kitchen doorway, his gaze going to where Hayden sat at the table. "This is a bit of a surprise."

"You're always telling me to get out of the bedroom," Hayden said. "Want some coffee?"

"Uh... sure," Craig said as he moved to the table.

Paige quickly grabbed another mug and carried it to the table, along with the coffee carafe. She filled Craig's, then refreshed Hayden's, before getting the cream and sugar.

The men thanked her, and she headed out of the kitchen, leaving the guys to talk. She'd return to finish cleaning up once they went to Hayden's room.

It felt a bit weird to be stripping the sheets off his bed and gathering up the dirty towels in his bathroom now that they had interactions that didn't relate to her job at the apartment. She couldn't put her finger on why she felt that way exactly, and rather than dwell too much on it, she shoved the thoughts aside and focused on the job they paid her to do.

Chapter 17

Hayden waited near the front door of the church, keeping his gaze averted from everyone passing by him as they walked in for the children's program. Heather and Ash and Hunter and Carissa had taken the girls to where the children were being gathered. His mom, Essie, and George were already in the sanctuary, hopefully saving seats for all of them.

Normally, he'd be with them, sitting down rather than leaning on his crutches as he waited for Paige, her mom, and Rylan. But he'd told Paige that he'd wait for her, so there he was... waiting.

Shifting on his crutches, Hayden let out a sharp exhale as he lowered his gaze to the floor. He was sure that people were looking at him, and that made him antsy. There was a reason he stuck to his apartment and rarely ventured out to places where he'd draw attention to himself.

But for the second weekend in a row, he was putting himself in a position that was decidedly uncomfortable. All because of Paige and Rylan. And he had no idea what to do about that.

He would have been at the program regardless, because it made his mom and the girls happy. But in the stretch of time starting from the anniversary date of the accident and his dad's death in mid-November, he really didn't want to be out and around people. Even his family, if he was going to be perfectly honest. But he forced himself to do it.

Truthfully, he hated everything about the holidays, starting at Thanksgiving all the way through the New Year. He wished that he could just not have to participate in anything because it *all* reminded him of his dad and how they'd lost him. The hole he'd left behind was enormous. Far bigger than any hole Hayden would have left had he been the one to die in the accident.

"Hi Hayden!" Rylan's cheerful greeting had Hayden lifting his head and pushing aside his dark thoughts once more. They'd be there waiting for him later. The little boy waved excitedly as Paige pushed him toward where Hayden waited.

"Hey, buddy." Hayden let go of the handle on his crutch and held out his hand for Rylan to smack. Rylan pulled off his glove and gave Hayden's palm a light smack.

"Glad you could make it," Hayden said as he greeted Paige and Leta. "Do you want to take your jackets off?"

At Paige's nod, he led them to the coatroom off to the side of the front doors. It didn't take long to get their stuff hung up, and then they made their way into the sanctuary and down the aisle to where his mom was.

He noticed that they had switched up where they usually sat, choosing the rows around the one that had space for a wheelchair at the end of it. As Paige and her mom greeted the others, Hayden maneuvered his way into the row.

After he was seated, he realized that Leta had settled onto the pew behind them where his mom and Essie were sitting, along with George. Once Paige had gotten Rylan's wheelchair situated in the space at the end of the pew, she sat down next to him. Since Hayden had left room for Leta, there was space between them now. It was a bit awkward to be so far apart from her, so he shifted closer to her on the pew.

"How has your weekend been?" Paige asked.

It had been boring, but she didn't need to know that. Their plan to decorate gingerbread houses on Friday night had fallen through, which he'd felt surprisingly disappointed about. They hadn't even considered that the girls would have rehearsals for the kids' program.

"It was fine. Yours?"

"Well, we picked up some groceries. I did laundry. Lots of exciting stuff."

"Where are Rachel and Isla?" Rylan asked, his wheelchair situated so that he was forward enough to see Hayden past Paige.

"They're with the other kids who'll be in the program tonight. We'll see them afterward."

Rylan looked around, then back at Hayden. "They're going to be in front of all these people?"

"Yep."

"Won't they be scared?" Rylan asked. "I'd be scared."

"I don't think Rachel is, but Isla is a bit nervous. She and Rachel are going to sing together. Rachel has sung by herself before, so she's used to it. This is Isla's first time."

Hayden shifted, glancing over to see Hunter leading Carissa and the others into the pew from the opposite end. "Girls ready to go?"

Hunter sat down beside him and nodded. "I admire the people organizing this thing. Those kids are acting like they've been sucking on pixie sticks all day. Should be interesting."

"They were like that last year too," Carissa said. "But they were fine once they got on stage. I'm sure that will be the case this year too."

"For every parent here, I hope that's the case," Hunter said with a shake of his head.

Once the program started, Hayden kept glancing at Rylan, glad to see him watching the kids on the stage with a smile. From what

Paige had said, the pair had attended church in Chicago, which was probably why Rylan seemed comfortable being there.

When Hayden saw Rachel and Isla's smiling faces on the big screens at the front of the sanctuary, he had such a dichotomy of emotions that his chest hurt. While he was happy to see the girls enjoying themselves, the knowledge that this was something that would have thrilled his dad hurt so much.

Rachel sang the first verse of the song, with Isla joining her for the chorus. The words of the song seemed to be God's immediate response to his thoughts on Christmas without his dad. *Christmas isn't Christmas Til it Happens in Your Heart.* It was a song he'd heard before, but it had been ages ago.

Rachel and Isla's childish voices rang clear as they sang about needing to have Jesus in their hearts to truly experience Christmas.

Hayden had invited Jesus into his heart a long time ago, so Christmas should have been a time to celebrate. But since the accident, there had been no celebration of Jesus' birth in his heart. His focus had been on the absence of his father, and how it had changed everything for him regarding Christmas.

Caught up in his grief, Hayden had forgotten that even though his dad had dressed up in Santa and threw Christmas parties, he had always made sure that they knew the *real* reason for Christmas. Every year, for as long as Hayden could remember, his dad had gathered them together each Sunday evening in Advent, and they'd read Scriptures and talk about what it meant.

His dad wouldn't have wanted his death to overshadow what Christmas was really supposed to represent. Hayden knew that while the other members of his family had grieved the loss of his dad, they hadn't come to hate the holiday the way he had.

Emotion threatened to choke Hayden as grief rose up within him, but he forced himself to listen as Rachel and Isla finished their song. He did it for his dad. He did it for the girls. And yes, he even did it for himself because he'd lost so much by allowing his grief and despair to overwhelm him. He needed to not let it rob him of special moments like this one.

Once Rachel and Isla finished their song, Hayden tuned everything out in an effort to get his emotions under control. It was something he'd perfected over the years when he was forced to be somewhere he didn't want to be. He had come to think that attending things to make his mom happy was the price he had to pay.

He breathed a sigh of relief when the program was over, and he focused once again on the conversation around him. Rylan excitedly recounted parts of the program that he'd really enjoyed, and Paige listened as if she hadn't just sat through it with him.

The two couples left as soon as the program was over to get the girls. Hayden knew from past years that there would be cookies and treats in the fellowship hall. Since he'd come with his mom, Essie, and George earlier, he would have to hang around until they were ready to go.

"They're serving some refreshments in the fellowship hall," his mom told Paige. "You're welcome to join us."

Paige glanced at Rylan, then at Hayden, before she nodded. "That sounds nice."

They waited until the crowd in the aisle had thinned enough for Paige to turn the wheelchair. Hayden adjusted his crutches, then walked beside the pair as they followed his mom and the others to the doors at the back of the sanctuary.

Hayden braced himself for the crowd in the fellowship hall, wishing that he could have just gone straight home. It was impossible for him to pick up any food or drink from the long tables that were set up.

"Which ones do you want?" Paige asked as she pushed Rylan's wheelchair along the table filled with trays of cookies and other treats. Rylan pointed to a couple of things, which she picked up and gave him on a small plate, then she turned to Hayden. "What about you?"

"What about me what?"

"Which ones would you like?"

Hayden wanted to insist that he could take care of it himself, but that would be a rather stupid protest when she clearly knew better. "Uh... I'll have a chocolate crinkle and a couple pieces of fudge."

She gave him a smile as she picked up another plate and put his requests on it before handing it to Rylan to hold. After doing the same for herself, she pushed the wheelchair over to where Rachel and Isla were standing with their parents.

Paige managed to rescue their cookies before Rylan's enthusiastic movements dumped them on the floor. The girls greeted Rylan with smiles, each of them holding a cookie.

Hayden positioned himself next to Ash, then balanced himself on the crutches so he could accept the plate with his treats on it from Paige. She stood talking with Heather and Carissa.

"Big plans for the week?" Ash asked after they'd both finished eating.

"You know it," Hayden responded. "Big plans like I have every week. Physio with Craig. Work. Although most of our projects have wound down for the holiday. You busy at the garage?"

Hayden kept an eye on Paige as she conversed with the others there. Though she seemed to lead a fairly quiet life, much like he did, watching her with Heather and Carissa made him wonder if that was what she preferred. Or was it because of Rylan and what had happened with her ex that her life had narrowed down to just her family and her job?

His life prior to the accident had definitely included more people than just his family. But since then, things had swung the opposite way. He wasn't sure if he'd ever end up at a happy medium, or if his life would forever be just his family. And maybe... hopefully... Paige, Rylan, and Leta.

"This was a lot of fun," Paige said as they put on their jackets a little while later. "I didn't really think about the fact that Rylan has missed going to church, but I think tonight has shown me he has."

"Well, as you've seen, the church is accessible, so if you wanted to come here with Rylan, you'd be able to."

"Maybe." She looked contemplative as she zipped up her jacket. "You don't attend here?"

Hayden shook his head. "Not really. Just for special stuff like this."

"I'll talk to Mom and Rylan about it. See what they say."

"I think the girls would be happy to help him in the children's church if you worried about leaving him."

"I'd probably stay with him for the first few classes, just to see how he does and how it works. It would be easier if he had a powered chair."

"Did he have one before everything happened with your ex?"

"No. I'd been looking at them and had plans to buy one, but then..." She shrugged, and Hayden could finish her thought.

Maybe it was something he could do. A Christmas gift that he could give to the pair. The only problem was that he didn't know anything about wheelchairs. But the good thing about having money was that he could find people who did, and they'd be happy to help him, especially if he told them he wanted the best kids' powered wheelchair that money could buy.

"Ready to go, darling?" Leta asked as she tugged on her gloves.

"Yep." Paige turned back to Hayden and gave him a smile. "I'll see you in the morning."

He nodded, then said goodbye to Rylan. Watching them leave the church, his mind was already moving forward to what he needed to do the next day to get the ball rolling on the getting his hands on a wheelchair.

"I really like them," his mom said, wrapping her hand gently around his bicep. "Do you think they'd spend Christmas with us?"

Hayden recalled the past two years, and how Carissa and Rachel, then Ash and Isla, had spent the holiday with them. "Why didn't you invite Leta to spend Christmas with us last year?"

"Oh, your brother did."

Hayden turned to frown at his mom. "He did? He never said anything to me."

"Yes. She'd mentioned that her daughter and grandson had unexpectedly had to move in with her. Hunter issued the invitation, but she declined."

He wondered if there would be a different answer if the same invitation was extended that year. "I suppose if you wanted to ask them, that's your prerogative since it's your home."

"You wouldn't mind having them with us?" She looked up at him. "I want you to be comfortable."

"I'm fine with it, Mom."

"I've always liked Leta," his mom said. "She took such good care of you boys, and I think Paige is doing the same for you now. Right?"

Hayden thought of all the stuff she did. Of the food she'd prepared for him. Of the work she did to keep his apartment clean. True, he hadn't really been focused on that over the past several months. He'd just taken it all for granted. Like food and clean clothes had magically appeared. He'd thanked her each time she'd done something for him—his mom had raised him right—but he was struggling so much with his own issues that he hadn't thought beyond that.

"Right."

"I'm so glad to hear that." His mom smiled. "I think I'll speak to Leta and see if they'll join us."

As they left the church and he climbed into the front seat of the SUV alongside George, Hayden tried to imagine what Christmas would be like with Leta, Paige, and Rylan present.

The Christmas that Carissa and Rachel had joined them had been a turning point. While he hadn't really been all that keen on having strangers in their lives, Rachel and Carissa had fit so well that he hadn't really felt a ripple of unease around them. When Ash and Isla had shown up, Hayden had once again felt comfortable around them.

He'd been around a few men who had dated Heather, and Ash was the first one she'd been interested in that Hayden had actually liked. He'd appreciated that Ash hadn't pushed him for conversation. Hadn't tried to suck up to him like others had.

Hayden was sure that Christmas would be as enjoyable with Paige and her family as it had been with the others. Not that they would be there in any capacity except friends. Even though he might have some sort of feelings for Paige, he dismissed them as gratitude and an appreciation for the type of woman she was.

Prior to the accident, if he'd been interested in a woman, he wouldn't have hesitated to express that interest. He would have flirted with her, confident in his charm and looks. Now, he definitely didn't have his looks and his charm was non-existent.

"I'll call Leta tomorrow to invite them," his mom said as George pulled to a stop in front of the house, since it was closer to the church than his apartment building was. "I think we'll have another wonderful Christmas." His mom opened his door and leaned in to give him a kiss on his cheek. "Love you, my boy. Sleep well."

"Love you too, Mom."

George left the SUV running as he walked the women to the front door and unlocked it for them. As he waited for the man to return to the SUV, Hayden pondered the idea of trying to drive once again.

There had to be a point where he made a decision on whether he was going to pick up a few pieces of his life, or if he was going to keep living his life inside the four walls of his apartment.

Chapter 18

"Your mom called mine," Paige said as she set a plate of French toast down in front of Hayden on Tuesday morning.

He glanced up at her. "Yeah?"

"Yeah. She said that your mom invited us to come for Christmas."

Hayden nodded as he lifted his mug of coffee, then took a sip. "She mentioned that she was going to."

"How do *you* feel about that?" Paige wasn't sure how she felt about the invitation, but she was curious about what Hayden thought. She assumed that he'd be at his mom's home for Christmas, so if he didn't want them there, she didn't want to intrude.

"I have no problem with it," Hayden said. "Having people join our family for Christmas was something that my dad used to like to do. It's taken awhile, but we're getting back to it."

"Would it just be us with your family? Or are the others who will be there?"

Hayden grimaced as he shook his head. "These days, my family only invites people who they think I'll be comfortable around. And for me, the fewer non-family members, the better.

So yeah, the past few years, we've had people with us, but only a couple."

"So, you're comfortable around us?"

Hayden gave a huff of laughter as he gave her an incredulous look. "Of course, I'm comfortable around the three of you. I mean, your mom was a part of our lives for a long time, and you've been part of mine for the past several months. And Rylan, well, you know I enjoy hanging out with him."

"Mom said Hunter invited us last year, but she'd refused."

"Yeah. My mom mentioned that."

"Last year, I wasn't in a good place to be around people. I think my mom knew that, which is why she didn't even ask me about it."

"I understand that. I think that's why it took four years for us to get to that point again after my dad had died." He cut a piece of French toast and forked it up, but he didn't eat it right away. "Are you going to come?"

"I think so. Your mom said we could spend Christmas Eve night at her house, but I don't think we'll do that."

"Heather will be so disappointed," Hayden said, then took the bite of French toast.

"Why's that?" Paige asked as she returned to the kitchen and began to clean up the dishes.

"She has a passion for making everyone wear matching pajamas on Christmas morning."

Paige grinned, having a hard time imaging Hayden, Hunter, and Ash wearing festive pajamas. "Do you actually go along with it?"

Hayden shrugged. "She's my sister, and I don't like to disappoint her. But I do put up a token protest, just so she'll think twice before she'll try to talk me into something else."

"You're a good brother."

"Eh. Sometimes." He shrugged. "And she'd agree with that."

"Well, as much as I hate to disappoint Heather, it's just easier to sleep with Rylan in our own beds."

"That's understandable. I'd actually prefer to sleep in my own bed too, but because it involves my mom, I can't say no. She asks so little of me that I figure it's the least I can do."

"I guess you're a good son too."

That observation brought a frown to Hayden's face, and Paige wondered why that was. She wasn't sure she should ask him about it, but the question was there on the tip of her tongue.

"Not sure my dad would have agreed."

Paige set a dirty bowl in the sink, then turned to face Hayden. "Why would you say that?"

He sat slumped in the chair with his gaze on his food. "My dad was often aggravated by my behavior. I wasn't like Hunter, who was more serious about his work and focused on his job. It was why my dad was training Hunter to take over for him and not me."

"Did you want that job?"

"No," Hayden said with a scoff. "Boring."

"Did your dad ever ask you if you wanted the job?"

"Sort of. During high school, he sat down with each of us to have a conversation about where we saw ourselves in the future and what we hoped to be doing." He paused and took another bite of his food, but Paige didn't say anything. "I told him that I would love to just tool around the States on my motorcycle."

"How did he react to that?"

"With some exasperation and disappointment. *Hayden Philip King, let's be serious.* He used to say that a lot to me."

In the time she'd known Hayden, Paige had always found him to be serious, so it was a bit harder to imagine that he hadn't been that way once. "I think being exasperated at times is normal for parents."

Hayden nodded. "But does Rylan disappoint you?"

"Not really, but he's young. I would imagine that there might be moments of that in the future. We only ever want what's best for our children, and for them to learn from our mistakes. Unfortunately, sometimes they have to make their own mistakes, which usually results in some disappointment. But none of that would ever make me love Rylan less. So maybe you felt like you disappointed your dad, but I'm pretty sure that he still loved you."

"He did," Hayden agreed readily enough. "But the last thing he expressed to me was his disappointment."

"You mean before the accident?"

"Yeah. He wanted to talk to me without everyone around, so he was taking me out to eat. I'd missed a couple of project deadlines, and he wasn't happy—rightfully so—about my work ethic. Unfortunately, the conversation started before we got to our destination, so he was distracted."

"But it wasn't like he blew through a stop sign or a red light and got into an accident," Paige said. "My mom said that the pile-up involved a *lot* of cars, and that there were many injuries. I'm sure not all of those drivers were distracted. Everyone has said that the road conditions contributed to the pile-up."

"I know, but not everyone involved in the accident died. Maybe the only reason my dad did was because we were arguing."

Paige had a growing understanding of why Hayden was living his life the way he was. It didn't take a degree in psychology to see that he carried a huge amount of guilt, and perhaps even felt like he had deserved everything that had happened to him.

She'd never been one to believe that bad things happened as a punishment for something. Her dad's sudden death over a decade ago had been a horrible event for her family, but she hadn't thought that they'd done something wrong that had brought it about.

Rylan also had done absolutely nothing bad and had ended up confined to a wheelchair. She didn't view what had happened to Rylan or even what had happened with the settlement money as punishment for anything she'd done. Plus, there were plenty of awful people in the world who seemed to be flourishing.

Trying to make it make sense was a waste of time. She did believe that everything happened for a reason, but that sometimes the reason wasn't obvious. And though she might have been upset with how things had turned out, especially with regards to the settlement, she did still believe that God was in control.

That wasn't to say that she didn't question why stuff happened, and she *had* struggled with her relationship with God following Glenn absconding with the money. But God had provided. She could see that now.

"Sorry. Didn't mean to offload all that onto you," Hayden said as he reached out and grasped his mug, though he didn't lift it to take a drink.

"I don't mind. It sounds like maybe you need to talk to someone about how you're feeling."

He grimaced at that suggestion. "I've been to a therapist."

"But let me guess... they didn't want you to shoulder all that guilt. They wanted you to work toward freeing yourself from it."

He looked over at her, his frown deepening. "I suppose that's pretty standard practice."

"I think most counsellors and therapists want to help people move forward in their lives. Letting someone stay mired in guilt—especially if it is unwarranted—would go against what they're trained to do."

Hayden sighed. "I stopped seeing my therapist."

Though Paige wanted to tell him that maybe he should start with them again, she once against stayed quiet. Clearly, he'd been told to go to counseling when he hadn't been ready to do the work. And it wasn't her place to judge if he was or wasn't at that point yet.

"I should probably start seeing him again."

Paige stifled a laugh at how quickly that had come about. "As long as you feel ready to embrace what the therapist wants you to work on. It won't be any more effective this time around if you aren't."

He began to eat again, so Paige returned to her cleaning. She hoped she hadn't overstepped, but he had been the one to bring up the subject initially. Though she might have agreed that counseling was a good idea just on principle for someone in Hayden's position, now that she'd gotten to know the man on a more personal level, it felt even more imperative.

She'd come to care for him far more than she probably should. And when she cared about someone, she hated to see them hurting, especially if there was nothing she could do to help them. She had that helpless feeling when it came to Hayden. All she could do to help him was what she'd been doing for the past ten months.

"Has Rylan ever gone to counseling?"

Paige paused, and once again turned her attention to Hayden. He was watching her with a serious expression on his face. "Yes. I thought he might need it after the divorce."

"And did it help him?"

"Maybe? The therapist told me that he didn't seem to be upset about his dad leaving. She said that he appeared to not have any sort of attachment to his dad, but that she wasn't too worried because it didn't stem from abuse, and though Glenn had neglected him, I hadn't. That meant that he was well-adjusted and thriving, despite being without his dad."

"He does seem to be a happy child."

"I'd like to think so. I've done everything I can to give him a stable, happy home. Having to move back here threw a wrench in my efforts, but we've adjusted."

"Do you think he'll be ready to go back to school next fall?"

The thought made Paige's stomach clench. "I'm... I'm not sure. I know I could get him into a good school, but I still... worry."

"You really think he'll be teased or bullied?"

Paige sighed as she prepared to make a confession of her own. "I worry that the more he's around kids his own age, seeing what all they can do, the more he'll see his own limitations. He knows what happened to him. I've always answered any questions he's asked me as honestly as possible. I just don't want him to become angry and unhappy."

"Because he can't do what other kids can do?"

Paige nodded. "I want him to be happy. I want him to be able to focus on the things he can do, and not on the things he can't."

"Hiding the world from him won't be good in the long run. At some point, you'll have to let him out. I would think that helping him accept his limitations at a younger age would be easier than doing it when he's older."

Tears stung her eyes, forcing her to turn away and focus on the wiping down the counter so that Hayden wouldn't see if they spilled over. "I love him so much. It didn't matter to me that he couldn't walk. As soon as they put him in my arms, he owned my heart completely. From that point on, I've tried to do everything to protect him. Especially since I hadn't been able to protect him during his birth."

"Rylan is fortunate to have you as his mom," Hayden said. "But even as you pour love into his life, you need to also prepare him for life beyond the four walls of your home."

Paige couldn't help but see the irony of their conversation that morning. Just like she had advice for him about his life, he had advice about hers. Clarity appeared to be a bit farsighted. It seemed to work best when used at a distance, viewing someone else's life and problems as opposed to the ones closer to home.

"Maybe if you're thinking about going back to therapy, I should consider broadening Rylan's horizons."

"Maybe."

She heard the clink of his silverware against the plate and glanced over to see that he was eating once again. The weight of their conversation seemed to lift, and she took a deep breath and blew it out.

Craig showed up just as Hayden finished his breakfast, and the pair once again disappeared down the hallway. She focused on cleaning the kitchen, then started her chores for that day.

As she worked, she thought over the conversation she'd had with Hayden, wondering how she could broaden Rylan's horizons without actually sending him back to school. She needed to find a way to get him a powered wheelchair, because otherwise, he was too reliant on people to help him. Once he had a powered wheelchair, she might consider school for him once again.

She was trying to save up, but the small amount she managed to set aside from each paycheck meant it was going to take a very long time to get enough to buy one that would meet Rylan's needs. The Kings paid her well for what she did, but she was still supporting three people on that salary.

Maybe it was time to call the police in Chicago again, to see what—if anything—they'd discovered about Glenn and her money. Unfortunately, she wasn't holding her breath. They'd told her not to. The police had said it was unlikely they'd be able to find her money, and it was best to just accept that and move on.

It was hard to accept that. But did she have any choice?

Chapter 19

Saturday dragged on. Every hour felt like three, and Hayden was restless. He needed something to do, but there was nothing that needed doing in the apartment.

Finally, he shut off the movie that had been playing on the screen in the theater room and picked up his laptop. He opened a browser window and started to do some research on driving. He knew that he could drive with a prosthesis, plenty of people did, but he wondered if it would be any different if he didn't have a prosthesis on his non-dominant leg.

He couldn't find anything, which just added to his frustration, so he shifted his attention from that.

He'd contacted a place about a wheelchair after his conversation with Paige, and they had been happy to speak to him. He would love to have a wheelchair to give Rylan at Christmas. Paige would probably object to such a pricey gift. Still, he hoped she didn't reject the gift outright.

And just in case he wasn't able to get the wheelchair in time, he'd done a little online shopping for Rylan and the girls. He'd paid extra for fast shipping, so everything should be there for

Christmas, which was just a few days away. He hadn't known what to get for Paige, and still wasn't sure.

In previous years, his siblings had purchased electronics for the people joining them for Christmas. In Paige's case, while she didn't have the newest and largest phone available, she did have one of the newer models. The tablet Rylan used was also not that old. He supposed those items had been purchased before the settlement money had been stolen.

In the end, he bought a bunch of gift cards for places he thought she'd be able to buy stuff for herself. Hopefully, she wouldn't get upset about the amount of money he'd spent. It felt like it was all he had to offer these days.

His phone rang, and Hayden frowned at it. Most likely, it was Hunter or Heather calling to bug him about something. He knew that they would only keep calling if he didn't answer.

With a sigh, he picked it up, but then he noticed that it wasn't any number he recognized. For a moment, he contemplated ignoring the call. But he was bored, so he swiped to answer it.

"Hayden King?" The voice on the other end of the line was impossible to place. He couldn't tell if it was a man or a woman, or even how old they were. All of that made him leery to confirm that's who he was. "Kent is a mutual friend."

"Oh! Yes. I'm Hayden King."

"Wonderful. Kent passed on some information to me. I'm happy to say that I've been able to empty the pockets of someone who had money that wasn't rightfully his."

Hayden sat in stunned silence for a moment. "Really? Like… you seriously were able to track him down?"

"I was."

"I mean, I'd hoped, but honestly, I wasn't sure. The cops, you know, hadn't been able to get anything."

The person gave an indignant huff. "The cops? They could *never* do what I do. *Never.*"

Hayden was afraid that he'd offended the person. "Uh... sorry. I wasn't sure what Kent was going to do with the information I gave him."

"Much as Kent is talented in his own right, he also can't do what I do." The voice hesitated. "I'm sure you realize that if this could have been done through official channels, the cops or even Kent, would have found what they needed."

Hayden got what he was saying. *Un*-official channels. *Illegal* channels.

"I don't care how you got it, only that you did. Did Kent tell you who that money belonged to?"

"Yes, he told me about how the money was stolen from a single mom and her disabled child." The person gave a growl. "Because of that, I was tempted to wipe his accounts completely. Instead, I just took the amount that had been taken from her plus my finder's fee, which he'd never have had to pay if he hadn't taken it in the first place."

Hayden chuckled. "I'd be happy to match that fee."

"No need. I try only to take money from people who have gotten their cash by nefarious means."

"Robin Hood?"

The person laughed. "You could call me that."

"Can I call you at this number if I need you for something else?"

"Nope. This number will be gone once our call is over. If you need something else, you can let Kent know. Where do you want me to transfer the money? It's sitting in one of my accounts at the moment."

"Well, I don't know her account number, so I'll have to get it from her. Can I let Kent know? Could he get that information to you?"

"I could find her banking information, but I'd rather not take the risk of hacking a bank at the moment. Especially when it's possible to get the info in a less risky way."

"That's makes sense," Hayden said. "This is wonderful. Just wonderful. Thanks so much for this."

"You're welcome. Take care."

The line went dead, and Hayden stared at his phone for a long moment. He hadn't expected to be contacted directly. And if he was going to be perfectly honest, he hadn't really thought that they'd be able to track Paige's ex down. Especially not so quickly.

His goal had been to get the money back for Paige, and that had been accomplished. Now, the money needed to be officially returned to her. He hoped that it helped to ease any stress that she might be under.

He stared unseeing, the site on the browser window blurring as he considered that perhaps returning the money would mean that Paige would quit working for him. The money would mean she could go back to being a full-time mom, staying home to care for Rylan like she had since his birth until her ex robbed her of the ability to do that.

The idea of not seeing Paige on a nearly daily basis filled him with sadness. Would she want anything to do with him if she didn't have to work for him?

On the heels of that came the thought that maybe the only reason she'd been spending time with him had been because she worked for him. While technically Hunter had hired her and paid her, at the end of the day, she came to the apartment where he lived in order to work. And everything she did to help him was done to earn a paycheck.

He didn't like the idea of her only agreeing to spend time with him—both at work and socially—because she feared it would affect her job if she didn't do it. But if that truly was the case, he understood. It wasn't like he was someone that most people wanted to hang around with these days.

Frowning, Hayden lowered his gaze to his laptop and clicked back to the movie he'd been watching. He started it up and set his laptop on the table beside his recliner. With a sigh, he focused on the screen, eager to escape his confusing reality.

Monday morning, Hayden was moving slowly. He'd sunk into a funk over the weekend that he still hadn't pulled himself out of.

The only thing he'd done of any merit over the weekend had been to call Kent and give him Paige's contact information. He'd decided that he preferred she not know that he'd been involved in the return of her money. So, he'd told Kent not to reveal how he'd come to know about her issue, only that he had and that it had been taken care of.

Hayden didn't want one more thing that might make Paige feel beholden to him. It was bad enough to think she might only be tolerating his presence because of her job. Getting her money back was such a huge thing that he could see her feeling like she owed him big time. He didn't want that.

It was tempting to let himself slide back into the mindset he'd been in just a few short weeks ago. He'd been unable to ignore the idea that he was falling for someone who might only be with hanging around him because she might be worried about losing her job.

But even as he'd spent the weekend wallowing in self-pity, there was a part of him that resisted being pulled back into the emotional quagmire that had been his life since the accident. That part was why he dragged himself out of bed, rather than staying there until Paige appeared to wake him up.

It frustrated him that nothing happened quickly anymore. Something as simple as pulling on a pair of sweats and a long sleeve T-shirt took far too long.

Finally, he sat on the edge of his bed and braced himself for what was to come. Kent had called to let him know that he had contacted Paige, so things were going to change whether or not Hayden wanted them to. Yet one more thing outside of his control.

Grabbing his crutches, Hayden got himself up and headed out of his room. The smell of bacon greeted him as he walked down the hall. Though he wasn't overly hungry, he'd eat the food she'd made him.

"Hey!" She greeted him with a smile that made his heart skip a beat. "Ready for breakfast?"

"Yes. Please." He made his way to the table and sat down.

"Did you have a rough night?" she asked as she set a mug of coffee and a plate with eggs, bacon, and some toast.

"Not really. Just trying to... work through some stuff."

"If you want to talk about it, I'm here," she said, her voice soft.

He murmured his thanks, but he didn't take her up on the offer. What he wanted was to hear her news, but he couldn't exactly ask about it.

"How was your weekend?"

"It was kind of an up and down thing," she said.

"What was the down?" Hayden asked, worried something had happened with Rylan.

She grimaced. "It might be better to tell you that after you're done eating."

Hayden looked down at his plate, then back at her. "Why's that?"

"It involved a trip to the ER because of a possible infection."

He frowned. "For you or Rylan?"

"Rylan, but it was nothing serious. He's fine."

"Okay. We'll come back to that," he said. "How about the up?"

Paige came and sat down across from him at the table. "Honestly, I'm not entirely sure it was an up. I got a really weird call from a guy who said that he'd tracked down the money Glenn had stolen."

"Really?"

"Yeah. But then he asked me for my bank information so that he could transfer it back into my account. That's when I thought it was a scam, even though he insisted it wasn't." She gave a huff. "But that's what a scammer would say, right?"

Hayden hadn't even considered how it might seem to Paige if she was contacted out of the blue and asked for her banking information. "What did you do?"

"I told him to give me a number, and I'd call him back. I figured a scammer wouldn't give me his number. I thought I'd go set up a new account with no connection to my real account, so if they're after my money, they won't get much."

Hayden realized that if he vouched for Kent, it would all be much easier. "Did he say how he found out about this?"

"When I asked him, he just said that a concerned person had passed the information on to him. I wondered if maybe one of the cops had contacted someone outside of the department, since they've not been able to make any progress on it."

"I guess then perhaps it might be worth setting up the account."

She sighed, grasping her hands against her chest. "I can't tell you how much I'm hoping this is true. It would be the best Christmas present ever."

"It would be a horribly cruel prank if it wasn't."

"It's not stopping me from hoping, though."

"If you need to take some time off to go to the bank, you can have it."

"Are you sure?" she asked, her expression so filled with hope that it made Hayden glad that it wasn't going to be for nothing.

"Definitely. Feel free to go now, if you want."

"I'll just clean up the breakfast stuff, then I'll go." She got back up and went into the kitchen. "How was your weekend?"

"It was fine." He didn't bother to tell her that he'd spent it watching movies and playing video games, turning down Hunter's invitation for dinner on Sunday evening.

"That's good. Are you excited about Christmas?" she asked as she began to wash a pan.

"Uh... sure."

She gave a short laugh as she shook her head. "That was kind of a dumb question, huh?"

"Well, most people probably are. And I'm not *not* excited, but it's just a lot more low key."

"So low-key it's barely discernable," Paige quipped.

"Maybe." The teasing exchange didn't do a thing to lessen how he felt about her. "Why don't you go ahead and tell me about the down. I think I'll be okay now."

She frowned a bit, then said, "If you're sure."

"I am." Anything to keep her talking to him, sharing bits of her and Rylan's life with him.

Chapter 20

Paige rinsed the pan she'd used for eggs and put it in the dish drainer. "Well, Friday night, when I gave Rylan his bath, I noticed that there was irritation around his stoma."

"His stoma?" Hayden asked, his brows drawing together. "What's that?"

"Oh, sorry. I guess I haven't explained that part of his care." She hesitated for a moment, trying to come up with a way to describe it without being too graphic. Most people might get a little squeamish. But she figured that with his own injuries, maybe he could handle it, so she gave the details of what had happened.

"Okay. I understand."

"Anyway, usually we don't have any issues with this. But every once in a while, the bag might slip and the skin around the stoma gets irritated. If we don't catch it soon enough, it can end up infected. So we went off to the ER, just to be safe. I tend to be over-protective when it comes to Rylan's health."

"I don't blame you for that. Infections are nothing to mess around with it."

Paige paused, having forgotten about the infection that had robbed Hayden of his leg until he made his comment. "Uh...

Well, I have to say that I'm very thankful for the health insurance that comes with this job. It gives me peace of mind to know that I can take Rylan to the hospital when I need to."

Hayden frowned. "Didn't your settlement include health insurance for the duration of Rylan's life?"

Paige sighed as the memory of that time pressed down on her again. "I'd been prepared for like a quarter of the amount we'd asked for and hopefully health insurance. They came back with an offer of almost three quarters of that number, but with no provision for health insurance. It seemed like a great deal, and of course, Glenn thought it was too. So we agreed to the settlement, figuring that if we were careful with the money, we'd be able to afford the health insurance Rylan needed."

Hayden stared at her for a long moment, a considering look on his face. "Is that why your mom retired? So that you could take the job here and get insurance for Rylan?"

Paige froze, a flutter of nerves in her stomach at the thought that maybe he'd get upset if she confessed that that was what they'd done.

As if reading her mind, Hayden said, "I wouldn't blame you at all if you did. Things have been just as good with you here as when your mom was, so we've never been unhappy with your work."

Paige gripped the edge of the counter as she faced him. "We didn't mean to, uh... take advantage of you. I've always tried to make sure that I did the job as well as my mom had."

"Paige," Hayden said, his voice gentle but firm. "I have no complaints about your work. If this is what you needed to do for Rylan, then I absolutely agree with your decision. What has your mom done for insurance?"

"We were able to find something that wasn't too expensive for her. Thankfully, she hasn't needed to use it much, and when she has, it's been good enough."

"I'm glad to hear that."

She'd thought the up and down of the weekend was over, but this brief exchange with Hayden had added another quick rollercoaster ride. At least she could afford insurance on her own should she need to, if she really did get the money back.

"Do you think that the person who called me about the money might be for real?" She didn't want to hope, but it would mean so much to have that security for Rylan once again. It probably wouldn't change much about their current situation, although maybe they'd move to a bigger house so that Rylan could have his own bedroom. But her goal was to keep as much of the settlement money as she could for him and his needs.

Hayden seemed to consider her question for a long moment. "My dad always used to say that God works in mysterious ways. Maybe that's the case here. As long as you safeguard your actual account, you've got nothing to lose, right?"

"I was pretty mad about what happened—what God allowed to happen—that I didn't pray much about it, believing that there was little chance of ever getting it back. I've only started to pray about it again more recently, though my mom said she'd been praying that it would be returned to me from the moment I told her what had happened."

"My parents believed—believe—strongly in prayer, and they always shared the answers to those prayers with us. They encouraged us to pray as well, telling us that nothing was too small to pray about."

Paige nodded as she walked back to the table to clear away his dishes since he'd finished eating. "My mom feels the same way."

"I'll... I'll pray that this is for real."

Paige's affection for the man swelled within her, understanding that prayer was likely a difficult thing for him, as it had been for her. And yet she knew that he would pray, just as he said he would.

"Thank you." Needing a connection with him for some reason, she rested her hand on his shoulder and gave it a light squeeze. "I really appreciate it."

He lifted his hand and covered hers for a moment, the warmth of his touch comforting against her skin. "I just want you and Rylan to be happy."

Paige stood there for a moment, letting his words sink and coming to a rather surprising realization. "We are happy. I didn't think it was possible to be really happy again after losing the money. But honestly? For the past several weeks, I can truly say we've been happy."

Hayden looked up at her then, his wavy hair falling back from his face. His eyes held emotions that she couldn't even begin to interpret. "I'm glad to hear that. You deserve to be."

"You deserve to be happy too," she told him softly, wanting to run her fingers through his hair and soothe the tension from around his eyes. "I know you don't believe that, but you do. You've helped make me and Rylan happy. I wish we could do the same for you."

The corner of his mouth twitched up in a small half-smile. "You have. It's not your fault that so much of my life recently has been mired in sadness and disappointment, making it hard to tell when I'm happy."

She didn't know what to say to this man who was wounded so deeply and yet wanted to help make others happy. "Rylan happens to think you're amazing, and I'm inclined to agree."

For a moment, the shadows seemed to fade from his gaze, and the smile that tugged at the corner of his mouth lingered a bit longer. "If you're angling for a raise, I'm afraid you'll have to talk to Hunter."

She tugged gently on a lock of his hair. "Not even close."

"Well, I know it's easy to impress a young boy when I've got unlimited movies and several game consoles. I would have thought that you'd be a little harder to impress."

Paige gave a laugh as she moved her hand and picked up his dishes. "You under-estimate your charm."

"Really?"

"Are you fishing for a compliment?" she asked as she loaded the last of the dishes in the dishwasher.

"Never. My mother taught me better than that."

Paige grinned as she wiped down the counter. "I'm sure she did."

The flutter of nerves in her stomach increased as she finished in the kitchen, then gathered up her things. "Are you sure it's okay for me to go?"

Hayden stood nearby, leaning on his crutches. "Of course I am. You hardly ever take time off during the day, so don't worry about it."

"I just hope it's not time wasted."

"I don't think it will be," Hayden said with a confidence that Paige didn't completely share.

Paige zipped up her jacket. "I guess only time will tell."

Hayden's mouth lifted into a half-smile. "Yep. But I have a good feeling about it."

"Hope isn't something I've had in a long time regarding this," Paige said as she opened the door. "So I pray you're right because I can't help but hope that this is for real."

"It'll be fine," Hayden assured her.

With a sigh, she gave him a nod, then stepped out of the apartment.

As she drove to the nearest bank, Paige played over the conversation she'd had with the man on the phone, then thought of how confident Hayden was that the call was genuine. It made her wonder... Maybe she'd been off in thinking it was related to the cops. Maybe... just maybe... it had been *Hayden* who had done something.

She didn't think he could have done anything himself, but he certainly had the money to hire someone. As the idea sank its claws into her mind, she really hoped that wasn't the case. She already felt like she owed Hayden and his family so much just from them having hired her.

She would ask him about it because she had to know. He'd appeared ignorant of what was going on, but then he'd also seemed strangely confident of the authenticity of the call.

That thought stayed with her through the process of setting up the account, then driving back to the apartment. Craig was still there working with Hayden, and after he left, Hayden had had to deal with some work stuff.

It was almost time for her to leave for the day before she got the time to talk to him about it again.

"Did you call the guy with your account information?" Hayden asked as she set his dinner on the table in front of him.

"Not yet," she said, then paused, trying to figure out if she really wanted to know if Hayden was involved. But in the end, she knew that she had to ask him, even though she wasn't sure she'd believe him if he denied being involved. "Did you have a part in this?"

His brows rose. "What do you mean?"

"I'm pretty sure it's not been you I've been talking to, and I'm also pretty sure you weren't the one responsible for actually getting the money back. However, it's possible that you funded the whole thing."

"Nope." Hayden said it so confidently that for a moment Paige was willing to accept that he wasn't involved.

However, she had one more question for him. "Did you ask someone to look into where my money went and to try to get it back for me?"

That question made him pause, his gaze dropping to his plate. Paige's heart pounded as she waited for an answer. She wasn't sure why it mattered, but it did.

Hayden looked up at her, his jaw clearly clenched. "Yes. Kent, the man who called you, works for us in our IT department. He specializes in computer security and has some... talented contacts."

Paige stared at him, her emotions warring within her. "Why would you do that?"

Hayden's eyes widened briefly, then his brows drew down as he frowned. "Why *wouldn't* I do that? After you told me what happened, I suspected that the police would have their hands tied with how far they could go to get your money back. You needed someone who could cross lines that the police couldn't. I didn't know if Kent had that capability, but I figured, from conversations I'd had with him, that if he didn't have the skill, he knew someone who did."

Paige stood there, staring at him and trying to figure out what to say in response to his revelation. Emotion surged within her, and she had to swallow hard to keep it from spilling out.

"You can't tell me that if you had the ability to help someone who really needed it, that you would walk away," Hayden said. "That's not who you are, and it's not who I am. And just so you know, it didn't cost me anything."

"It didn't?"

"No. The person who tracked your money down said that they took their finder's fee from your ex's account. They were tempted to wipe it out completely, but in the end, they took just what he'd taken from you plus their fee."

Paige let out a huff of laughter. "I suppose it's only right that he pays for their efforts to track him down."

"Did you want to tell the police where he is? I didn't ask the person, but I'm sure if you wanted to know, they'd tell us."

She thought about that for a minute, then shook her head. "I don't want anything more to do with him. All I want to know is that Rylan's money will be safe from him in the future."

"Once you have the money back, I can set you up with our financial advisor. He'll be able to help you figure out how to safeguard your money and to invest it in ways that will make sure that you and Rylan have what you need."

"Glenn was supposed to have done that. Because he was an accountant, I trusted him to make the right decisions for the settlement. All he did was make it easy for himself to move the money later on."

"Call Kent. Give him your banking information and get your money back."

"I want to be angry at you for interfering," she told him. "For not telling me what you'd done."

He shrugged. "I couldn't tell you because I had no idea if they'd actually be able to get your money back. I know what it's like to have your hopes up, only to have them dashed. I didn't want that for you. It was better you didn't know if it didn't work out."

Paige knew that he was referring to the experience he'd had with his surgery, and the dashed hopes that had come with the complications that had resulted in the loss of his lower leg.

"When you told me what happened, I couldn't just sit back. As much as you deserved the money back, he deserved to lose it. That a man could do that to his own child..."

Hayden's anger was palpable, and Paige found that it matched the anger that had burned inside her over the past year for what Glenn had done to Rylan. "I guess all I can say is thank you. Thank you for doing this for us. I'll forever be in your debt."

He began to shake his head before she even finished speaking. "No. This was why I didn't want you to know that I was behind this. If you want to be in anyone's debt, be in debt to the person who actually got the money back. But keep in mind that they paid themselves, and they ask nothing of you either."

Paige sighed, blinking back the tears that threatened to fall. "I don't think you comprehend the weight that's been on me ever since I realized that the secure future I thought I had for Rylan was gone. I knew that no matter what I did, it would never be enough to give him the life the settlement would have been able to. He's already been suffering because of the loss, but now... now I can make sure that he is taken care of, no matter what."

Hayden held out his hand, and after a moment's hesitation, Paige took it, gripping his fingers and absorbing the strength in them. "Even if the money hadn't been found, we would have made sure that Rylan was taken care of. I hope you know that. You, your mom, and Rylan... you're family now. Just ask my mom."

Paige clutched his hand with both of hers. "I really don't know what to say. It's just all so unexpected."

"Don't say anything. Just go home, make the call to Kent—tell him I said hi—then take the rest of the time off before Christmas to enjoy your family."

She frowned at that. "I can't do that. You need me here."

He squeezed her hand. "I'll be okay. You always make sure the freezer is well-stocked, and I'll be at my mom's for several meals, anyway."

"If you're sure..."

"I'm positive. You're all coming to Mom's on Christmas Eve, right?"

Paige nodded, hating the idea of not seeing Hayden for the next couple of days.

"I'll see you then."

It was harder than it should have been for Paige to let go of his hand and do what she needed to before she left him alone in the apartment. Leaving, knowing he was going to be alone, had gotten increasingly harder over the past several weeks. After months of leaving the apartment like it was any other job, now it felt more like she was leaving something... someone... important behind.

Chapter 21

Heather regarded him with a frown. "What do you need wrapping paper for?"

"I have a few presents to wrap." Hayden had anticipated that she'd be curious, especially since he usually just gave her money to help cover the costs of the gifts she bought for everyone.

"For who?"

"I bought some stuff for the girls and for Rylan." And Paige, but Hayden didn't mention her to Heather.

He'd missed seeing Paige over the past few days, but it had been for the best. He'd needed the distance to keep his feelings for her from deepening even further. Plus, it had made it easier to meet with the people regarding the wheelchair for Rylan, which they'd agreed to deliver on Christmas Eve morning.

His mom had been delighted when he'd called to let her know that he planned to come to her house two days before Christmas and stay through until the day after. He usually came to the house on Christmas Eve and went back to the apartment the night of Christmas Day, if he could manage it.

Staying more than one night was definitely unusual, but he felt the need to spend more time with his family. And less time alone with his thoughts and feelings.

George had picked him up mid-afternoon, and now Hayden was on the hunt for wrapping paper. He hadn't had any at the apartment and hadn't even thought to order some along with the gifts. So now he had to beg his sister for help and answer any probing questions she might have.

"I didn't know you planned to buy them stuff," Heather said as she plopped down on the couch beside him. "What did you get?"

"I got Rachel a new bookcase that I hope matches what she's told me about her room, along with several new books. For Isla, I got her an art desk and some art supplies."

Heather smiled at him. "I'm impressed. I'm sure the girls will be thrilled. And Rylan?"

"I got him a racetrack," he said. "And a new wheelchair."

Heather's eyebrows rose. "A... wheelchair?"

"I've got people delivering a child's powered wheelchair tomorrow."

"Paige might object to that," Heather said. "I mean, I'm assuming that we're not talking about a couple hundred dollars here."

Hayden thought of their conversation on Monday. "I think she'll be okay with it."

Or if she wasn't, at least he now knew that she could afford to get one for Rylan if she wouldn't accept this one. The company had assured him that he could return it if it didn't work for Rylan. They'd also made him aware of a division of their company that worked to match low-income children with donated wheelchairs. Hayden planned to make sure that there was a wheelchair donated—whether it was the one he'd originally picked for Rylan or another one.

"Where are all your gifts?" she asked.

"George carried them downstairs for me."

"Let me go find some wrapping paper, and I'll meet you down there."

Hayden got to his feet and left the office and went down the stairs to the rec room. When Heather joined him, she carried several rolls of paper as well as a couple pairs of scissors and some tape. "Okay, brother dear, let's wrap some presents."

"You're going to help me?" Hayden asked as he settled onto one of the overstuffed couches.

"Of course. I don't want presents under the tree that look like they were wrapped by a three-year-old."

Hayden wanted to object, but honestly, it had been quite a few years since he'd last wrapped a present. He'd probably been a teen when his dad had insisted that they wrap presents for their mom.

Heather pushed the coffee table closer to Hayden, then cleared everything off of it. She got everything organized, then proceeded to boss Hayden through the process of wrapping each of the things he'd bought.

"You're lucky that I bought a ton of wrapping paper," Heather said when they finally finished with the last one. "Next year, give me a head's up. Or buy some smaller stuff."

"It was kind of a last-minute thing," he admitted. "I just got some of them on Monday."

"I bet you loved the online shopping experience."

"Better than the one I would have had if I'd had to go into a store," he muttered.

"Even I prefer shopping online. I mean, I can do it in my pajamas from the comfort of my bed. What's not to love?"

"Did you buy us all pajamas again this year?"

Heather fixed him with a look. "Does Santa have a beard?"

"I don't know. I kind of think the guy shaves it off the day after Christmas so he isn't so recognizable for a few months."

"Nope. He lives at the north pole. He'll want the beard to keep his face warm."

Hayden stared at her for a moment before starting to laugh. "That sounds like something Dad would say."

Heather's lips parted a bit, and she blinked rapidly, her eyes taking on a sheen. Was she… crying?

"Oh, Hay. I don't think I've heard you laugh like that in so long, and for you to mention Dad? That's just amazing." She flung her arms around him and hugged him tightly. "I love you so much."

Hayden froze for a moment, then wrapped his arms around her, remembering how he had once been much freer with his hugs. That had changed after the accident, and most of his hugs since then were reserved for his mom. But right then, he found that he didn't mind Heather's arms around him.

"Love you too, sis." Emotion made his voice rough, forcing him to clear his throat.

"I think that this might be one of the best Christmases we've had."

Hayden wasn't sure that was true. In his mind, no Christmas that didn't include his dad would be one of the best, though he did think it would be a good one. It was just hard not to imagine how much better it would have been if his dad was there with them.

But maybe it was time for him to set in his mind that he couldn't keep comparing things to how they'd once been. His dad was gone, and nothing could change that.

"He said he loved you."

Memory washed over him, and cold invaded his bones, leaving him chilled and hurting. He felt Heather take his hand, but it wasn't enough to pull him back from that cold, dark, painful night. Once the car had come to a stop, his dad had taken his hand, gripping it tightly as he'd prayed for protection.

"Hayden?"

"He said to tell Mom he loved her and wanted her to be happy. Then he said to tell you and Hunter that he loved you and was so proud of you. Then…" Hayden squeezed his eyes shut and pressed his lips together to stop their trembling. "Then another vehicle hit Dad's side of the car."

And within the blink of an eye, his dad's grip had gone slack. Hayden had never felt so alone as he had that night, trapped in the car, bones crushed, pain in every part of his body, and having to accept that his dad was no longer with them. His loss of consciousness had been a blessing.

"We'd been arguing right before we hit the ice that sent us sliding into that semi." Hayden hated having to make that confession, but they deserved to know. "He was mad because I'd missed some deadlines, and I wasn't listening well to my supervisor. He was so disappointed in me. He never told me…"

Heather's grip on his hand tightened. "He did, though. You know that no matter how many times we disappointed him, he never stopped loving us."

Hayden shrugged. "But he wasn't proud of me. He died disappointed in me."

"I'm sure that in those last moments, he let all of that go," Heather said, her voice soft, but confident. "He never held onto those feelings after he discussed them with us. His priorities would have shifted once the accident happened. He didn't die disappointed in you, even if he wasn't able to voice that before he passed away."

She might believe that, but even though it had been six years since the accident, Hayden still wasn't convinced. His father's disappointment was his cross to bear.

"I wish you could accept that Dad would have wanted you to be happy. It would crush him to see how you're living your life so many years after his death. If he'd be disappointed over anything, it would be that."

Heather spoke the words gently, but the bluntness of them stabbed at Hayden's heart. She wasn't wrong, and it wasn't the first time she or Hunter had hinted at something like that. But this was the first time it had been so starkly pointed out, as if his revelation of those last moments in the car with their dad had given Heather the right to say it the way she did.

"I would never say that you owe it to Dad to live your life differently, but you know that this would never have been what he'd want for you."

"My life is fine."

"No, it's not," Heather stated. "You're punishing yourself, even though you haven't done anything wrong. As long as you don't have a prosthesis, you won't be able to convince me differently."

Hayden rubbed a palm over his thigh, remembering the pain that used to shoot up his leg from his crushed ankle. The ankle that was no longer there.

Though he wanted to tell Heather that he didn't need to convince her of anything, Hayden didn't, because he knew that every word that she spoke to him came from a heart filled with love.

"That accident robbed us all of a wonderful man, and it would have been doubly horrible if we'd lost you both," Heather said. "Honestly, though, there are a lot of days when it feels like we *have* lost you both. The brother we had is no longer here."

"You can't honestly have expected me to come out of that accident unchanged."

"No, I wouldn't have expected that at all. But it would be easier to accept the changes in you if we could see signs that you were at least trying to move forward and live life in some way."

Hayden knew she was right, but he wasn't going to admit to that. He'd learned to never let his siblings know they were right, simply because it usually meant he was wrong. That was a definite no-no in sibling rivalry. He may have changed in a lot of ways, but the fundamentals of being a sibling were still firmly entrenched inside him.

"Okay. I'm going to stop lecturing you."

"Thank God for small mercies," Hayden muttered, which earned him a fist to the shoulder.

"I could tell Hunter and Mom about this conversation."

At one time, he would have objected to that. But after having spilled it all to Heather, the idea of the others knowing didn't seem as daunting. "Do what you've got to do."

She put her arm around him and rested her head on his shoulder. "I'm going back upstairs. Thank you for talking to me. I love you."

"Love you too."

After giving him a squeeze, she got up and headed for the stairs. "I'll get George and Hunter to help carry the presents up later."

Alone in the rec room, Hayden slumped back into the cushions of the overstuffed couch and stared across the room at the unlit fireplace. He wasn't sure if he'd made a mistake in sharing what he had with Heather, but a weight had been lifted from him.

Maybe he should have told them sooner about those last minutes he'd spent with his dad and everything he'd said. But because of his own hurt from that time, he'd tried his best to not think about it. Hopefully, they'd forgive him.

"I'm sorry, Dad," he murmured. "I know that you're not focused on us anymore. But just in case, I want you to know I'm sorry. For everything."

Hayden knew that he wouldn't get any sort of answer, but he just needed to have said the words aloud. He'd thought them plenty of time over the years. However, that day, he said them with the knowledge that his dad would have accepted his apology without hesitation and then moved on from it.

He let out a sigh, knowing that as they celebrated his dad's favorite holiday, he needed to make a choice. Did he live in the hurt and regrets of the past? Or did he honor his dad's legacy by living his life in a way that honored the man, letting Christ have a place in his heart once more?

There wasn't even a choice, Hayden realized. There was only one path to take, and he felt like he was finally brave enough to take it. The small flame of hope that had fizzled out when they'd told him he was going to lose his foot flickered to life within him once again.

Perhaps God had a plan for him still. As that thought flitted through his mind, so did the thought that maybe he could find a place, not just in life in general, but possibly in Paige and Rylan's lives as well.

However, it was likely she wasn't going to work for him anymore, which meant that there would be no reason for them to be in his life any longer. That very idea filled him with sadness, and a sense of loss was there inside him, even though he didn't know for sure what was going to happen.

Hayden hoped that even if Paige wasn't interested in a romantic relationship, she'd still be willing to be a friend because he had precious few of those. And he'd willingly take Paige as a friend, if that's all that she'd offer him.

It was so much better than nothing.

Chapter 22

Paige guided the wheelchair far enough forward that Rylan could push the doorbell. It didn't take long for the large wooden door to swing open to reveal Heather standing there with a welcoming smile on her face.

"Merry Christmas!" she sang out as she motioned for them to come inside. She wore black slacks and a green and red sweater that somehow managed to be festive without looking cheesy.

Paige maneuvered the wheelchair into the large foyer of the mansion. Her mom stepped in behind her and greeted Heather. Over the next couple of minutes, they removed their boots and jackets.

"Come on into the living room," Heather said after she'd hung up their jackets. "We'll be eating in a little while."

Before following Heather, Paige ran the wheelchair back and forth across the large rug in front of the door, hoping to get any wet and dirt from the outside off the wheels. The last thing she wanted was to track that stuff through the elegant King home.

As she pushed Rylan through the opening into the living room, Paige's gaze swept the room. Though the room was beautifully decorated, the only thing she noticed was that Hayden wasn't there, and her heart sank a bit. She hoped that his absence didn't mean he was having a bad day.

Rachel and Isla ran in behind them and greeted Rylan with smiles. Paige moved the wheelchair off to the side, then left it there while the three talked and laughed together. She went to the couch and sat down beside her mom. Heather had taken a place beside Ash on the loveseat.

"Has your week gone well?" Heather asked.

Paige nodded. "It was a great week, and Hayden was very generous to give me most of it off."

"That's great. Did you have Christmas shopping left to do?"

"No. Mom and I made sure we got everything we wanted well ahead of time. Neither of us are fond of crowds, especially since it's not easy taking Rylan out with us. I do online shopping, mostly."

"I prefer that too," Heather said. "And when Ash asked me for gift ideas, it's easy to just send him links."

Ash nodded. "I've never really done much Christmas shopping in my life, but I have to say that doing it that way was surprisingly easy."

"I used to enjoy going into the stores for the Christmas atmosphere," her mom said. "But now it seems to be more stressful for people, so you're more apt to run into someone in a bad mood than one in a festive mood. I figured I can get my Christmas atmosphere in other ways."

Heather's mom walked into the room then, a smile on her face. She wore a pair of black slacks and a red silk blouse that suited her coloring quite well.

As Eliza approached them, Paige and her mom got to their feet and accepted the hugs the woman offered. "We'll be eating in a couple of minutes. I hope you're hungry. Essie has outdone herself yet again."

Paige went to get Rylan, pushing the wheelchair behind the others as they walked to the large dining room. The table was set with dishes that had a Christmas pattern on them, and there was even a tree in the room along with many other decorations on the sideboards and the mantle of the fireplace.

There was a space for Rylan's chair next to the one where Eliza told her to sit. Her mom was seated on the other side of Rylan. Hunter was there with Carissa, and as they were all finding their seats, Hayden finally made an appearance.

He wore a pair of dark gray pants and a white button-up shirt with long sleeves. His hair actually looked like it had been trimmed. As he made his way around the table to the empty seat next to her, Paige noticed that his expression seemed more relaxed than usual.

He smiled at her with that half-smile that she'd come to love as he settled into the seat beside her, then he leaned over to put his crutches on the floor beside him. Before he said anything, Eliza got their attention, then said a prayer for the food.

As the woman had promised, it was quite an amazing spread. Even when they'd been more well-off, they hadn't eaten things like prime rib dinners. Rylan hadn't been too sure about the meat, but he dug into the potatoes and vegetables with relish and managed to eat two of the fluffy, soft dinner rolls.

"How's your day been?" Hayden asked as he passed the gravy to her.

"It was good. We just stuck close to home. We spent a good chunk of it watching Christmas movies."

"I bet Rylan enjoyed that," Hayden said.

"He really did. But honestly, Mom and I enjoyed it, too. It isn't often that we have nothing to do. Thank you so much for giving that to us. I hope you weren't too inconvenienced."

"I'm glad you were able to enjoy your time off. I came here yesterday afternoon, so I wasn't inconvenienced at all." He hesitated, then said, "I actually enjoyed spending time with Mom and Heather. Essie even let me help her a bit in the kitchen this afternoon. So no, it was an inconvenience at all."

"Did you watch Christmas movies too?" Paige asked.

Hayden rolled his eyes. "Yes. But not fun ones like *Elf*. Nope, I got stuck watching the romantic Christmas movies with Mom and Heather."

Paige had asked the question as a joke, but at his response, she had to laugh. "We didn't think Rylan would find the Christmas romance movies very entertaining. We should've switched places."

"I would have agreed to that for sure."

"You can't tell me that you didn't enjoy those Christmas romance movies, though. They're very feel-good movies, after all."

He leaned closer to her, lowering his voice as he said, "I can't admit to that with my mom and Heather so close. They'll make me watch them all the time."

"I see." Paige mimed zipping her lips. "They won't hear it from me."

He winked at her. "You have my eternal gratitude, and I'll owe you one."

Paige's cheeks warmed at the interaction, and she picked up her glass to take a drink of the icy cold juice. She knew that she shouldn't be letting her emotions get so wrapped up in this man, but she really couldn't seem to stop herself.

Once the main meal was done—a meal filled with smiles and laughter, along with the good food—they all pitched in to clear the table. Essie and Carissa then carried in platters of Christmas goodies. Cookies. Brownies. Fudge and other candies. Rylan's eyes grew as he took in the wondrous sight.

"How many can I have, Mama?" he asked in a loud whisper.

"Why don't you start with two, and then we'll go from there."

He nodded his acceptance of her terms, and when the platter came to them, she held it so that he could select the two items he wanted. He carefully picked up a piece of fudge and a cookie that was shaped like a star with a layer of yellow frosting.

Paige also took a piece of fudge and a cookie that was coated in icing sugar. Along with a cup of coffee, it was the perfect end to the meal.

Unfortunately, they couldn't linger too long over their desserts since they were going to the Christmas Eve service at the Kings' church. She hadn't been sure if her mom would have preferred to go to her own church that night, but she'd said she didn't mind going with them. Paige was glad because she wanted them to go together.

Though she might have enjoyed riding with the Kings, Paige knew that she needed to take her own vehicle. They were going back home afterwards, though they'd return to the Kings' home the next day for their Christmas festivities.

Like the last time they'd been at the church, they sat in a row that had room for Rylan's wheelchair at the end. Sitting there surrounded by the Kings, Paige felt the truth of Hayden's words to her earlier in the week that she, Rylan, and her mom were family to them. It was a feeling she wanted to cling to and never lose.

The service included Scripture and poetry readings, along with the beautiful music she loved about the season. Rylan sang loudly with the Christmas carols that he knew, which were quite a few since in the past, she'd always started playing Christmas music around the middle of November. She'd made sure to include kids' versions of the songs along with the versions she enjoyed. For the more upbeat songs, she'd take his hands in hers and they'd "dance" together.

They hadn't done that for the past couple of years, and it made Paige sad. She'd allowed a terrible man to rob her and

Rylan of happy memories and traditions, and she should have put a stop to that right away. Instead, she'd harbored anger and let it impact their lives too much.

Throughout the singing, Hayden didn't join in. But when Paige glanced over at him, he seemed to enjoy the service. At least, he was focused on what was happening on the stage. Well, unless he'd developed the ability to be present physically while his mind was somewhere else.

She wouldn't be surprised if that was the case, since there had been plenty of things he'd had to be present for physically that he probably wouldn't want to be present for mentally. But Paige really hoped that wasn't the case. She wanted him to be able to enjoy the service and the time spent with his family through the holiday.

The service ended with the congregation singing *Silent Night* a cappella. The sanctuary lights had been dimmed, and candles flickered, held by people who were walking down the aisles toward the stage. As the person leading each line reached at the front row, they stopped.

Rylan gazed up at the woman standing next to him in the aisle as she stood there holding her candle and singing. It was a beautiful moment, and Paige absorbed it and thanked God for being faithful in her life. For being gracious and forgiving as she stumbled her way through the last year, blinded by anger and frustration. For answering the prayer she'd struggled to put into words because she couldn't handle the disappointment if it wasn't answered.

When the service ended, it didn't take long for the sanctuary to empty, people obviously eager to continue their holiday celebrations. As they stood at the doors of the church, Paige wished that they could have been going back to the Kings'. But she knew it wasn't going to happen that night, so she pushed the desire aside.

"Will we see you tomorrow, Hayden?" Rylan asked as he reached out to touch the man's hand.

Hayden let go of one of his crutches and ran his fingers through Rylan's hair. "I think you, your mom, and your grandma are going to come over to the house."

"But it's not your house," Rylan said. "Will you be there?"

"Yep. I'll be there."

"Yay!" Rylan grinned up at Hayden. "Rachel and Isla will be there too?"

"They will be."

"I'm so excited," Rylan told him. "I can't wait."

"We'll have lots of fun," Hayden said. "And lots of good food."

When Paige saw that Hunter and George were heading out, she joined them, since she had to bring her car up to make it easier for Rylan. It was cold, so she pulled her collar up, then tucked her hands into the pockets of her jacket. They had all parked in the same section of the lot, so she ended up following them as they drove their SUVs to the front of the church.

Everyone exited the church, her mom pushing Rylan's chair. Paige got out and went around to put Rylan in the backseat. When she straightened after buckling him in, she found Hayden standing near the back of the car.

"I'm glad you could join us tonight," he said.

"Me too." She shut the back door as her mom climbed in the front. "It was a beautiful service."

"I'm looking forward to seeing you all at the house tomorrow."

"Well, as you can see, Rylan is excited about it."

"And are you?" he asked.

"Am I excited, too?" He nodded. "I am. Very much."

"Good." The corner of his mouth tipped up, and his smile lingered. "I think it will be fun."

"Hey, Paige," Heather called out as she hurried over to them, a bag in her hand. "These are for you guys."

Paige took the bag when she held it out. "What is it?"

"Christmas pajamas. You can wear them over in the morning."

"I *can*?" Paige asked. "Or I'd *better*?"

Hayden chuckled. "Oh, she's got your number, sis."

Heather frowned at Hayden, but then turned a smile on Paige. "Well, it would be nice if you would. But if you'd prefer not to, that's fine as well."

"You're so lucky," Hayden said with a dramatic sigh. "She threatens Hunter and I—and now Ash—with no presents if we don't wear her pajamas."

Heather crossed her arms. "Well, I still need to make a good impression on her, so she gets a choice."

"Enjoy it while you can," Hayden said with a wink in Paige's direction.

"I'm freezing," Heather announced. "See you tomorrow." She hurried off toward one of the SUVs, turning back to wave her hand. "Merry Christmas."

"Merry Christmas," Paige called back.

"Guess I'd better join them," Hayden said. "Drive safe."

"I'll try." She watched him walk away, then rounded the car to the driver's side.

Smiling, Paige held the bag out to her mom, then slid behind the wheel when she took it.

"What's this?" her mom asked as she peered into the bag.

"These are our pajamas for tomorrow. Heather said that she'd like us to wear them, but she'll understand if we don't want to."

Her mom chuckled as Paige guided the car from the church. "Oh, I think we should wear them. It seems like a fun tradition."

"Are there pajamas for me too, Mama?" Rylan asked.

"Yep. There are pajamas for all of us, and we're going to wear them when we go to the Kings' house for breakfast tomorrow."

"I can't wait," Rylan crowed. "This is going to be great!"

Paige found that she agreed with him one hundred percent.

Chapter 23

Hayden wore his pajamas without complaint, and he was up in the living room with the rest of the family when Paige arrived with Rylan and Leta. He smiled as Rylan made sure everyone saw his pajamas, and he was delighted that Rachel and Isla had similar ones, only they were red instead of green like his.

He had no idea where Heather got the pajamas. For all he knew, she put in an order with Santa for some elves to specially sew them for the family. That would explain how the sizes all seemed to be perfect. They were magic Christmas pajamas. That was the only explanation.

"Can we open our stockings now, Auntie Heather?" Rachel asked.

"Yep! Would you like to help me hand them out?"

Both of the girls went to join Heather at the mantle. Over the next little while, the girls skipped around the room, handing out the stockings. When they gave Rylan his, he clutched it to his chest, a huge smile on his face.

"Go ahead and open your stockings," Heather said, gesturing to everyone.

Hayden didn't. The last couple of years had proven that it was more fun to watch the young ones open their stockings and presents. This year, his gaze bounced around between the three, but it lingered on Rylan. As he watched the little boy express so much delight over the things he pulled from his stocking, Hayden couldn't imagine how Paige's ex could just walk away from him.

But that man's loss was definitely their gain. If he hadn't been blind to the blessings in his life, Paige and Rylan wouldn't be there with them. Leta had been a blessing for years too, a quiet but steady fixture in his life beginning even before the accident.

Essie had been the one to hire Leta, telling them all that she was the best person to determine who could take care of him and Hunter since they were moving out on their own. And she'd been right in her decision that Leta would be the best one for the job.

That decision by Essie had started them on the journey to this point, and Hayden decided he needed to be sure and thank her for that. Maybe even buy her a new kitchen appliance, since he knew she wouldn't be happy if he bought her a diamond necklace or other piece of jewelry.

Paige pushed Rylan's wheelchair closer to the coffee table where the girls were sitting with the contents of their stockings. The three of them showed off their stocking loot, and Hayden had to admire Heather and Carissa's efforts to make sure that the stockings were filled with equal amounts of practical and fun items.

Not that that seemed to matter to Rylan. He seemed as excited by the *Cars* toothbrush and toothpaste he'd received as he was for the *Hot Wheels* cars that had also been in his stocking.

When Rylan looked over at him, his smile grew even brighter, and Hayden knew in that moment that he loved the little boy... just like he loved the boy's mama. The feelings had been there, floating around inside him like mists in the morning. But right then, they solidified, becoming something real and bright and stunning.

For a moment, he could barely breathe.

Before his injury, Hayden never would have imagined he'd fall in love with a single mother. His younger self wouldn't have been interested in a woman with a child. After all, there had been plenty of women without children that had been interested in him. He'd had lots of options of women to date.

Following the accident, dating and falling in love had dropped so far down in his priorities that he hadn't even thought about them. He'd had no interest, and he'd been sure no woman would have been interested in him.

He hadn't realized that all it would take to drill through the hardness of his heart were two little girls who'd made him realize how great kids were and prepared him for a little boy with big brown eyes and his strong, capable mom. So maybe it wasn't a real surprise that he'd lost his heart to the mother and son.

"Your family really does go all out for Christmas," Paige observed as she sat down beside him on the couch. "Are there any presents left in the store?"

Hayden looked at the tree that seemed to have even more presents spilling out from underneath it than it ever had before. "Dad set a good—or bad—example, depending on how you look at it. I think that was one of the reasons he started the Christmas party for the kids. He could only buy us so many presents. As Santa, he could buy for even more children."

"Who is responsible for all of that?" Paige asked, gesturing to the mountain of gifts.

"I would say that ninety percent is probably the result of Heather's and Carissa's efforts. They have picked up Dad's mantle... or maybe it's his Santa sack. And they have done it with great relish."

"I'm sorry we weren't able to add much to the pile," she said.

"You didn't have to add to the pile at all," Hayden assured her.

"We brought a few things, but it's hard to buy for people you don't know super well."

"I understand that," Hayden said, trying to give her a reassuring smile. "And just a head's up, Heather tends to go *very* overboard."

Paige laughed and gestured to her pajamas and then to his. "I never would have guessed."

Hayden looked down at himself. "I used to think she did it to humiliate Hunter and me. But now she's got the man she loves wearing them, so I just don't know anymore."

"It might be overboard, but it is kind of cute."

"If you say so."

Paige laughed as she leaned against his shoulder for a moment. "Is the big handsome man threatened by having to wear cute Christmas pajamas?"

"I don't know," Hayden muttered. "You'd have to ask Hunter or Ash."

"Oh, stop." Paige straightened and gave his arm a squeeze. "You're as handsome as they are."

"I used to be," Hayden said. "My body is a bit too broken for that now."

"Nope. Not going to listen to talk like that today. God kept you alive, and I believe He has a purpose for you. Just like I've realized He has a purpose for me and for Rylan. I lost sight of that over the past year because I felt, in a lot of ways, that He'd abandoned us. You know, if it had just been me impacted by what Glenn had done, I probably wouldn't have gotten so angry. I would have picked myself up and moved on. But because it impacted Rylan, I let anger fill my heart and held onto it tightly."

"It was justified," Hayden told her.

She shrugged. "Maybe at first. But I let it go on too long. I'm surprised that God allowed the money to come back to me while I still harbored any anger in my heart."

"I wish you hadn't had to go through what you did, but I have to say that you've always been so good about helping me, and meeting Rylan has been amazing."

Paige regarded him for a moment. "Meeting Rylan was life-changing for me too."

"How much did everything change when he was born?" Hayden asked, realizing he didn't know anything about her life before Rylan.

Her gaze shifted to where the little boy sat with the girls. "Completely. I was in school at the time, and though Glenn and I had planned to have kids eventually, my pregnancy with Rylan was a surprise. The timing was still good, though, because I was due with him early in the summer, so I wouldn't miss school. Once classes started up again in the fall, I planned to put Rylan in daycare."

"What were you going to school for?"

"I was a year from getting my bachelor of science," she said, her brows pulling together. "I had hoped to get a job in genetic research."

"You're a smarty," Hayden said.

"To some degree, I suppose. But I was also just really interested in the subject, which made it easier to work hard."

"But you had to stop when Rylan was born?"

"Yeah. Glenn was more than okay with still putting him in a daycare, but I couldn't do it. Not that I didn't think there were experienced people out there who could have taken care of him. I just... after he had such a rough start, I didn't want to be apart from him."

"And your ex was okay with that decision?"

Paige sighed. "He had been supportive of me going to school, but he wasn't as supportive of me taking time off when I only had a year to go. He wanted me to graduate so I could get a job."

"Your ex wasn't in school too?"

She shook her head. "He was ten years older than me, so he'd already graduated and had a good job when we married."

"Do you hope to go back to school to finish your degree?"

"I don't have any plans for that right now. I've just been focused on creating a stable life for Rylan after the upheaval of the divorce."

"Your options have definitely opened up now that you got the money back, though, right? That should help you with stability."

"Yes, it will. But that money isn't just for now. I need it to last Rylan for as long as possible, so probably the only thing that will change now is that we'll move to a place that has three bedrooms. He and I share, so it will be nice for each of us to have our own room."

Hayden took in her words, then cautiously asked, "Are you still planning to work for... uh... Hunter?"

She looked at him with an arched brow. "Were you planning to fire me?"

He gave a huff of laughter at the very idea. "Not a chance. I just thought since you got the money, you wouldn't need the job anymore."

"I don't want to use the money to support us when I'm capable of working. I also trust Mom to take care of Rylan more than I ever trusted my ex."

Hayden's relief at her response filled him from head to toe. "I am so glad to hear that."

"You just don't want to have to train someone new to cook your meals and clean."

"To be honest, that wasn't even in my mind." Hayden paused, rubbing a hand across his face. "I just wasn't looking forward to not seeing you and Rylan as much."

Paige's brows drew together. "Are you saying you'd miss us?"

He cleared his throat as he nodded. "I really would."

Her gaze dropped to her hands for a moment. "Well, we'd miss you too."

Hayden knew he wasn't a great catch anymore, especially right then, but boy, did he want to flirt as easily as he once had in his life. The choices he'd made in the past five years—and especially the past ten months—continued to haunt him.

He could have chosen to take a more positive approach to his life, even as he'd been grieving his dad's death. Instead, he'd allowed negative thoughts and emotions to pull him so far down that he was drowning in them. In some ways, Rylan and Paige felt like lifesavers, dropping down into his emotional waters. He'd grabbed onto them, and whether they'd realized it or not, they'd supported him, even as they'd pulled him closer to the shore.

He was within sight of the shore now, thanks to them and to his family, who had faithfully stood by him through everything. It was his choice whether he was going to make that final push—that final effort—to reach the shore and pull himself up onto it, freeing him from the negative waters that had threatened to drown him over and over again.

It was his choice to get the help he needed to stand solidly on that shore and begin to live again.

He scrubbed his hands over his face, then ran his fingers through his hair. It was the first time he'd really looked at his life and how he'd been living—or not living, as it were—for the past year. He'd been aware of it in bits and pieces, but he hadn't put the complete puzzle together in a way that made him really see how far he'd fallen physically and mentally.

There was no way he'd ever be the man he'd once been. Even if he'd had a more positive outlook following the accident and his dad's death, he'd gone through a traumatic experience, which impacted him on every level. But he still could have taken the steps that his family had encouraged him to in order to deal with it all.

But the one thing that had apparently stayed the same in him was his stubbornness, and as much as it had been a trait that had hurt him over the past few years, he could use it now to change the direction of his life. He could embrace the joy, love, and hope of his dad's favorite holiday and open his heart to everything he'd been closed off from for far too long.

"Are you okay?" Paige asked, laying her hand lightly on his arm.

Hayden let out a long breath as he turned to look at her. "Actually, I'm fine, and I really mean that. I feel better than I have in a long time."

Her eyes widened. "Really? What's brought this about?"

"A lot of different things, but you and Rylan have played a big role in that."

"We did?"

"I know it seems a bit strange." Hayden gave a huff of laughter and rubbed the back of his neck. "But over these past several weeks, you two have brought light into my life. I don't know why it took me so long to see that about you, but finding Rylan in the kitchen that day opened my eyes in a way they hadn't been in… forever, really. Rylan had such a positive attitude, even though he clearly had difficulties of his own. It made me look at my own attitude."

Paige's smile was soft and affectionate. "He is an amazing little boy. I've felt like that from the day he was born."

"I think he's that way because of you. If you'd had a negative attitude toward his disability, the way his father did, I think he'd have a much different outlook on life. And though you never said anything one way or another about my situation, you also had expectations that got me up every day. I might have gone back to bed afterwards, but at least my days had a starting point, thanks to you."

"I did feel bad for what you'd experienced," Paige said. "I couldn't imagine going through something like that. But honestly, I also felt like you were wasting your life."

"I was," Hayden agreed. "But prior to these past few weeks, I probably wouldn't have received that observation positively."

A smile ghosted across her face. "I was aware of that."

"But you don't have a problem telling me now?"

She shrugged. "I don't want to hurt you by saying things you don't want to hear, but I feel like I've become invested in you, and I want you to be happy in your life."

"I didn't think that happy was ever a possibility for me because I didn't want to *be* happy," Hayden murmured. "I mean, I wasn't willing to do what my therapist wanted me to in order to move past the accident."

"Has that changed?" Paige asked, her voice soft.

He glanced at her, then at Rylan, then at the rest of his family gathered there. He found Hunter watching them, a contemplative look on his face. Their gazes met for a moment, and Hayden saw love and support in his brother's eyes.

"Yeah. I think it has." He thought of the song that the girls had sung during their Christmas program. "I thought Christmas would never be happy again without my dad being here. But God reminded me recently that *He* is who will make me truly happy. He may use other people to bring that joy and happiness into my life, but ultimately, I need to let Him back into my life."

Paige nodded. "I understand that. For far too long, I thought it would take me getting the money back in order to be content again. I was so focused on the money providing security that I forgot that God should be the one I trusted with our future. He provided for us in ways that I didn't really want to acknowledge."

"Guess we both needed to learn things."

Paige frowned as she let out a sigh. "It's kind of disheartening how easily I let my frustration with what happened come between me and God. I guess that's what happens when we become focused on things to provide us with security and happiness rather than God."

Hayden felt a touch on his shoulder and looked up to see his mom standing beside him. She gave him a gentle smile. "Are you ready for some breakfast, darling?"

"I am," he said with a nod, suddenly starving. "I hope Essie made lots."

His mom beamed at him. "Oh, you know Essie. She's cooked *plenty*."

Hayden grabbed his crutches and got to his feet, and Paige did the same. He waited as she went to grab the handles of Rylan's wheelchair, then walked beside her as they followed the others out of the living room.

The table in the dining room was set beautifully, and there were platters of food spread across its surface. They all settled into the same seats they'd used the night before, which meant he was seated by Paige again.

After his mom had said a prayer of thanks for the food, Hayden looked around the table, taking in the cheerful faces of those he loved. And while he wasn't feeling ecstatic or anything, he was content with the low hum of happiness inside him.

For the moment, that was enough.

Chapter 24

Paige looked around the living room, feeling a little shellshocked. The number of gifts that had been handed out—including to her, Rylan, and her mom—was unreal. She'd seen how the presents had spilled out from under the tree when they'd first arrived, but when they'd started to hand them out, it had seemed like they'd never end.

She had figured that there might be a gift or two under the tree for her and her mom—maybe a few more for Rylan—but there had been far more than a couple of gifts. There had been way, way, *way* more than that for each of them. It had truly overwhelmed her.

But really, she shouldn't have been surprised at the generosity of the Kings. The previous year, her mom had come home with a huge hamper of food that had included everything they'd need for a Christmas dinner and then some.

On top of that, they'd given her mom a new top-of-the-line tablet and, even more surprisingly, they'd sent cards with money for her and Rylan. Even though she'd been so angry at how things had turned out for her and Rylan just weeks before, it touched her that they had done that for her mom.

It was one of the reasons she'd taken the job when she and her mom had decided it was the best course of action. She'd felt like it would be a safe place for her to work. And they'd proven their generosity even more that day.

Paige glanced at her mom, and when their gazes met, she could see the shock she felt reflected in her mom's eyes. Even having been the recipient of their generosity in years past, her mom was clearly still impacted by what they'd given them that year.

Hayden had also added to the gifts from "Santa" with a few gifts that he'd evidently picked out himself. Paige was speechless by it all. Saying *thank you* felt so... insignificant.

When the couch where she sat with Hayden shifted a little, she looked over to see him getting to his feet with the aid of his crutches. He glanced at her and gave a small smile before heading for the door of the living room with Hunter following him, both carefully picking their way around crumpled wrapping paper and gift boxes.

Paige stared after them for a moment before looking at Rylan. He'd been thrilled with the presents he'd gotten, especially the remote-control cars and helicopter, the perfect toys for him since he could control them from his wheelchair.

"How're you doing?" Heather asked as she dropped down on the couch beside her.

"Thank you," Paige said instead of any other response. "I just don't know what else to say. It's so much."

Heather grinned. "Santa must have had fun picking all that out."

Paige gave the woman an exasperated smile as she shook her head. "Yeah. Santa. Sure. And maybe Santa's helpers."

"Yep. Probably them, too."

"In all seriousness, thank you. The generosity you've shown us is unbelievable."

"You and your mother have gifted our family with the care you've given Hayden. Yes, I know that we've paid you. But you've gone above and beyond in your care for him, and we appreciate that. Hayden is important to us." Heather gave her a curious smile. "And maybe a little to you?"

Paige knew that she could have denied it. Maybe *should* have denied it. But something must have tipped Heather off, so Paige didn't bother. "Yes. He is."

"I'm pretty sure you and Rylan are important to him, too." Heather glanced at the doorway where Hayden had reappeared, hovering in the opening. "And I think perhaps Santa isn't finished just yet."

"What?" Paige frowned as she watched Hayden move out of the way, and Hunter appeared pushing a wheelchair. A child-size wheelchair.

"Can you bring Rylan over here, Paige?" Hayden asked. "It might be easier to do this in the foyer away from all the paper and stuff."

Feeling even more overwhelmed than she had been earlier, Paige slowly got to her feet and went to Rylan, who sat staring at the bright blue wheelchair. She carefully pushed him to where Hayden and Hunter waited. Once there, she looked at Hayden for an explanation.

"You'd mentioned that a powered wheelchair would be easier for Rylan, so I reached out to some contacts to see if anyone had a lead on people working with children's wheelchairs. One of those contacts ended up being a company who has been working on making powered wheelchairs as accommodating as possible. This is one of their latest models."

Paige stared at Hayden for a long moment, struggling with her feelings about everything, before shifting her attention to the wheelchair. She'd been planning to buy him one since they'd gotten the money back, but something told her that this particular model wouldn't have been within the budget she'd set for the purchase.

"Mama!" Rylan clapped his hands as he stared at the wheelchair. "This is so *cool!*"

Well, there was no way she could refuse the gift, since Rylan was already in love with it.

"Do you want to give it a try?" Hayden asked. "If there's anything that doesn't work for Rylan, we can have it adjusted. That's something that they've tried to do with this model. Make it as customizable as possible for the child, since they know that not every kid's needs are the same."

Paige nodded, well aware that she wouldn't be able to say no without disappointing Rylan. It took her a couple of minutes, but she got Rylan transferred from his old wheelchair into the new one.

Hayden talked to Rylan about the controls on chair, then Paige watched in concern as Rylan guided the chair around the foyer. There were plenty of fragile things in the area, and the last thing she wanted was for Rylan to break one of them. Thankfully, Hunter walked beside him as he circled around the foyer, which made Paige breathe a bit easier.

"I know this is a lot," Hayden said as he maneuvered himself to stand next to her. "But I hope that you'll accept it for Rylan."

She crossed her arms as she looked at him. "I think you know there's no way I can say no now that he's actually tried it out."

Hayden's shoulders slumped. "I know. I just wanted to do something that would make life easier for you and him the way you've made life better for me."

"But that's my job," Paige pointed out, though when Hayden's expression fell, she wished she could call her words back. "I didn't mean—"

Hayden waved his hand. "I get it. Still, I hope that you'll accept this for him. No strings attached, of course." He paused then said," I mean, it's not like I can't afford it."

In the space of a few minutes, the connection they'd formed earlier disappeared. As Hayden moved away from her, Paige's heart hurt, knowing she'd started it with her dismissal of any personal reason for helping him.

But it had been the truth. For the most part, the things she'd done for him had been because that was her job. It was only more recently that her care and concern for him came from a place of personal interest.

Instead of letting Hayden think that everything that had transpired between them had been strictly business, she should have told him that she did care for him—more than she should, considering her position in his life. And there was no denying how much easier life would be, and how much better it would be when Rylan went to school if they had a powered wheelchair.

She watched the brothers as they stood side by side, speaking together in voices too low for her to hear. Was Hayden telling Hunter how ungrateful she was? She wouldn't have blamed him if he had.

Rylan came to a stop in front of her. "This is so *great*, Mama! Did you see how good I can drive it?"

"I did," she told him. "It was really great of Hayden to get this for you. Be sure you thank him."

Rylan nodded vigorously. "So this is mine? For real? We can take it home?"

"I think so." She didn't think Hayden had brought it there just to tease Rylan. "If we can fit it in the car."

She had no idea how the wheelchair would fit in her vehicle. Even though the SUV had plenty of space with the third row folded down, this one didn't look like it would collapse like his current one did.

Hunter approached them, a smile on his face. "This model is made so that it can be broken down into two pieces."

Paige watched as he showed how the wheelchair could be taken apart so that it would fit in the back of her vehicle. She hoped that she could remember how to do it, even though it didn't seem like it was overly complicated. What *was* complicated right then was the situation with Hayden.

While she'd been paying attention to Hunter's instructions, Hayden had disappeared, and she had no idea where to in the large house. She felt sick at how quickly things had spiraled downward because she'd been so overwhelmed and had spoken without thinking first.

"Is this really for me?" Rylan asked, his eyes rounded as he gazed up at Hunter.

"Absolutely." Hunter gave him a smile. "Hayden thought it might be something you'd like."

"I *love* it. I've never had anything so amazing in my *life*! I love Hayden!"

Hunter reached out and ruffled Rylan's hair. "I have a feeling he feels the same way about you."

Paige's stomach clenched, and she swallowed hard at Hunter's words. That was what she'd wanted for Rylan... a man in his life who cared about him. Who loved him. That man should have been his father. Instead, the man showering him with care and affection was someone who didn't *have* to pay him any attention.

That day Hayden found Rylan in the kitchen, he could have just said hi and then gone back to his room. Instead, he'd taken the time to interact with him. And because of that, his interactions with her had changed as well.

"I need to thank Hayden." Rylan looked around. "Where is he?"

"He'll be back in a bit," Hunter said as he glanced at Paige. "You can thank him then. Do you want to show the girls your chair?"

Rylan nodded, then with Hunter's help, guided the wheelchair into the living room. Heather came with a couple of black garbage bags in her hands and gave her a quick smile.

Paige watched how easily Rylan handled the wheelchair, and she knew he was absolutely going to flourish with it. Even though Hayden had known she could buy a powered wheelchair for Rylan since she had the money back, he had still wanted to give it to him.

Having not done any exploring of the house, Paige had no clue where Hayden might have gone. She needed to make things right with him. The ache in her heart made it imperative. Hurting him hurt her, and it should never have happened. But since it had, it was important she fix it. If she could...

"Hayden's gone downstairs."

Paige looked over to see Heather approaching her. "Uh... where exactly is that?"

Heather hesitated a moment, her gaze a bit wary, then she said, "I'll show you the stairs."

"Thanks," Paige murmured as she followed the other woman.

"Head down there." Heather pointed to an open doorway. "He'll be in the rec room."

She gave Heather a nod of thanks before starting down the carpeted stairs to the basement. Looking around, she could see that it wasn't your average basement. The wide hallway at the bottom of the stairs was beautifully decorated with plush carpet, pocket lights in the ceiling, and artwork on the wall that had probably cost a fortune.

The carpet muffled her footsteps as she made her way toward a large doorway. As she stepped into the dimly lit rec room, Paige noticed how comfortably it was decorated. There was a stone fireplace, which was currently lit, as well as a huge television on the wall opposite one of two large overstuffed couches in the room.

The Christmas decorations hadn't just stayed on the main floor. In the corner of the room, there was a tree covered in colored lights and red plaid decorations. The Christmas décor was of a more rustic sort when compared to the elaborately decorated main floor.

The light from the tree and the fireplace allowed Paige to see the figure sitting hunched forward on the large, overstuffed couch. He had his elbows braced on his knees, and his head was bent.

"I'm sorry, Hayden," Paige said, keeping her words soft so that she didn't surprise him too much.

Maybe she hadn't surprised him at all, because he didn't even look in her direction. In fact, he didn't show any reaction at all to her words.

She rounded the end of the couch, then sat down next to him. "I'm really sorry for what I said. I..."

"It's fine," Hayden said gruffly with a wave of his hand.

"No. No, it's not," she said. "There's no excuse for what I said. I was just so overwhelmed that I didn't think."

He still didn't look at her. "You were right, though. It's your job to take care of me. I know that."

"That's how it was for a lot of months, yes," she agreed. "But that's changed. For both of us, I think. You hadn't focused on me as anything more than an employee before that day with Rylan."

Hayden rubbed his hands over his face. "Yeah. You're right."

"But things have changed for me," she told him. "Maybe for us both?"

He gave a single nod, still not looking at her. "I feel... different now. Rylan was like a bolt of lightning, shocking me and opening my eyes to help me see my life in a new way. See you in a new way."

"He did the same for me too, you know. Seeing how you interacted with him helped me to see you as more than just the man I cooked and cleaned for."

Hayden sniffed and cleared his throat. "And you weren't just the person who cooked and cleaned for me after that day either."

Paige shifted closer to him. "I didn't mean to hurt you, Hayden. It hurts me to think I did."

"I shouldn't be so sensitive."

"Don't say that. I actually appreciate that you have a sensitive side to you. I see it when you're dealing with Rylan, and I appreciate it so much. He needs a man like you in his life, who is sensitive to his situation and his emotions. So please, don't ever change that about yourself."

"I didn't use to be so sensitive to things." Hayden gave a hoarse laugh. "Ask Hunter and Heather. They'd tell you that I was an insensitive idiot a lot of the time."

"Not sure we can take the word of a sibling," Paige said. "I prefer to see who you are today. I don't know who you were before the accident, but the man I see in front of me now is one worth knowing. One worth... caring for."

He angled a sideways glance at her, holding her gaze for a moment before looking back down at his hands. "I'm still not so sure about that."

"That's because ever since the accident, you've believed you aren't worth loving. That you don't even deserve to be alive. But there are people who love you who believe differently."

He sighed, then gave a nod. "I've just felt so broken. Like I was shattered into a million pieces that day, physically, emotionally, and spiritually. But it felt like it was my burden to carry. That I deserved to be broken in all those ways and so many more."

"But you didn't. I'm not sure why God allowed that accident to happen. Why He allowed so many people to be injured and killed that day. But sometimes we just have to accept things without understanding why they happen."

She thought of her father's unexpected death that had left them floundering. Of Rylan's birth. Of everything that had happened with Glenn. None of it made sense.

There was a high probability that there would be more unexpected things ahead, but there could also be love, joy, and hope. She wanted that for herself. For her mom. For Rylan. For Hayden and for his family.

With that in mind, she reached out and rested her hands on his that were clenched together. "My dad used to tell us that God's specialty is broken people. That we didn't have to have it all together before God would accept us and use us."

"Dad used to tell me when he was lecturing me that there was nothing wrong with the aspects of my personality that kept getting me into trouble. My enthusiasm. My love of adventure and life. My desire to make people laugh. He said that God made me the way I was, but that I needed to use those things to give Him glory. I never really figured out how to do that, though, so I felt like those things brought about his death, you know."

"He wouldn't want you to cut those parts of yourself out," Paige said. "Did you ever make him laugh? Did he ever smile about something you did?"

He gave a huff. "Yeah. All the time."

"You brought him joy, Hayden. Just like you brought that joy to your mom and your siblings." She squeezed his hands. "Just like you've brought joy to me and Rylan."

He glanced at her again. "I don't know about that."

"Rylan has had so much fun with you. Watching movies. Going swimming. You've made him smile. You've made me smile."

"You've both done the same for me."

They sat there in silence for a few minutes, then Paige said, "Did I ruin everything?"

"What?" Hayden turned more fully toward her then, his brows pulled together.

"Did my careless words ruin everything?"

Hayden moved one of his hands and sandwiched hers between them. "Nothing is ruined. Everything is fine."

Paige knew then as she gazed into Hayden's eyes that she wanted everything with him. She didn't know if he felt the same way, but she really hoped that he did. However, she had a feeling that as long as he saw himself as undeserving of love, there wasn't much hope for them.

"I hope so," Paige said. "I don't want to hurt you. Ever. I'm so sorry that I did."

One corner of his mouth tipped up, and his expression softened. "Even though I don't think there's anything to forgive, I forgive you."

She let out a sigh at his words, then smiled as he lifted her hand and pressed a kiss to the back of it.

Chapter 25

Hayden kept hold of Paige's hand, not wanting to let go even though he was sure that he should. But she hadn't pulled her hand away, even after he'd kissed it, so maybe it was okay.

He couldn't believe how much Paige's words had hurt him, even though he'd tried to deny that to her. Those words shouldn't have hurt that much, because like he'd told her, they were true. He *had* been a job for her for a long time. Just like she'd been an employee for months longer than she'd been a friend. His feelings for her—both friendship and beyond—had only developed in the past several weeks.

"I'm glad you and Rylan could spend Christmas with us," Hayden said. "It has made it extra special for me."

"You've made it extra special for us, too," Paige said. "And not because of all the gifts you and your family have given us. You've opened your life to us, and I know that hasn't been an easy thing for you to do."

Hayden gave her hand a light squeeze. "Actually, it was easier than you think. I trusted you already because you'd never given me a reason not to. You were... someone who had been there steadily for me, even if it was just your job. And then Rylan was a ray of sunshine. Both of you made me care about things in my life again."

Opening up that way with Paige set him on an edge a bit. Being vulnerable had never, ever been a part of his personality. Before the accident, vulnerability wasn't even a word in his vocabulary, and even after the accident, he'd shared precious little with his family. Something about Paige and Rylan, however, reached into a part of him he usually hid from everyone.

He might have been a risk-taker in life before that fateful day, but the thought of making his heart vulnerable to Paige and Rylan was scary. Partly because he knew they'd both been hurt already, and he was worried that he'd inadvertently add to their pain. Plus, it had been proven earlier that Paige could hurt him in a way no one else had been able to.

Apparently, his heart was already in a vulnerable position, so that left him with two options. Either pull back completely and protect himself, or open right up to her and accept the risk that came with loving someone outside of his family.

"I've definitely seen a different side to you recently," Paige said, not making any attempt to pull her hand free of his. "I felt bad for you when everything happened with your leg. It was hard to see you basically lose your will to live."

Hayden nodded. It wasn't like he could deny that when she—more than anyone—had been there to witness his state of mind most days. But he didn't need to continue to live that way. As with all things in life, he had choices. It just seemed that every decision he'd made, even before the accident, had been the wrong one. Was he even capable of making good decisions?

"Why haven't you gotten a prosthesis?" Paige asked, daring to go where few had dared before.

"I suppose because then it meant I was accepting what had happened to me. I've just been so angry because, after all I'd been through, it seemed unfair to then have one more thing taken from me. That surgery on my foot should have been the one that left me almost back to normal. I knew that I'd still walk with a bit of a limp, and I'd never be completely free of pain, but it would have been more tolerable."

"But the only person you're hurting by not going getting a prosthesis is yourself," Paige pointed out, her tone gentle even as her words held weight. "You need to stop punishing yourself."

Hayden nodded as he stared down at their hands. "I realize that. No one ever said I was the smart one of the bunch."

"Hayden," Paige said reprovingly. "You're far from dumb. You say that your eyes were opened, which I hope means that you are able to see yourself for who you truly are. Who the rest of us see you as."

Hayden swallowed, his throat tight with emotion. "I have been dumb over the past several months, though. Not accepting the help that was offered to me was really stupid."

"But the damage isn't permanent. You can still get the prosthesis. You can still get the help you need."

"I think it's time." Long past time, actually. But it had taken a little boy with a bright smile and a positive outlook on life to shine a light on his attitude toward his own situation. "I need to grow up."

Paige bumped her shoulder against his. "For what it's worth, I think that you made a lot of decisions in the midst of terrible pain and grief. Pretty sure that most of us would struggle in circumstances like those."

"I appreciate you making excuses for me, but we both know that I could have come to my senses a few months ago."

"Better late than never," Paige said. "Right? I doubt your family would be mad if you suddenly decided to go for the prosthesis and got the help you needed. I know I wouldn't be."

"No, they'd be thrilled, and they would tell me that they told me so. You know, like siblings do."

Paige gave a little laugh. "Yeah. But you know, I think they would say it with all the love they have for you. And from what I've seen, they love you a *whole* lot."

"Yes, we do." Hunter's voice had them both turning to the door, watching as he walked over to face them. "I don't mean to interrupt, but I heard what Paige said, and I wanted to let you know that she is absolutely right. You mean the world to us, and all we want is for you to be happy. For you to know that you're loved and supported in every way."

He held out his hand to Hunter, and when Hunter took it, Hayden used it to leverage himself up to stand on his foot. Hayden put his hand on Hayden's shoulder to keep his balance as he met his brother's gaze straight on. In Hunter's eyes, he saw what had always been there. Love. Support.

He pulled Hunter into a hug and held onto him. "Thank you for never giving up on me."

"I never would have done that. You're my baby brother."

Hayden gave a huff of laughter as he thumped Hunter on his back. "Baby brother. Ha."

When they ended the hug, Hunter said, "I'll leave you two. Rylan was just wondering where you were."

Paige got up. "I should probably go upstairs."

"He wasn't upset. Just wondering. Stay down here as long as you need," Hunter said. "I'll let him know you'll be up in a little while."

Paige's brows drew together for a moment, but then she nodded. "Okay."

"Dinner will be in about an hour, Essie said."

Hayden held onto Hunter as he lowered himself back down on the couch, acknowledging in that moment that he had always known that his family would be there for him. Not once had he reached out and been slapped away. He'd taken that for granted, even as he'd rejected doing what he should to move forward with his life.

"I love you, bro," Hayden said, looking up at his brother, at the face that had once been so similar to his. "Always."

"I love you too," Hunter replied with a small smile. "Forever."

Hunter left the room then, and silence settled over them. Hayden wanted to take Paige's hand again, but it kind of seemed like the moment had been broken. He didn't want it to be, though. He felt like they'd moved in a direction that he hadn't been sure they could, and he didn't want to backtrack.

But how did he prevent that?

It wasn't as straightforward as it might have been if they'd just been two people who met. Her working for him—and yeah, they might say it was Hunter who was her boss, but she was still doing work for *him*—made the situation a bit more complicated. And it was a complication he wasn't sure how to deal with.

He wanted to be able to just ask her out on a date without wondering if it was awkward because of their situation. And to think that he'd been worried about her quitting, only to turn around and wish that she would.

But if she wanted the job, he wouldn't take it away from her, even if it meant he couldn't ask her out without it being awkward. Or was he just making it awkward when it didn't need to be?

"Uh, penny for them?"

Hayden realized then he had just been sitting there in silence for the last minute or so. Could he pass it off as emotion from Hunter's visit?

Shifting to face her more directly, Hayden said, "I can't decide if they're worth way more than that, or if they're not even worth a penny."

Paige smiled. "I would imagine that they're actually worth way more."

"Doubt it."

"Only way to know is for you to tell me," Paige said. "Either way, I'm going to have to go with an IOU since I have no cash on me at the moment."

Hayden had never thought of himself as lacking courage—at least where women were concerned. However, right then, he was definitely wary of broaching the subject. Because even as much as dating would be awkward, being around each other if she turned him down or if it didn't work out would be even more so.

What he felt like he needed right then was a little Christmas miracle. Though maybe he'd already had one with the change of heart he'd undergone.

He tried to draw forth the bravado he'd once had, but it was non-existent. "I was trying to figure out if it would be awkward to ask you out on a date."

"Oh. Well." She gave a little chuckle. "Did you figure that out?"

"Not really. Do you have any thoughts on the matter?"

He hoped that she didn't offer the solution of just not dating, though that response would make it pretty clear that she wasn't interested in something more than the friendship they'd built so far.

"I'm guessing this has to do with me working for you," she said.

"Yeah. I would like to ask you out, but I'm not sure how you feel about that."

She stared at him for a moment, and Hayden held her gaze, wanting her to see how serious he was about it.

"I'd like that too," she said, a small smile briefly lifting the corners of her mouth. "But yeah, I can see that there's potential for problems given our situation."

Hayden hoped that a date with Paige would be the start of something lasting, but he hated that it seemed rather clinical to be troubleshooting stuff before even going on one date. It wasn't like they were strangers, though. They knew a lot about each other already. They just hadn't gone on a date yet.

It was definitely not a situation that he had experience with. Most of the time, any dating he'd done had been with women he hadn't known very well initially. He'd gotten to know them as they'd dated.

"I care about you," Hayden said, hesitant to voice his deeper feelings. "That's why I want us to go out. However, I don't want you to feel awkward or worried about your job."

Paige nodded. "I care about you, too. Which I have to say is something I never saw coming."

Hayden gave a huff of laughter. "Yeah. Same for me. I guess we have Rylan to thank for changing things up for us."

"I think he'd love to know that," Paige said.

"Do we just throw caution to the wind and go for it?" Hayden asked. "That's how I used to do things."

"And how did that work out for you?"

Hayden grimaced. "Sometimes better than others. It was one of those things my dad kept trying to caution me about. That I needed to think things through a bit before acting or speaking."

"I can understand why he'd encourage that, because it's how I've lived most of my life," Paige said. "But there are times when I believe you can overthink things. I mean, after what happened with Rylan, I didn't spend weeks, or even that many days, thinking about what I should do. I threw caution to the wind and made the decision to put off school and stay home with him. I might not currently be staying home with him, but it was the best decision at the time."

Hayden rubbed his hands along his thighs. "It's been awhile since I've thrown caution to the wind. I feel a little out of practice."

Paige laughed. "We'll throw caution wind together, and then do our best to make it work."

"You really want to do this?" he asked. "With me?"

"If you had asked me when I first started working for you if I could see us getting to this point, I'd have said no way. I wasn't exactly viewing men in a positive light."

"And I changed your mind?" Hayden asked, a bit skeptical of that.

"Even on your worst days, you treated me respectfully," she said. "Plus, my mom always spoke highly of you and Hunter. The icing on the cake, however, is how you treat Rylan."

"Well, one lesson I did learn from my dad was to treat people with respect, and I've tried to do that, especially when it's someone who hasn't given me any reason to not treat them that way."

"You've already shown me that you're a good man, so honestly, it doesn't feel that much like I'm taking a chance."

"I'm not a perfect man, though," Hayden reminded her, feeling the weight of expectation.

Paige gave him a gentle smile and reached out to take his hand, threading her fingers through his. "I know that. I don't expect you to be because goodness knows that I'm certainly not perfect either."

Hayden wanted to be the best man possible for her and for Rylan, and he would pray every day that God would help him be that man.

"Guess I should head upstairs, so Rylan knows I'm still here." Paige gave his hand a squeeze. "We can talk more about this later."

Hayden smiled as best he could. "You can count on it."

With a laugh, Paige got to her feet, then helped him up onto his crutches. Hayden followed Paige upstairs, resolving to make a call to see about a prosthetic leg as soon as that office was open again. Now that he'd decided to go that route, he wanted to get it underway as soon as possible.

Later that evening, Hayden stood in the foyer while Paige, Leta, and Rylan got ready to leave. He wished they didn't have to go, but he understood why they had to. Instead of bemoaning the fact they couldn't stay, he chose to be happy that they'd been there at all. And it looked like they'd be back the next day to spend more time with them.

"Mama?" Rylan said as Paige took the jacket Heather held out to her.

"What's wrong?" Paige asked, then bent down to him when he motioned for her to come closer. As she listened to him, she glanced up at Hayden for a moment. "Sure. I can do that."

Hayden watched as she hung the jacket on the handle of the wheelchair, then unbuckled the belt that held Rylan securely in the chair. Once free, she lifted him up and turned toward where Hayden stood.

As she neared him, Rylan held out his arms, and emotion tightened Hayden's throat when he realized that the little boy had asked his mom to help him give Hayden a hug. Hayden settled his weight on the crutches so that he could let go with one hand. As Rylan wrapped his arms about Hayden's neck, Hayden put his arm around both the little boy and Paige.

"Merry Christmas, Hayden," Rylan said. "I love you."

Tears pricked at Hayden's eyes, forcing him to close them so tears didn't form. "Love you too, bud. Thank you for spending Christmas with us."

Rylan's arms tightened for a moment before he let go. Hayden opened his eyes as Rylan settled back against his mom, a huge smile on his small face. "We're coming back tomorrow, right?"

Hayden looked at Paige and saw that she wasn't as successful at keeping the tears from her eyes. He kept his hand on her back, since she wasn't moving away from him just yet.

"Yeah. We'll be back tomorrow. I wouldn't want to be anywhere else."

Hayden couldn't help but smile, feeling the pull of his scar as he did. "I can't wait."

Paige stepped closer and wrapped her arm around Hayden, pressing her cheek to his shoulder. "Thank you for today. For everything. It's been a wonderful Christmas."

"It has been for me too," Hayden said, his voice low. "I look forward to seeing you both tomorrow."

She nodded against his shoulder, then stepped back. His arm fell to his side, so he gripped the handle of his crutches again. The front door opened, letting in a blast of cold air as Hunter and George came back inside from taking all the gifts out to Paige's car.

Though he was sad to see them leave, nothing could squelch the joy and hope in Hayden's heart. It had been a long time since he'd felt either emotion so strongly. He really hoped that no matter what might come, he didn't lose that joy or hope.

Chapter 26

Paige paused at the top of the wooden steps and looked out at the man standing on the dock that ran out over the ocean. The sun was slowly sinking toward the horizon, already casting streaks of red and orange across the sky. She wasn't sure she'd ever seen a more beautiful sunset.

Of course, she could honestly say she'd never been in a more beautiful location to watch a sunset. Considering that just a few days ago they'd been in frigid Minnesota, she was doubly appreciative of their current location.

The light breeze coming off the water pressed the skirt of her sundress against her legs as she walked down the steps. As soon as she stepped onto the dock, Hayden turned on his crutches to face her. Though Heather had insisted that he get his hair trimmed for the wedding, it was still long enough to be ruffled by the breeze.

He wore a white short-sleeve button-up shirt with a pair of linen shorts. She was sure that the main reason he'd been comfortable enough to wear shorts was that it was just family and staff on the private tropical island.

"You look beautiful," he said, his mouth tipped up in a lopsided smile.

She returned the smile as she approached him and took the hand he held out to her. "And you look very handsome."

Hayden looked down at himself. "Hunter vetoed the T-shirt and basketball shorts I planned to wear."

Paige laughed because she was quite certain that he hadn't planned on wearing anything of the sort. While it was true he tended to wear T-shirts and sweats at home, she'd seen what his closet held over the months she'd worked for him, and it contained plenty of fashionable items.

"Shall we sit down?" Hayden said, waving his hand to the end of the dock where a table and chairs had been set up.

The round table was covered by a white tablecloth with a candle surrounded by glass to protect it from the breeze. There were also tiki torches along the edges of the dock, their flames flickering brightly.

It was certainly the most romantic date she'd ever been on.

Once they were seated, one of the staff approached them with a chilled bottle of sparkling juice. Another followed behind them with a tray.

As the first person poured the juice into their glasses, the second set plates with appetizers onto the table, as well as a plate with some bread. Now that she'd been on the island for almost a week, Paige was used to the incredible food. Well, maybe she wasn't used to it, but she was less in awe of it, while still appreciating its tastiness enormously.

"Did Rylan want to come with you?" Hayden asked as they began to eat.

Paige laughed softly. "Not just him. Rachel and Isla both tried to convince me that you would be fine with them coming along too."

"I love them all to death, but tonight is just for us," Hayden said. "I wanted at least one evening with you before we head back, and since we leave tomorrow, tonight was the night."

"I still can't believe that Heather wanted us to come along for this."

Hayden smiled. "She was most insistent, and surely you've come to realize that when she puts her mind to something, you just don't argue."

"Yes. Yes, I have realized that." Paige laughed. "And it was a bonus that I didn't need to convince my boss I needed to take time off."

"Hah," Hayden said with a grin. "And you didn't need to take Rylan out of school."

"Although considering Rachel and Isla are both out of school, that probably wouldn't have been a big problem."

When Heather had first broached the idea of her coming, Paige had said no. After all, there was no way she could afford the airfare or the hotel room. Of course, then she'd found out that they were taking a private plane and staying on a private island that belonged to a family friend. All of that meant that it wouldn't cost them anything to join the family for Heather and Ash's wedding.

So, she, Rylan, and her mom had joined them just a week and a half into February to wing their way to an island with a spacious home that had an amazing mix of luxury and beach house amenities. It was a sharp reminder of the social circle that the Kings moved in. They might not own an island in the Pacific themselves, but they obviously knew people who did.

"Heather got the wedding she wanted," Hayden said as they ate their appetizers. "The one she thought Hunter and Carissa should have gone for."

"Something in the tropics? Or a Valentine's Day wedding?"

"The tropics thing. I think she wanted an escape from winter, so she'd tried to talk Hunter and Carissa into a destination wedding. They said no."

"Well, she certainly picked an amazing destination for her wedding."

"It is nice," Hayden said, leaning back as one of the servers came to clear away their dishes. "But even though I have enjoyed the break from winter, it's a bit over the top for me. Or maybe I just didn't enjoy the beach as much because I couldn't walk very well on the sand."

"Thank you for arranging this tonight," Paige said, waving her hand at their surroundings. "It's a better way to enjoy the beach, right?"

"I'm definitely enjoying it more than trying to maneuver my crutches on the sand."

The sky was even more alive with color as the sun slowly sank into the far horizon, but Paige found her gaze drawn to the man across the table from her. Since Christmas Day, when they'd agreed to go on a date, her feelings for him had continued to grow.

She'd braced herself for things to be awkward as she'd continued to work for him, but it hadn't turned out that way. Hayden had made some changes in his life that had helped to draw some boundaries.

When she arrived each day now, he was already up and ready to face his day. He usually sat at the kitchen table while she made him breakfast, drinking his first cup of coffee. After Craig had been and gone, Hayden disappeared into a room she'd rarely seen him use before, which was the office. He'd work until lunch, then the two of them shared that meal before he went back to work again. Though she hated to leave him to eat dinner on his own, he assured her that he was fine.

On Fridays, she brought Rylan with her, and he and Hayden hung out together. Sometimes, they went swimming. Other times, they watched movies or played video games.

In the midst of it all, Hayden had been attending appointments with his therapist and, more recently, with the clinic where he was being fitted for his prosthesis. She'd thought he'd pursue it immediately after Christmas, but he'd taken his time for whatever reason.

Seeing the difference between how he was right then and how he'd been a few months earlier just amazed Paige. Once he'd made up his mind to move forward, he'd done just that. She was seeing depth in him that hadn't been apparent in the months following his amputation, and she was so thankful that God had brought him to that point. Brought them both to that point.

~*~

"So, are you okay with this?" Hayden asked.

"Sitting on the end of a dock overlooking the ocean with you?"

Hayden chuckled. "Not exactly. I was thinking more about us dating."

They had finished their meal, relishing the dessert of flaky pastry and fruit, and then moved to sit on the end of the dock, their feet dangling over the water. The sun had long since set, but the tiki torches cast flickering light around them.

When Paige leaned against him, Hayden put his arm around her shoulders, taking that as a good sign.

"I'm more than okay with this," she murmured. "I really doubted that I'd ever be interested in another relationship after what happened."

"That's understandable. I mean, I had no plan to ever date again."

"Then there was Rylan," Paige said.

"Yes. Then there was Rylan," Hayden agreed with a chuckle. "I guess he was the great eye-opener for us both. Such an amazing little boy."

"I've always thought so, but it's nice to have other people see beyond his wheelchair to who he really is."

"He showed me that I don't have to be defined by a tragedy. Losing my leg seemed to just be the terrible frosting on a horrible cake. Meeting Rylan put so much into perspective for me. I needed that." Hayden hesitated. "Thank you."

"For what?"

The water lapped quietly in the background as they spoke softly together. The darkness making him feel like it was just the two of them on the island.

"For so many things," Hayden said. "But mostly for trusting me with Rylan. Not many would have."

"You were never a bad man. Stubborn, maybe. But you hadn't given me any reason to think you'd be mean to Rylan. Even as you struggled with what had happened, you were always respectful to me. That didn't mean I wasn't worried when I brought him to work with me. Not that I thought you'd be mean to either of us, just that I might have crossed a professional line in bringing my son to work with me."

"I would never have fired you over something like that," Hayden assured her. "And neither would Hunter."

"I know that now," she said. "The more we've gotten to know each other these past few weeks, the more I've come to admire you." She hesitated for a moment. "I don't know who should be the first to say it, but I'm just going to dive in here—well, not literally dive in because I'm not wearing my swimsuit—but you know."

She shifted toward him, lifting her hand to rest on his cheek. The one with the scar marring it, and for a moment, Hayden had to fight the urge to flinch. But Paige knew about the scar—how could she not?—and it didn't seem to bother her. So why did he let it bother him? He lifted his hand to hers, pressing it against his cheek.

"I love you, Hayden."

Hearing her give voice to the words that had been lingering in his heart for a little while now filled Hayden with warmth. He cherished her love for the gift that it was because he didn't feel particularly worthy of it.

"I love you too," Hayden said, his voice raspy with emotion. "My heart is yours."

As she leaned closer, Hayden did the same, pressing his lips to hers in a gentle kiss. He poured all of his love into that kiss, wishing that the moment could last forever.

The hope that had first bloomed at Christmas took root firmly with him. And for the first time in forever, Hayden wasn't afraid to let that hope grow alongside the love he had for Paige and for Rylan. There was joy within him as he looked forward to the future. The one he hoped to spend with the mother and son who had helped him open his eyes and his heart to hope and love once again.

Epilogue

Eliza King sank down into the recliner in the corner of her bedroom. She drew the blanket that lay on the arm of the chair around her, tucking it up under her chin.

For a moment, she closed her eyes and took several deep breaths, bracing herself for the emotion that was sure to come. She welcomed it, even though it made her feel like her heart was being ripped from her chest every time it came.

Seven years... It was hard to believe that it had been that long already. Seven years since the call had come that her beloved husband was gone, and that her youngest son might not make it.

Grief had come hard on the heels of the panic she'd felt when she'd first heard the news. But all of it had had to be pushed to the side so that she could help her—their—children cope with everything that had happened. She had needed to be strong for them, especially since their pillar of strength was gone.

Her support. Her best friend. Her lover. Her heart.

All gone in the blink of an eye.

Her hardest moments had come in the darkest hours of the night. A time when he should have been there to hold her. But those hours had been spent alone, her pillow often soaked with the tears she held back all day for the sake of her children.

The soul-crushing grief had eased over the years, and though her tears still fell, it was no longer the nightly thing that it had once been. Happiness had helped to soothe the grief as reasons to smile—things that would have made her beloved smile—crept back into their lives.

Opening her eyes, Eliza reached out and picked up the framed picture that sat on the table beside the chair. It was the last picture taken of the two of them. Heather's Christmas tradition might involve pajamas, but Eliza had a tradition of her own. Each year in early December, she had them all show up for family pictures.

Up until the triplets were ten, she had dressed them in identical outfits for the pictures. But as pre-teens, they refused to wear the matching clothes, so she'd had to settle for similar colors.

This photo, however, was of just the two of them, and her memory of it being taken was as clear as the day it had happened. It was a pose of them looking at each other rather than at the camera, and Eliza cherished it more than any other because of the love she knew was in their gazes for one another.

Though the sense of loss had been intense at first, now it was tempered with the knowledge that not everyone had a love like they had shared. And even knowing how it would end and the grief that would follow, Eliza would still want to experience that love with him.

"Well, my darling," she said, running her finger over the photo. "Tomorrow is the last of the weddings. You would be so happy for Hayden. The love he and Paige share is wonderful to see. He has come on such a journey from where he was a year and a half ago. He's going to make a great husband and a wonderful father. You'd be so proud of him, darling. I know that I am."

Though she always missed him, she missed him most acutely at Christmas and at the weddings of their children. That meant she was feeling the grief a bit more intensely since Hayden and Paige's wedding was happening on the afternoon of Christmas Eve.

Aching loss swept over her as she clutched the picture frame to her chest. The tears began to fall then, and Eliza let them. There would be more shed the next day, but they wouldn't be as raw as the ones she wept alone in the quiet and darkness of her room, mourning the man who would hold her heart forever.

~*~

Hayden stood at the front of the same hall where Hunter and Carissa had gotten married. The group gathered there was smaller than it had been for their wedding, but the most important people to them were present.

"You nervous?" Hunter asked as he nudged Hayden with his elbow.

"Nope. Still not nervous."

Hunter had been asking him that since they'd arrived at the church. If Hayden had to pick a word to describe how he was feeling, the word would be *excited*.

Like his siblings, he and Paige hadn't had a long engagement. After he'd proposed at the end of summer, Hayden had left picking the wedding date up to Paige. If he'd had his way, they would have eloped. However, when she'd suggested a Christmas wedding, he'd readily agreed.

Heather and Paige had gone all out for the decorations for the ceremony, hiring someone to transform the room into a winter wonderland. All around the outside of the small gathering of chairs were piles of fake snow and Christmas trees. The trees were of varying heights, decorated only with tiny white lights and a light dusting of "snow" on the branches. Meandering around through the trees was a white picket fence.

At the front, where he, Hunter, and Ash waited, were more Christmas trees as well as a white arch with spruce branches, poinsettias, and white lights decorating it.

His dad would have loved the Christmas theme.

As the string quartet off to the side played *Ode to Joy*, the back doors opened to reveal Heather in a red velvet dress. Behind her came Rachel and Isla, both in white satin dresses with dark green velvet sashes that matched the suit coats he, Hunter, Ash, and Rylan wore.

Rylan came next, his wheelchair making slow progress down the aisle. He had a broad smile on his face, which was no surprise, as he'd been extremely excited about the wedding. When he joined Hayden at the front, he held out his hand for a high five, which Hayden happily gave him.

Then, finally, the woman he loved stepped into the doorway with her mother at her side. Hayden took a deep breath to expand his chest that had grown tight with emotion. He'd been waiting for this moment ever since that night on the beach.

His gaze followed the women as they made their way toward where he waited. He could see the emotion on Leta's face, which had been mirrored on his mom's earlier when he'd accompanied her down the aisle. Both women were missing the men they'd loved, and no doubt each felt their absence keenly.

Though his mom sat in the front row with Essie and George, Leta would join them on the stage as Paige's matron of honor. As the women came to a stop just feet away, Hayden met Paige's gaze and smiled. The smile he got in return showed him that, like him, she wasn't nervous about what they were doing there that day.

Soon the ceremony was underway with the minister moving them through it with a casualness that he and Paige had both requested. They'd debated writing their own vows but had ended up going the traditional route, simply because neither of them felt comfortable voicing their feelings to an audience.

All that mattered was that they made it to the point when the minister pronounced them husband and wife. "And now you may kiss your bride."

Hayden was more than happy to gather Paige into his arms and press his lips to hers. "I love you, sweetheart."

Paige smiled up at him. "I love you too."

Then, hand in hand, they walked up the aisle with their wedding party following behind them. Once at the back of the room, Hayden swept Paige into his arms and spun them around, something he wouldn't have been able to do if he hadn't gotten his prosthetic leg earlier that year.

"Yay!" Rylan cheered as he stopped his chair close to them. "You're my dad now!"

"Yes, I am," Hayden said as he bent to give him a hug. "And I am thrilled about that."

"Me too! And I get to be a King like Rachel."

Hunter had adopted Rachel, and Heather and Ash had officially adopted Isla. Now, all that was left was for him to adopt Rylan. Their family had grown by leaps and bounds in the past few years, and it was set to grow again in a couple of months, when Carissa, who was currently seven months pregnant, gave birth to her and Hunter's first child together.

For the next hour, they mingled with the people who had been present there. Instead of a reception, they had hors d'oeuvres and drinks for their guests. Since it was Christmas Eve, they knew that most people wouldn't want to be away from their family for the evening. Having their wedding early in the afternoon allowed them to still have their own family festivities later in the day.

After their guests had left, the family made their way to where they'd booked to have their pictures taken. Then it was back to the house for the wedding/Christmas Eve dinner that Essie had prepared.

~*~

Paige waited as her mom unzipped her dress, then helped her out of it. Though she'd loved her dress, she was eager to get into something more comfortable for the rest of the evening.

"Thanks, Mom," she said as they worked together to get the dress into its protective bag.

"You're welcome, darling. This was such a wonderful day." Her mom came and gave her a hug, hanging onto her tightly. "Your dad would have loved it. He would have loved Hayden. More than he would have liked Glenn, that's for sure."

"Yeah. I love Hayden more than I loved Glenn. But then, Hayden makes it so easy to love him because he is such a wonderful man."

Her mom nodded. "I'm glad to call him son-in-law."

After they were dressed in more comfortable clothes, they went downstairs. She'd planned to help Rylan change, but Hayden had said he'd take care of doing that for him. He'd already stepped into the role of father, doing things for Rylan that Paige usually did.

Early on, he'd asked Paige to show him how to care for Rylan and the special needs he had. She had total confidence in Hayden's ability to care for him now.

Downstairs, she found Hayden with the others in the living room. Her mom had veered off toward the kitchen to help Essie with the meal. For some reason, her mom and Carissa were the only two people that Essie tolerated helping her out in the kitchen. However, with Carissa currently pregnant, even she was banned now.

"Hello, wife," Hayden said with a smile as she curled up next to him on the couch.

She gave him a kiss, then returned the smile. "Hello, husband."

"Are you happy with how everything went?"

"It was perfect. Heather certainly outdid herself."

"Or the people who hired her did," Hayden said with a laugh.

"Yeah. Or them."

"Hey now," Heather protested from where she sat with Ash. "I had a vision."

"And paid people to carry it out."

"Well, yes. They were definitely more talented than me in carrying out that vision."

"It really was beautiful, darling," Eliza said. "And everyone looked amazing. I wasn't sure about that dark green velvet jacket for the guys, but they all looked very dapper."

"I'm just glad to be married," Hayden said. "And now we can focus on Christmas."

Paige was glad the stress of planning the wedding—even a small one—was behind them. They weren't going on a honeymoon until after the New Year. That night, her mom was going to be staying at the King home with Rylan while Paige and Hayden went to spend their wedding night in the home they'd be living in together now that they were married. In the morning, they'd be back for all the Christmas festivities—wearing the pajamas Heather had bought for them. Once they'd decided they wanted a future as a family, they'd had a house built that was accessible for Rylan and had a small, attached apartment for her mom. Hayden had insisted that she return to school, and her mom had supported that by offering to help as needed with Rylan in order to make that happen.

Rylan had gone back to school for grade two in the fall, and he seemed to be doing fine so far. He was in the same school as the girls, and there was an aide available to help him with anything he needed. All in all, it seemed to be a good situation for Rylan, which made Paige breathe a sigh of relief.

"This has been the best day of my life," Hayden said, his voice low as conversations went on around them.

"I think I speak for Rylan when I say that we feel the same way. I never dared to hope that we could be part of a family that loved the way your family has loved us. They've accepted all of us—even my mom—in a way that they didn't have to, and that's been a huge blessing."

"So you're saying you married me for my family?" Hayden asked, a smile lifting the corner of his mouth.

"Yep. Has nothing whatsoever to do with the fact that you are an amazing man who I love with all my heart. You are a man that I can say without hesitation that I want Rylan to look up to and to emulate."

Hayden sobered at her words. "I'm glad that God opened my eyes to what I had in my life, and that you and Rylan came along to add so much more to it."

They had both lost hope, discouraged by things that had happened in their lives. But God had been gracious and faithful to them, bringing people alongside them to offer them support and hope. As they'd attended a Bible study group that had included Hunter, Carissa, Heather, and Ash over the past few months, they'd both come to realize that their hope was in the Lord. Regardless of their circumstances, they needed to keep their hope in Him.

Though there was grief for those who weren't there, they took comfort in knowing where their loved ones were and that they'd see them again one day. All because of the birth of a baby who had brought with Him the love of God, the joy of salvation, and the hope of glory.

"Mama, my heart feels like it's gonna burst with happiness," Rylan said as he came to a stop in front of them. "Can that happen?"

"Mine feels the same way, buddy," Hayden said. "Why don't you come sit with us for a few minutes, and we can be happy together?"

As Hayden carefully freed Rylan from the wheelchair and settled him between them on the couch, Paige had to agree. Her heart was going to burst with happiness that had a whole lot of love, joy, and hope mixed in with it.

~*~*~ The End ~*~*~

ABOUT THE AUTHOR

Kimberly Rae Jordan is a USA Today bestselling author of Christian romances. Many years ago, her love of reading Christian romance morphed into a desire to write stories of love, faith, and family, and thus began a journey that would lead her to places Kimberly never imagined she'd go.

In addition to being a writer, she is also a wife and mother, which means Kimberly spends her days straddling the line between real life in a house on the prairies of Canada and the imaginary world her characters live in. Though caring for her husband and four kids and working on her stories takes up a large portion of her day, Kimberly also enjoys reading and looking at craft ideas that she will likely never attempt to make.

As she continues to pen heartwarming stories of love, faith, and family, Kimberly hopes that readers of all ages will enjoy the journeys her characters take in each book. She has no plan to stop writing the stories God places on her heart and looks forward to where her journey will take her in the years to come.

Printed in Great Britain
by Amazon